# HOUSE OF WHISPERS

ELLIE JORDAN, GHOST TRAPPER,
BOOK FIVE

by

J.L. Bryan

Published 2016
JLBryanbooks.com

Copyright 2015 J.L. Bryan
All rights reserved.

This book or any portion thereof may not be reproduced or used in any manner whatsoever without the express written permission of the publisher except for the use of brief quotations in a book review.

All characters appearing in this work are fictitious. Any resemblance to real persons, living or dead, is purely coincidental.

# Acknowledgments

I appreciate everyone who has helped with this book. My beta readers include authors Daniel Arenson and Robert Duperre (try their books!), Annie Chanse, and as Isalys Blackwell from the blog Book Soulmates. The proofing was done by Thelia Kelly and Barb Ferrante. The cover is by PhatPuppy Art.

Most of all, I appreciate the book bloggers and readers who keep coming back for more! The book bloggers who've supported me over the years include Danny, Heather, and Heather from Bewitched Bookworks; Mandy from I Read Indie; Michelle from Much Loved Books; Shirley from Creative Deeds; Katie and Krisha from Inkk Reviews; Lori from Contagious Reads; Heather from Buried in Books; Kristina from Ladybug Storytime; Chandra from Unabridged Bookshelf; Kelly from Reading the Paranormal; AimeeKay from Reviews from My First Reads Shelf and Melissa from Books and Things; Kristin from Blood, Sweat, and Books; Aeicha from Word Spelunking; Lauren from Lose Time Reading; Kat from Aussie Zombie; Andra from Unabridged Andralyn; Jennifer from A Tale of Many Reviews; Giselle from Xpresso Reads; Ash from Smash Attack Reads; Ashley from Bookish Brunette; Loretta from Between the Pages; Ashley from Bibliophile's Corner; Lili from Lili Lost in a Book; Line from Moonstar's Fantasy World; Lindsay from The Violet Hour; Rebecca from Bending the Spine; Holly from Geek Glitter; Louise from Nerdette Reviews; Isalys from Book Soulmates; Jennifer from The Feminist Fairy; Heidi from Rainy Day Ramblings; Kristilyn from Reading in Winter; Kelsey from Kelsey's Cluttered Bookshelf; Lizzy from Lizzy's Dark Fiction; Shanon from Escaping with Fiction; Savannah from Books with Bite; Tara from Basically Books; Toni from My Book Addiction; Abbi from Book Obsession; Lake from Lake's Reads; Jenny from Jenny on the Book; and anyone else I missed!

# Also by J.L. Bryan

## The Ellie Jordan, Ghost Trapper series
Ellie Jordan, Ghost Trapper
Cold Shadows
The Crawling Darkness
Terminal
House of Whispers
Maze of Souls

**The seventh Ellie Jordan book will be available in May/June 2016**

## The Jenny Pox series (supernatural/horror)
Jenny Pox
Tommy Nightmare
Alexander Death
Jenny Plague-Bringer

## Urban Fantasy/Horror
Inferno Park
The Unseen

## Science Fiction
Nomad
Helix

## The Songs of Magic Series (YA/Fantasy)
Fairy Metal Thunder
Fairy Blues
Fairystruck
Fairyland
Fairyvision
Fairy Luck

*For Sherri*

# Chapter One

During autumn in Savannah, you can feel the spirits everywhere, watching from the shadows under the shifting trees. Leaves stir on the ground when there seems to be no wind, and footfalls echo down empty alleys between crumbling antique mansions.

Sometimes the ghosts come right up to your window and look in at you while you're sleeping.

That happened to me the night before we began our investigation at the Lathrop Grand Hotel. My cat, Bandit, woke me with a low growl, one paw resting on my face. It was late, almost three in the morning.

Normally I sleep with my blackout curtains drawn tight, because normally I sleep during the day. Ghost hunting is nocturnal work. Between cases, though, I sometimes get crazy and decide to sleep at night instead.

So I awoke to my cat growling, his ears flattened back, his little black nose pointing at the glass door to my balcony, where I'd left one of the curtains wide open. The door looked out onto a dark night, full of the crooked shadows of old oaks and magnolias dimly lit by streetlamps.

"Sh," I said, groggily patting my cat's head. "There's nothing..."

He growled again. I eased him away from my face and leaned far over the edge of my bed to drop him down onto the floorboards, since I generally try to keep some distance between my eyeballs and the claws of panicky cats.

As I pulled myself back up, I saw it looking at me from the balcony.

The face was pale white—not transparent or filmy, but a solid opaque shape, smooth and bloodless as a plastic mask, with none of the wrinkles and hairs of living flesh, nor any expression on its white lips. It was female, fading into shadows at the edges. The eyes were dark and empty.

I lay rigid with fear in my bed, caught entirely off-guard, hoping this was a dream but not really believing it.

The face floated just outside the window, disembodied. I wanted to blink it away but didn't dare take my eyes off it long enough to close my lids. Besides, blinking only works if you're dealing with something imaginary.

I had a tactical flashlight within reach, just under my bed, but I didn't want to make any sudden moves. I told my rapidly-beating heart to calm down a bit, which it failed to do, and I waited to see if my defenses would hold.

My apartment is a long, narrow studio, a somewhat refurbished loft in a small, long-disused factory. I hang the walls with folk remedies against malevolent spirits—dreamcatchers, witch balls, and so on—the trim around the windows and doors is painted haint blue, a local tradition to protect against the countless ghosts in the area.

Whether any of that helps with any particular ghost is little more than a matter of random chance, but I'd also replaced my windows and the balcony door pane with thick leaded glass, as ghost-proof as it gets. They should hold out any entities trying to slip inside my apartment.

I stared at the face, trying to identify it. I have any number of malevolent ghostly enemies out there who might want to stalk me in search of revenge, but this face didn't particularly match any of them. It was female, but because of the plaster-mask quality of the skin, and the ghost-white hair color, it did not appear any specific age.

The face remained. I eased my hand down toward the floor again, keeping my gaze locked with her dark, empty eyes. Her dead-white lips remained as flat and expressionless as the rest of her face.

I reached under my bed, and something sharp grabbed my wrist, snarling. Cats, always there to help.

"Let go!" I whispered, shaking my cat away. My fingers closed around the reassuring solid aluminum surface of my flashlight. I raised it toward the balcony door, but the face melted away before I could blast it with light. I hesitated, leaving the flashlight off, waiting to see if the face was really gone.

In moments like these, just after your glimpse of the supernatural has ended, when your skin is still cold with sweat and shock, the rational mind is sometimes desperate to assert itself. It was possible I'd imagined the apparition. I was alone, there were no other witnesses, and I'd captured no images of the strange face. I'd just awoken from a troubled sleep—of course, all my sleep is troubled, filled with nightmares of fire and the flat voices of the restless dead.

Actually, there had been one other witness.

"Thanks for the warning, Bandit," I whispered. The cat let out a quick snarl, keeping himself hidden below the bed.

I slowly sat up and placed my bare feet on the creaky old floorboards. Flashlight in hand, I crossed to the glass balcony door and looked out.

My light revealed nothing on the shallow balcony outside, except the usual folding lawn chair that took up more than half the floor space out there. The balcony was just big enough for one person, one cat, one cup of coffee, one paperback or magazine. Nice black iron railing, though.

I was tense, expecting the face to jump out at me as I stood close to the glass.

Encountering nothing, I hurried to close the thick blackout curtain across the balcony door. I tied it to the matching one on the opposite side—none of those inch-wide gaps of darkness between the curtains for me. I usually keep them shut tight at night, but I'd obviously forgotten to do it before falling asleep.

Once the curtain was in place, I checked my other windows to make sure their curtains were completely shut, too. I didn't want Lady White Mask looking in at me again. I even covered my mirror with a spare bedsheet just to be safe.

I didn't sleep well. The face kept appearing every time I closed my eyes, floating in the darkness behind my eyelids just as it had floated in the darkness beyond the glass door.

Resisting the urge to call another human being for comfort at four in the morning, I turned on the television instead. Waking up

Michael or Stacey to tell them I was scared of a ghost would just make me look silly. I hunted ghosts for a living. If ghosts had heads, my walls would be covered with mounted ghost heads. Okay, that sounds pretty scary and kind of gross, but anyway, I could handle a little late-night fright by myself.

I searched for some programming that would definitely not make me think of the unhappy dead or strange faces peering into windows. I landed on a PBS show about meerkats, little adorable fuzzy creatures that build elaborate tunnel warrens. Perfect.

As meerkats eventually gave way to orca mating songs, I still couldn't shake the creepy feeling inspired by that face, nor could I figure out who it might have been.

The next morning, as scheduled, Stacey and I traveled to the home of one of the city's most famous ghosts, the sweet-faced, golden-haired young lady named Abigail Bowen—or, more colloquially, "Stabby Abby." The site was one of the must-see locations on any major ghost tour of Savannah, but I'd never investigated it before. I wondered if Stabby Abby was the same entity who'd showed up on my balcony the night before. I hoped not. That ghost had a bit of a reputation, as her nickname would suggest.

## Chapter Two

"So we're trying to catch a really big fish this time, huh? I wonder why they'd want to get rid of such a famous ghost. Seems like it would be bad for business," Stacey said as I eased the van down Gaston Street, alongside the sprawling tree-shaded green space of Forsyth Park. A number of sizable antique homes lined the street, most of them residential, a couple of them converted to bed and breakfasts or schmancy office space.

"We don't know that they want us to get rid of her," I said. "There could be other problem ghosts. Plus, it's almost October, so they could be bringing us in for some kind of Halloween publicity stunt. Maybe they'll want us to find some video or audio evidence of Stabby Abby they can share with tourists."

"And you're okay with that kind of publicity-stunt work?" Stacey asked.

"I'm always okay with working for a five-star luxury hotel. At least the checks probably won't bounce."

We parked in an alley a few blocks from our destination and hoofed it up the shady, tree-lined sidewalks, passing mansion after mansion, garden after garden.

The Lathrop Grand dominated most of a city block, a four-story behemoth of faded brickwork with prominent verandas and balconies on the second and third floor, their wrought-iron columns and balustrades brimming with intricate black curls. The hotel was one of the city's oldest and had been featured as a haunted and/or historic destination all over the basic-cable spectrum, from SyFy and Chiller to the Travel Channel and Destination America. It was a beautiful and genteel old place believed to house a number of ghosts, including Stabby Abby herself. She was a famous murderer, but her ghost was said to be mostly benign, though over the years she'd terrified a number of guests into taking a very early check-out time, like two or three a.m.

The hotel attracted guests from all over who hoped for a glimpse of the ghost. Maybe it would be our job to provide that. I couldn't say for sure, because the hotel manager had been very cagey on the phone, asking for discretion while disclosing no details.

We were walking into this meeting fairly blind. Fine with me—as I'd told Stacey, I didn't mind the whole whisper-drama routine on the manager's part as long as the hotel could afford a sizable fee. Many of our clients are people struggling financially, trapped in their haunted homes by mortgages or the simple cost of moving. Consequently we can't realistically bill them too much, and our fees tend to arrive in small, irregular payments here and there.

Stacey and I passed window boxes full of pansies and snapdragons, mounted under large spotless panes that offered glimpses into the spacious hotel lobby. A brick archway marked the front entrance to the weathered but stately old hotel. The glass double doors under the arch didn't make a sound when we pushed them open.

The lobby was two stories high, with a grand staircase sweeping up to the second level, all of it glowing in the late-afternoon sunlight and echoing with soft piano music. The floor was marble tile, mostly white but interspersed with the occasional square of pink or black. A huge, empty fireplace loomed at one side of the room, its mantle decorated with bowls of bright flowers and baskets of miniature pumpkins and Indian corn.

We made our way past a sitting area with straight-backed chairs and a Victorian-style sofa arranged on a muted rug—overall, the lobby looked like the parlor at somebody's wealthy grandma's house. There were more flowers, plus mirrors and fragile china and porcelain decorations, including a few creepy dolls in stiff dresses perched on one bookshelf.

"Of course, we cannot guarantee that any guest will see a ghost," said a voice with a lilting accent that immediately conjured images of sunlight and sparkling ocean water. The smiling young man behind the front counter, dressed in a black blazer and tie with his hair in a number of short braids, sounded like he was from somewhere in the Caribbean. He faced a middle-aged couple across the counter.

"We asked for the most haunted room you've got," said the male half of the couple—denim vest, faded Black Sabbath t-shirt, gray ponytail and beard. His wife wore heavy black eyeliner and dark gray eye shadow, and her long, poofy salt-and-pepper hair looked as if it had been glued in place with half a bottle of hairspray. She wore Doc Martins and tight black jeans with a studded metal belt under a crop top, clearly happy to let her belly muffin out all over the place.

"Room 208 itself has been reserved for months, of course," the clerk said, smiling a little wider. "It's our most requested room. We have you in 212 on the same hall."

"What about the fourth floor?" Big Hairspray Lady asked, her voice hushed, as if speaking of an ancient curse, or maybe somebody who was expected to die in the very near future.

"The fourth is still closed for renovations," he told them.

"But we can explore around? Take all the pictures we want?" Ponytail Man asked, thumping a camera bag strapped over his shoulder.

"Of course," the clerk replied. "Except for the fourth floor. But you're welcome to photograph the library, the art gallery, the courtyard—"

"We want the *haunted* areas," said Big Hairspray Lady.

"Ghosts have been seen in every hall, on every floor," the clerk explained. "And in the stairways."

"Have you ever seen one?" Ponytail Man asked the clerk.

"I've heard them," the clerk said with a grin. "They like to walk around late at night."

"I bet you're more sensitive because of your background," Big Hairspray Lady said.

The clerk's eyebrows rose just a hair. According to the little gold bar on his lapel, his name was Steve. "My background?" he asked.

"Aren't you Haitian? Or Jamaican?"

"Crucian," he said, his professional smile beginning to falter a bit.

"What does that mean?" she asked.

"It means I'm from Zimbabwe," he replied, keeping his face perfectly straight. I tried not to laugh, since "Crucian" refers to someone from the Caribbean island of St. Croix, thousands of miles from Zimbabwe.

"Oh, well, Africa is very spiritual, too," the woman said. "Lots of people who still talk to the spirits of nature and ancestors—"

"Let's get moving, Carla," Ponytail Man nudged her, glancing back at us. "There's a line."

"We'll talk later," Big Hairspray Lady said to the clerk, whispering loud enough for the whole room to hear.

"I look forward to it," the clerk replied, smiling as Ponytail Man and Big Hairspray Lady walked off to the elevators.

Steve the clerk gave Stacey and me the same broad, professional smile and said, "Welcome to the Lathrop Grand...y'all." The last word came after half a beat, as though he were still learning to tack it onto the greeting, a mismatch for his island accent. "What can I do for you?"

"I'm Ellie Jordan with Eckhart Investigations," I said. "We have an appointment with Madeline Colt."

"Of course. Just a moment, please." He picked up a phone from behind the counter, punched a button, and turned slightly away to murmur into it. His accent might have been fresh from the sparkling waters of the Caribbean, but he clearly wasn't new to the hospitality industry, with such powers as speaking low enough that we couldn't hear him from two feet away, while apparently his boss on the other end could hear him fine. He nodded before hanging up. "She's on her way," he said.

"Thanks," I said.

"So, Saint Croix sounds nice," Stacey said, giving the young man a big smile. "I think my cousin has a house there. That's the one with Blackbeard's Castle, right?"

"You mean Saint Thomas," he replied. "Saint Croix is the one with the nicer beaches and prettier girls."

"Oh." Stacey blushed a little.

"Have you really seen ghosts?" I asked. "Or is that something you're supposed to tell the tourists?"

"That depends," Steve said. "Are you a tourist?"

I laughed a little, and he was saved from having to give a real answer by the arrival of the hotel's general manager. I'd spoken with her on the phone the previous day, but only very briefly. She looked to be in her mid-forties, carefully styled platinum blond hair that just grazed the shoulders of her black blazer. She had a quick smile, but her eyes seemed cold and distant as she examined Stacey and me. They were a green hue that made me think of bottle glass. Sharp little chunks of bottle glass. Her accent was from somewhere deep in Texas.

"It's so nice to meet you! I'm Madeline. Which one's Ellie?" she asked, glancing between us.

"That's me," I said, then quickly introduced Stacey Tolbert, my tech manager, protege, apprentice, and person who's in charge of making coffee at the office.

"Come along this way. Any trouble finding the place?" Madeline asked. We passed around the grand front stairs and into a broad hallway paneled with dark old wood and softly lit by sconces near the twelve-foot ceiling. Paintings of gardens and women in antebellum dresses adorned the walls, overlooking antique high-backed chairs, upholstered benches, and potted trees.

"No, ma'am. The Lathrop is famous," I said.

"Oh, goodness, you don't have to call me 'ma'am.' Here we are." Madeline touched the dark wood paneling, and a door-sized rectangle of the wall swung inward. She gave us a knowing smile as she led us through the hidden door into a narrow hallway. The marble tiles on the floor gave way to scuffed hardwood as we passed through, and the ceiling dropped a bit. Bland fluorescents lit the concealed passage, glowing dully on its plain white plaster walls.

"That's pretty cool," Stacey said, while we passed closed doors and turned down another narrow, windowless hall.

"Jib doors are everywhere in the hotel," Madeline said. "The design philosophy was for the staff to appear and vanish as quickly as possible. This inner cluster of rooms and stairways would keep guests and workers from rubbing too many elbows." She opened what looked like a tall, narrow cabinet, but turned out to be the doorway to steep wooden stairs leading up to the next floor. "The staff can move invisibly through the hotel, even from floor to floor."

"Like ghosts," Stacey said, grinning.

"These inner rooms must have been dark in the days before electricity," I said.

"I'm not sure how they handled that. The hotel's been remodeled a few times in its life. To be altogether honest, I'm just beginning to learn the history of this place. I've only been GM for three weeks—they transferred me from the Burlingame House in Asheville—have you ever been to Asheville? It's so pretty. Of course, Savannah's pretty, too, in so many ways, and I couldn't be prouder that the partners chose me for this opportunity..."

As we passed through the narrow, dark inner passageways, I glanced through an ajar door and saw a man in a starched white chef's jacket loading a covered tray into a stainless steel dumbwaiter. A busy kitchen area lay behind him. The tantalizing smell of fresh-baked bread wafted out, reminding me that I'd only had a cup of yogurt for breakfast.

Madeline pulled open another door and waved us into a spacious office. Early-afternoon sunlight filled the office through a pair of tall windows. The décor was similar to the hotel lobby, with lots of antique furniture and bowls of flowers on the mantel above the old brick fireplace, which was spotless, and so probably hadn't been used in decades.

The panel of wall through which we'd entered, including chair rail and baseboard, silently closed behind Madeline as she stepped into the room. Another, more traditional door was built into another wall.

"Please have a seat." Madeline indicated a few high-backed chairs facing an old ornate desk with sculpted, bowed legs, carved to look like stern women in Victorian dresses. "Sorry to take you through the shortcut, but otherwise it's a long way around."

"It was fun!" Stacey said. "I've wanted to explore this hotel since I saw it on *Haunted Places*."

"Can I get you ladies anything? Coffee, tea, sparkling water?"

"We're fine, thank you," I told her. I brought out my notepad while she took her seat across from us. "Why don't you tell us a little bit about the problems you've been having?"

"Oh, honey, I will, but first I just need y'all to sign these little old non-disclosure agreements." Madeline fished a couple of thick documents and pens from a drawer and slid them over to us. The logo at the top of each document read BLACK DIAMOND PROPERTIES. "The bigwigs don't want to risk any rumors leaking out."

Stacey glanced over the document, then looked at me for guidance. I rifled through the pages for a minute.

"It looks pretty standard to me," I said, as if I'd reviewed heaps of such agreements in the past. "If you're worried about people discovering this hotel is haunted, though, I don't think you'll ever get that horse back into the barn." I thought a Texas lady might appreciate horse-related metaphors.

"Oh, I don't expect to, and we surely welcome all of our guests who want to come and try to see our resident ghosts. This is just something to make the partners feel a little more in control of the situation. You know how men are," she said, tossing me a wink with her long, thick, very likely artificial eyelashes.

"I should probably have *our* boss check this over before we sign anything," I said. I wasn't sure Calvin Eckhart, the retired homicide detective who employed Stacey and me, would be thrilled if I signed such a contract without a more careful review.

"Do what you need to, honey, but we can't proceed until those are signed."

I nodded, wondering whether this was just standard procedure for her corporate masters or if there was something specific they wanted to keep secret. Naturally, I was eager to find out what she was trying to hide, if anything. My curiosity was stoked, but I tried to tell myself there was probably nothing more than overcautious lawyers behind this.

Madeline continued smiling at us, but again I had the impression of cold, sharp green glass when I looked at her eyes. She remained silent, waiting for me to make a decision.

"I'll just call the office, if that's okay," I said, bringing out my phone.

"Oh, you just go right ahead. I would hate to waste your time coming all the way out here." The way she said it, I got the impression she was really telling *us* not to waste *her* time. Her overlarge smile seemed to confirm this.

I called the office, but Calvin didn't answer. I couldn't reach him on cell, either, but that's not surprising since he regards cell phones as the most irritating invention since the lava lamp.

That left me sitting there awkwardly, contract in front of us, Madeline's impatience growing with every second. I could tell by how her smile kept getting wider and wider as we regarded each other in silence.

I flipped through the NDA again. I told myself to stop worrying. Calvin was considering selling the detective agency to an out-of-state company called Paranormal Solutions, Inc., which I absolutely didn't want him to do. A nice infusion of cash from this high-end hotel might convince him to delay selling out a little longer.

"Okay," I said. "We'll keep your secrets. Where do I sign?"

"Just here...and here..." Madeline flipped through the pages, pointing. "And right here, sugar, just your initials is fine for that one..."

Stacey and I signed here, here, and right here, and I assumed we weren't unknowingly buying a timeshare in Weeki Wachee or transferring our savings to some Nigerian prince.

"That's all settled, then." With a quick sweep of her arm, Madeline made the contracts vanish into a drawer, then she hopped to her feet.

"We should probably get copies of those," I mentioned, standing up with her.

"Oh, I'll just email them, sugar," Madeline said, waving a dismissive hand at the closed drawer. "Lawyers worried about covering their own backsides, is all that is. I suppose I'd better show you where it happened." She pushed open the jib door in her office and stepped into the narrow service corridor behind it.

"I'm sorry?" I asked, as we followed after her. "Where what happened?"

"The..." Madeline began in a hushed voice, then spoke louder as a lady in a blue and white maid uniform passed by, pushing a custodial cart down an intersecting hallway, also narrow and windowless. "Black Diamond Properties invests in only the highest caliber of historic hotels. We bring the most advanced, modern comforts into the most beautiful antique buildings for a peak luxury guest experience."

"Oh...how interesting," I said, adjusting to her sudden change in tone. It sounded like she'd panicked at the sight of her employee and retreated into some memorized sales pitch.

"Historic hotels in historic cities, all over the Southeast," she said, while leading us to a pair of steel elevator doors. These were no-nonsense industrial doors, nothing like the embossed golden-brass doors to the guest elevator in the lobby.

"So you go from hotel to hotel, then?" I asked. "Flipping them?"

She winced a little. "Not 'flipping,' sugar, but updating, rehabbing, and beautifying. And I personally consider it an honor to help bring these historic properties back from the dead."

"The Lathrop Grand wasn't out of business, though," Stacey

said. "It wasn't dead."

"Not out of business, but certainly out of date. And the fourth floor..." She shook her head as the elevator doors opened, revealing an equally unadorned gray freight elevator car big enough to carry heavy furniture between floors.

The doors closed, and the elevator ascended to the fourth floor. I noticed that this elevator, accessible to staff only, had a basement button. The polished mechanical indicator above the guest elevator hadn't included a B.

"I promise I'm not trying to smuggle you two around by using this freight elevator," she said. "The fourth-floor button on the guest elevator has been disabled for safety. The fourth floor is not open to guests until we get it nice and fixed up."

"Is it open to us? I notice the doors are still closed," I said.

"Oh, goodness. I'm sorry." Madeline inserted a keycard into the elevator's control panel, and the doors finally opened, giving us our first view of the forbidden fourth floor.

Already it looked in disarray. Empty dark doorways in the service corridor offered glimpses of sawhorses and sheet plastic. Lumber, wood chunks, and sawdust littered the floor. A hanging strip of fluorescent stuttered reluctantly to life after Madeline jiggered the light switch a few times.

My strongest first impression was the cold, clammy air as we entered the room. The light above continued flickering, lending a strobe-like quality to our movements.

The area looked like an abandoned construction site, wires hanging from the ceiling, loose nails and screws strewn across the warped old hardwood floors. Portions of paneling had been removed from the walls.

I glanced at Stacey. She was shivering, and she nodded back at me, letting me know she felt the unnatural cold, too. I drew my flashlight from my purse in case the spotty fluorescent lighting decided to die on us altogether. My tactical flashlight is my sidearm, my first defense against unpleasant specters. A good ghost hunter never goes anywhere without one.

"It happened through here," Madeline said, her voice barely above a whisper as she led us down the corridor.

"What happened, exactly?" I asked, matching her hushed tone.

Instead of answering, she pushed open a section of wall, leading us through another of those nearly invisible jib doors meant to keep the hotel staff out of the sight of wealthy guests.

It opened onto an expansive dark space, just as cold as the first room. Madeline worked at the light switch panel and managed to bring a pair of hanging bulbs sputtering to life, though most of the bulbs in the room remained dark.

Here, the floor was tiled with dark marble, and two rows of thick columns ran the length of the room, one on either side, casting deep shadows along the walls. There were no windows. My flashlight found intricate little figures carved into the walls—men with goat horns and goat legs, women with tails, and people who looked as if they were part tree, with branches for arms or a tree trunk in place of a leg. I considered that a tree-trunk leg would be fairly inconvenient, rooting you into place. At best, all you could do was walk in a hopeless circle. More friezes depicted a hodgepodge of Egyptian-style hieroglyphs and assorted occult symbols.

I couldn't say right off whether the elaborate wall carvings were meant to be ancient and pagan or a bit more demonic than that, but clearly some skilled artist had spent a great deal of time and effort to create them, and so someone else had probably paid a lot of money for them.

Likewise, they'd paid a great deal for the marble, including the big, dusty raised dais or altar at the western end of the room.

"Here," Madeline said, then sighed.

"I feel like there's something you're not telling us," Stacey said.

"I'm sorry. This was the upper ballroom. There's a bigger, nicer ballroom on the ground floor, of course, where we have weddings and such, and our annual Halloween ball. I can't see why anyone would want to make such a dark and dreary room up here, or anywhere." Madeline shook her head, frowning as if disappointed. "Someone went to great expense to make an ugly place."

I nodded, waiting for more. Madeline struck me as the type who would plunge right ahead and keep talking to avoid any moments of quiet in the conversation.

"From what they tell me, this whole entire floor has been closed up for decades," Madeline said. "The hotel itself was in and out of business through the twentieth century, of course, and this area's just never been restored. The last owner never even fiddled with it, as far as we can tell. Just kept it closed. Restoring the fourth floor was part of the big value-add I'm supposed to be bringing here. That was the idea..." Her lip trembled. Her eyes were shiny, too, as if she were about to cry. Either she got very emotional about renovations or there was something bigger going on. "Do y'all know much about the history of this place?"

"Everybody knows at least a little bit," I said. Of course, I'd Googled it before coming to meet with the client, so the major details were fresh in my mind. "It was built in 1851 by Dr. and Mrs. Uriah and Mabel Lathrop, who wanted it to be the finest hotel in the city. And it was, or pretty close to it. Society balls and wealthy travelers. During the Civil War, it became a hospital for Confederate soldiers, then for Union soldiers after they took control of the city. Dr. Lathrop was a Confederate sympathizer but treated all the wounded equally. I guess he was more devoted to medicine than politics. The hotel was used as a hospital during the yellow fever epidemic about a decade later, but the most famous ghost comes from the Civil War period."

"Abigail Bowen," Stacey whispered, glancing into a dark corner of the bizarre temple room, as if she expected the long-dead nurse to come charging out with a scalpel at the sound of her name. I've seen stranger things happen.

"Stabby Abby," I said. "We used to have a playground jump-rope rhyme about her when I was a kid. *Nurse Stabby Abby, made the boys cry. If you ever see her, you're the next to die.*"

"Cute," Stacey commented.

"But there are other ghosts, too," Madeline said.

"Sure," I said. "Soldiers. Children who died in the epidemic. A number of ghosts have been seen or heard walking late at night. Sometimes whispering."

"I've heard them." Madeline gave a tight nod, looking pale, her bottle-green eyes wide. "More than once, when I was working late, usually in one of the upstairs hallways. I hear heavy footsteps, like someone's right behind me, but there's no one there. It gets real cold all of a sudden. I tell you, it makes my hair stand right up on end every time." She shook her head. "I heard this place was haunted before I took it over, but you never think much of stories like that. People will say just about any big old place has a ghost."

"Ghosts are more common than most people realize," I said. "If you ask around, almost everybody has a story or knows somebody who has one. Maybe seeing an apparition, or just hearing a voice or a footstep where there shouldn't be one. Maybe feeling a cold hand touch you, or a cold breath on the back of your neck, when you're alone in a room."

"Oh, honey, I know it," she said. "There was a little graveyard back home in Abilene, an overgrown place where the graves were all from the eighteen-hundreds. It was abandoned, nobody kept it up. They said if you went and sat on this big cracked slab over one of those graves, you'd feel something reach up and grab you from behind."

"Did you ever go there?" Stacey asked.

"It sounded too scary for me, but my friend Ginny went one night with some boys. Full moon and everything. She said she felt it. I never knew whether to believe her or not, and to tell the truth, I always figured it was one of those boys that grabbed her in the dark. After working here, I'm more inclined to think she was telling the truth."

"Have you had any other experiences here at the hotel?" I asked.

"Well, the voices, the occasional footstep...I always try to tell myself it must be guests or staff. We do have a lot of hidden passageways, as y'all have seen. But I can't always bring myself to believe it."

"What about this room?" I gestured around at the dark, temple-like ballroom.

"Y'all did sign the nondisclosure agreements, so I'll go ahead and get to the meat of it, but you have to promise this information stays with you."

"Of course," I said.

She took a deep breath. "All right now. You see, I've had the toughest time keeping contractors at work up here. The first company just flat quit, saying the workers refused to come up here anymore. They said they felt like they were being watched and harassed, all their tools getting rearranged or disappearing, and they'd come in the morning to find their past day's work all wrecked. Then that second company I hired to replace the first..."

"Go on," I said.

"It was awful. One of their men was on a stepladder, up high near the ceiling—some of the wires look like they haven't been redone up there since the hotel was first electrified—and he fell right over. The whole ladder came down. He broke his neck and died on the spot."

"That's horrible!" Stacey said, and I nodded.

"The others said it looked like he was pushed," Madeline

continued. "Like something invisible came along and *shoved* that ladder over."

"It couldn't have just toppled over?" I asked, looking at the debris on the floor. "There's a chance it wasn't perfectly balanced, and he leaned over too far, something like that. It's a spooky environment, which might make the accident seem like something supernatural."

"These men were terrified," Madeline said. "They all refused to come back, even when I offered to pay them more. I tell you, if I don't get this place in shape and bring in more revenue, the bigwigs are going to nail my hide to the smokehouse door."

"I certainly hope that's a metaphor," I said. "We just need to consider other, less paranormal possibilities in these situations."

"This place is haunted," Madeline said. "Everybody knows it. Shoot, I saw a Travel Channel show about it."

"That's another reason people might tend to interpret events as ghost-related," I said. "But I'm not dismissing what the workers said. It's going to take some investigation. Can you give me any specific details? Things they heard or saw? Male, female, anything that could give us a lead on the ghost's identity?"

Madeline shook her head. "They didn't tell me much."

"Can you give me the contractor's contact information?"

"I surely will. It's important you keep it quiet about the poor fella dying. The bigwigs want the whole situation sealed up tighter than a Ziploc full of caviar."

"Understood," I said. "We'll be happy to look into this for you. Our usual process is to identify the ghost first, because that makes it much easier to trap it. In this case, we could be elbow-deep in ghosts at this hotel, so it might take a while."

"Don't you think Abigail Bowen did it?" Madeline asked.

"Stabby Abby is obviously a clear suspect, given what she did in life," I said. "But we don't want to jump to conclusions. From what I understand, people have been seeing her in this hotel for decades without being harmed by those encounters."

"Isn't she the one that grabs people's arms while they sleep?" Stacey asked.

"Hotel guests sometimes wake up with an arm extended away from the bed, held by cold fingers they can't see. Like a nurse checking their pulse," I said.

"Y'all seem to know more about it than I do," Madeline said.

"I'm just catching up."

"Abigail worked as a nurse for Dr. Lathrop during the war," I told her. "They say he treated Northern and Southern soldiers equally, but apparently Abigail was a devout Confederate. One night, she murdered a number of recovering soldiers in their hospital beds. She cut their throats with a scalpel. I think it was seventeen men she killed."

"My word!" Madeline said. "I didn't realize it was so many."

"Kind of makes that whole checking-your-pulse-in-your-sleep thing a little scarier," Stacey said. "Maybe she's checking whether she needs to kill you."

"This is just awful," Madeline said.

"She hasn't hurt anyone before," I reminded them. "Something has changed. Maybe it's the attempted renovations on the fourth floor."

"I can't give up on four," Madeline said. "The bigwigs would drench me in honey and throw me to the wolverines."

"You can assure them we're on the case," I said.

"Yeah...that brings me to another point. I need you to avoid speaking to anyone else about this. You see...my bosses back at the head office..."

"They don't know you're hiring us?" I offered.

"Exactly." Her shoulders slumped a little, and her smile wavered under her thick lipstick. "I know the problem is related to the haunting...or I *think* it is...but just try convincing those old men. I didn't even want to bring it up. I'm expensing your detective agency as 'security consultants.' Checking how secure our guests are against intruders and such. So maybe y'all could stick with that little story if it comes up somehow?"

"Absolutely," I said. "But we'll need to speak with some of the hotel staff. Preferably long-timers who can give us some insight on what's normal around here and what isn't."

"I'll see what I can do, but you'll have to be discreet and keep all that to a minimum," she said. "The staff say things have gotten much worse since we took over the hotel. Certainly a lot of complaints from guests, too. Whispers in their ears, scary things walking down the halls. Mirrors and drinking glasses just up and shattering right in front of them. The staff said it was never so bad before. I've had three people quit in the last three weeks."

"I understand. We'll have to figure out what kicked things up so much, but I'm betting the renovations have something to do with it," I said. "Our first step would be an overnight observation. We'd like to have some thermal cameras watching the haunted hotspots around the building."

"The hauntspots," Stacey said, nodding. I don't particularly like that term she coined, but I have to admit it saves a couple of syllables.

"You can do what you like up here on four, but we need to keep things calm and quiet for the guests on the other floors," Madeline said.

"Any chance we could investigate Room 208?" I asked. It was the most famous room in the hotel. "If we're trying to see what Abigail is up to..."

"I'm afraid we have guests there now," Madeline said. "People reserve that room months in advance hoping to see her ghost. I'll let you know if they leave early or switch rooms in the middle of the night. I hear guests in that room do it all the time."

"Maybe we'll get lucky and they'll run away screaming, then," I said. "I promise we'll keep things low-key. We'll need to set up a nerve center to monitor all our audio and video feeds. Usually we just park our van outside, but with this level of possible danger, I'd rather have Stacey somewhere inside the hotel in case I need help. That will help with the discretion aspect, too. Plus, your parking situation is not great here..."

Madeline nodded. "All right. How about I give y'all a couple of rooms on the third floor, maybe by the stairs?"

"That would be perfect," I said. "Thank you."

Madeline pushed open the wall panel, but I remained, looking around the room for a moment. Despite its size, it was hard to imagine it as a functioning ballroom. Those two rows of columns kept the room cluttered and claustrophobic. They were wide and built closely together, reminding me of the columns in ancient Egyptian temples whose architects hadn't yet discovered the magical power of the arch to help create open, airy spaces. Not that I've ever been to Egypt, but I do read *National Geographic*.

I couldn't picture a crowd of people dancing in this space, not without constantly bouncing like pinballs between the tightly clustered columns. The area at the center was long and narrow, terminating at the huge raised altar, big enough for a three-piece band, flanked by more of the thick columns. The wall behind the altar was intricately sculpted, but I couldn't see any details from where I stood.

"Ellie?" Stacey nudged me with her elbow, in a let's-not-space-out-in-front-of-the-client sort of way. Madeline, for her part, stood in the service hallway beyond the jib door, holding it open for us and giving me a puzzled look.

"I don't think this is really a ballroom," I said to Stacey as we walked out.

"What is it, then?" Stacey asked. "A skating rink? Bowling alley?"

"I'm not sure, but we need to figure it out."

After we left, the concealed door creaked its way shut, as though something unseen had lurked in the shadows, watching us, waiting for us to depart.

# Chapter Three

"Score!" Stacey said, just after opening the door to our hotel room on the third floor. As promised, it was close to a hidden service stairwell, giving us quick and discreet access to the closed fourth floor. We'd already gone to our office to stock up on gear, plus I'd fed and watered my cat. Now the sun had gone down and the sky was deep purple.

Stacey was clearly responding to the sight of the room—vases stuffed with flowers on the mantel over the brick fireplace, fine rugs on the hardwood floor, a four-poster bed dripping with lace curtains. An antique rosewood armoire stood in the corner, next to a matching writing desk with a deeply upholstered chair. Wrought-iron French doors soaked the room in orange late-afternoon sunlight and offered access to a veranda outside, which had a matching railing of spiraling, curling black iron. The open bathroom door revealed a clawfoot tub on a tiled granite floor. A connecting door led to another hotel room that Madeline had provided for me.

"Looks nice," I said.

"That was a stroke of genius, Ellie, getting us rooms here." She flopped back on the ornate bed, spreading out her arms. "It's so nice. Do you think we get room service? Spa privileges? I saw a sign offering mud masks and pedicures."

"I doubt those are included," I said, setting my armload of gear onto the nearest rug. Madeline had given us staff access cards so we could use the hidden freight elevator and windowless service hallways at the core of the building. She obviously wanted us to stay as invisible as the hotel's custodians and room-service waiters— probably even more so.

"How long do you think this case will take to solve? Please say months." Stacey hopped to her feet, then unlatched and opened the French doors to let in the cool evening air. The smell of roses wafted in from outside, probably from the window boxes elsewhere around the hotel.

"Close it up," I said. "We share that veranda with several other rooms. Madeline wants us to keep a lid on things, remember?"

"Or the bigwigs at the head office will whup her with an ugly stick and tie her to a wagon, or some other folksy form of torture." Stacey drawled out her soft Alabama accent into a deep Texas one. She closed the veranda doors again. "Okay, so where are you going to sleep? I call this room."

"We aren't being paid to sleep."

"If you think I'm not crashing on that sweet down mattress as soon as the sun comes up, you're crazy," she said. "I'm staying right here for the whole investigation, thanks."

"You might change your mind after Stabby Abby tries to slash your throat."

Stacey went a little pale, the color seeping away from her suntanned cheeks. "You just took, like, ninety percent of the fun out of this, Ellie."

"If we run into a murderous ghost, that other ten percent won't last long, either. Come on, let's go grab the rest of our gear."

Even with the rolling luggage rack we'd borrowed, it took a few trips to carry everything upstairs, and I was grateful for the freight elevator. By the time we were done, the pleasant, antique-filled hotel room looked more like a Radio Shack storage room, cluttered with video cameras, microphones, monitors, and spools of black cable.

Madeline had provided Stacey access codes to the hotel's system of tiny security cameras mounted in the corridors and stairwells, so we had plenty of basic black and white video to monitor. None of those cameras had ever been installed on the fourth floor, though. They'd only been installed in the most public areas of the lower floors, so naturally we didn't get views of any guest rooms or the spa that Stacey was so eager to try out.

"I'd like to get a couple thermals or something into the second and third floors, just the hallways," I said. "Do you think we can rig that up in a way nobody will notice?"

"No problem," Stacey said. She was already getting to work, opening up the armoire and setting up little monitors on the shelves. "I'll just have to grab a stepladder, my drill, and my secret undercover electrician's coveralls."

"You actually have those?"

"Nah, but it would be neat if I did, right? Let's go."

A few minutes later, after borrowing a stepladder from the custodial staff, we emerged through another jib door on the second floor into a spacious corridor with a hardwood floor and red carpet runner, softly illuminated by high sconces in the walls. Guest room doors ran along the wall across from us. Every floor seemed to be laid out this way—guest rooms and other guest areas along the outside of the building, where they could enjoy windows and light, while the hotel staff moved in the cramped hidden rooms and hallways at the center of the building.

"There it is," I said to Stacey, nodding as we passed the infamous Room 208, where Stabby Abby was seen most often. "That was Abigail's room when she was alive and working as a nurse here." I pointed to the hotel's small black ball of a security camera mounted high in the corner of the hallway, just below the ceiling, tucked away where most people wouldn't even notice it. "Here you go. Step right up."

Stacey climbed the stepladder, holding our smallest thermal camera. She set about attaching it to the mount for the existing security camera.

The guest elevator dinged softly, and a moment later a middle-aged man in a Brooks Brothers suit emerged from around the corner, accompanied by a young woman in a peach sundress. He paused to frown at Stacey and me, and I gave him an apologetic smile as Stacey's drill bit whined overhead.

He said nothing, just led the woman into a room—216, not the infamous 208—and slammed the door as if annoyed.

Less than a minute later, a portion of the wall paneling opened and a tall, broad-shouldered, borderline albino man in a dark blue suit stepped out, looking us over, his thin lips bent into a deep frown.

The name CONRAD was displayed on a brass name tag at his lapel.

"Security." He squinted up at Stacey, then pointed at the big luggage cart full of electronics. "What's all this?"

"Ah..." Stacey said, unhelpfully, then looked at me.

"We're security consultants from Eckhart Investigations." I opened my purse and passed him a card. "Madeline Colt hired us."

He nodded, but his facial expression didn't lighten up. "She mentioned you would be here. I was just expecting..."

"Males?" I asked.

"I assumed." He placed the card carefully inside his coat pocket, as if he meant to study it later. "What exactly *are* you doing?"

"Testing a few enhanced digital security measures," I said. "Just trying to make your job easier."

I meant for the comment to please him a bit, but it seemed to have the opposite effect. He narrowed his eyes, and a muscle in his jaw flexed as if he were biting down on some anger issues.

"Finish quickly," he said. "You must stay out of the guests' way at all times." Then he turned and stepped back through the door. The section of wood paneling closed, leaving the jib door all but invisible again.

"He's a friendly type," Stacey said. "Like Lurch from *The Munsters*."

"You mean *The Addams Family*."

"Pretty sure it was *The Munsters*." Stacey stepped off the ladder. No ghost had showed up to give her a shove. She checked her tablet, and there we were, two glowing red forms in the cool blue air-conditioned hallway. "So when do we bring Jacob in?" she asked.

"Whenever we have some idea of what's going on," I said. "Come on, let's wire the hallways approaching our room. I don't want any nasties sneaking up on us late at night."

After setting up a couple of cameras and a microphone on the third floor, it was time to head up to the fourth. Night had just fallen, but it was probably too early for any major ghostly activity yet. Then again, the workman had been killed during the daytime, so all bets were off as far as that went.

The freight elevator shuddered, almost making me lose my footing, then stopped with a metallic bang as it hit the fourth floor. The elevator hadn't given us any trouble on the lower floors, but it seemed to react poorly to being sent up to four. The lights sputtered as the metal doors screeched open.

"It's hard to imagine they want to turn this into luxury suites," Stacey said, her voice low as we emerged into the dark, chaotic construction zone.

"This is just the service area," I reminded her.

"It must have been miserable working here back in the day, without sunlight or fresh air..."

"Or air conditioning. It was probably boiling hot in the summers."

"So where do we start?"

"Let's try the Ballroom of Darkness." I led the way through the jib door we'd used earlier, into the strange dark-marble room with far too many columns. It felt much colder than it had during the daytime. All the light came from those two bulbs hanging from missing panels of the pressed-tin ceiling. Darkness shrouded every wall and corner. I clicked on my flashlight, but the gloom remained. I noticed some deep, rusty holes in the floor, like some kinds of poles or supports had once been mounted in a large circle at the center of the room.

"I have a bad feeling about this," Stacey whispered.

"A disembodied murderer may have killed a man here last week. You *should* have a bad feeling."

"Thanks for the reassurance, Coach."

Moving quietly, we set up thermal and night vision cameras on opposite ends of the room, as well as a high-powered microphone in the center. We wanted to keep close watch for any entities hanging around the possible murder scene. I had the feeling that something was there in the shadows around the room, watching us as we prepared to watch the room, but it could have been nerves.

"Now what?" Stacey asked, still whispering.

"We'd better poke around," I said. "See if we find any other creepy rooms up here."

"I don't think that will take very long..." Stacey turned a slow circle, her flashlight playing along the dark wood and marble of the walls. "Um, I'm not seeing any other doors out of here."

"There must be another jib door somewhere. I'll feel my way blindly along this wall, you feel your way blindly along that one." I indicated the two long walls, largely concealed from us by the densely packed columns. "If something grabs you, scream."

"Very funny."

We pressed our way along the walls, my fingers running over the raised texture of inscribed symbols that included stylized stars, spirals, and assorted symbols that reminded me of the sigils and pentacles found in the *Key of Solomon,* jumbles of curls and arrows that supposedly represent the names of angels and demons. The wall also featured open hands with eyes at the palm, clearly based on the Middle Eastern hamsa symbol that supposedly protects against the evil eye.

"Um, hey, Ellie?" Stacey said, speaking as low as she could from across the room.

I turned, but one of those columns blocked my view. I had to step around to see her leaning against her wall, studying the symbols.

"Did you find a door?"

"No, just wondering what's up with these weird symbols everywhere."

"They're a mishmash of Far East, Near East, and European religious and magical signs. If I had to guess, this room was designed by Ithaca Galloway, or some of her Spiritualist pals and hangers-on."

"And she was...?" Stacey rubbed her temple as if trying to remember.

"The Lathrop Grand Hotel closed with Mabel Lathrop's death in 1881," I said. "It sat idle for years, but was finally purchased by Ithaca Galloway, a wealthy widow from Boston. She was deep into the whole Spiritualist movement, with speaking to the dead and automatic writing and so on. Rumors of ghosts in the old hotel brought her here. She rebuilt and restored the hotel—electricity and running water, all the fancy stuff—and moved into it along with a small court of supposed mediums, psychics, hypnotists and palm readers, a crazy crew. The entire fourth floor was private apartments for her and her friends."

"So they built this freaky temple up here for their occult activities," Stacey said, looking around and shivering. "There's no telling what happened in here."

"Séances, rituals, conjuring evil spirits, blood sacrifice—" I began.

"I said 'no telling'!" Stacey snapped. "They seriously did blood sacrifices up here?"

"No one knows for sure," I said, giving it my best melodramatic movie-trailer voice-over imitation. "Seriously, though, Spiritualism itself didn't involve that...but it was a weird, culty time in American history, and we don't know what Ithaca and her psychics might have gotten themselves into. We'll need to hit the library pretty hard."

"Ugh. Let's find the next haunted room already." Stacey resumed poking and prying along the wall, and I did the same on my side. "So whatever happened to Ithaca what's-her-name?"

"Galloway. She died somewhere around 1920. The hotel changed owners a few times and had an upswing during Prohibition, when all the hidden passages and secret rooms probably came in handy. Remember Prohibition began in Georgia in 1908 and wasn't repealed until 1935. The Great Depression put the hotel out of business. It opened and closed throughout the twentieth century, slowly getting updated along the way."

"Except this floor," Stacey said. "Nothing about this says 'updated.' I didn't know we were stepping into such a crazy situation."

"This hotel, and this floor in particular, would have been a real hotbed of supernatural activity in its day."

"Yeah, I'm picking up on that, thanks. Next time I'll remember to do more prelim research and spend less time playing *The Sims*. I mean, um, testing and calibrating our gear..."

"Right. We're lucky so much was available online."

"Send me some links and I'll catch up—ah!" Stacey shouted as a heavy scraping sound echoed through the temple room.

I spun around with my flashlight to see her stumble briefly and regain her balance. Stacey had reached the end of the long room across from the raised dais. Two big rectangles had opened in the wall before her, a pair of concealed double doors leading into deep darkness.

"Are you okay?" I asked.

"Yeah...I don't think I'm going to like this, though." She pointed her light into the space beyond the door. "Hurry up, Ellie, I'm getting the creepy-crawlies pretty bad over here."

"What do you see?" I hurried to join her, merging my flashlight beam with hers.

The hallway beyond was in an exquisite state of decay, with crumbling molding and warped floorboards made of heavy dark wood. More marble trimmed the walls and corners. Somebody must have had the famous marble quarries in Pickens County working overtime when these rooms were built. The ceiling was arched but fairly low—I could just about reach up and brush my fingers along the heavy wooden beams.

Curved wooden doors were sunken at regular intervals along the walls, in shadowy alcoves, making me think of some medieval monastery. I looked through one and saw a cell of a room with brick walls, a chair, and a small writing desk, the meager furniture thick with dust and cobwebs.

We moved from room to room, rolling the cart of gear with us, opening the heavy, creaking doors when we could—many of them were locked with old-fashioned keyholes instead of modern card readers, so our staff keycards weren't much help. Of the rooms we could open, some were nearly empty, while others had a jumble of furnishings, mirrors, and trunks, as though they'd been hastily designated as storage areas. Dust and cobwebs were everywhere, and the lights in the rooms didn't seem to function. The air was thick and stale, with a tang of dry rot.

"Are any of these rooms creepy enough for you?" Stacey whispered.

"Ha ha," I said, but I was whispering, too. There was a heavy sense of presence in the hallway, the feeling of something malevolent nearby, stalking us, waiting and watching. The atmosphere was silent, despite the three floors of busy hotel below. The heavy walls and floors seemed to seal out all sound, except for our own footsteps and voices.

As we looked into one of the old rooms, decorated with an old bed frame, the sound of whispering echoed from somewhere out in the hall. It was like a group of people speaking to each other in low, hushed tones.

"What is that?" Stacey whispered. She looked ashen.

"I don't know." I gestured to the door and we stepped out into the hall. The voices stopped abruptly. It was that feeling of walking into a room and everybody goes silent, as if they were all gossiping about you.

Then the door we'd just left slammed shut behind us, making us jump. I may have cried out a little in surprise and fear. I'm not perfect.

"There was nobody in that room," Stacey whispered, pointing her flashlight at the closed door. "Right?"

More doors slammed shut, up and down the hall in both directions, every door we'd managed to open as we explored the fourth floor.

A wave of cold raised bumps all over my skin. It was

accompanied by whispers, multiple voices that seemed to scatter through the air around us, their words too low to understand. It was as though a flock of invisible birds blew past us on either side, cawing at us with throaty scratching noises. Something narrow and freezing, like a dead man's finger, brushed against my cheek, but I didn't see anything there.

The voices faded away down the hall. The coordinated slamming of the doors in both directions at the same time, and the multiple overlapping voices, made me think there had been two or more active entities involved.

Stacey gaped at me, her mouth open in shock. She didn't seem to be in the mood for more exploration—and neither was I, to be honest. I wanted to go somewhere with bright lights and lots of people. Even waiting in line at the DMV would have been more pleasant.

"Okay, let's set up some cameras right here," I said. "That should be enough to get us started. I'd rather wait until daylight before we come back to this floor. It's crazy active already."

"Are you still planning to spend the rest of the night up here?" Stacey asked. "Maybe I should stay with you."

"I'll think about it," I said. I certainly wasn't looking forward to it. As we got to work with the cameras and tripods, I remained wary, waiting for the presences to return. I'd never doubted that the hotel was haunted, but it was abnormal for the entities to start leaping out at us so quickly. Ghost hunting usually involves a lot of watching and waiting—and when it doesn't, you can bet there's danger ahead.

## Chapter Four

Our cheerful hotel room on the third floor was a welcome sight. I instantly found myself breathing easier, my overloaded heartbeat slowing to something approaching normal.

"I'm starving. Should we have supper at Mabel's? Scope the place out?" Mabel's was the restaurant on the first floor, named after one of the hotel's founders, itself a five-star restaurant with a Lowcountry-Asian fusion theme. I wondered what that entailed.

I didn't disagree with Stacey's rush to change the subject to something less ghost-related. Otherwise, we might have to talk about what we'd just experienced upstairs.

"Depends who's buying," I said. "If it's me, we can get take-out Chinese right down the street. Walking distance, even."

"Oh, come on! This is the fanciest hotel in the Historic District. We should take advantage." She looked at me for a long moment, then sighed. "Fine. My treat."

"Sounds great. I don't want to die on an empty stomach." I headed for the door.

"Uh...Ellie?"

I spun around, grabbing my flashlight. My eyes darted to the closet, the mirror, the dark space under the bed. "What?"

"I'm pretty sure they have a dress code," she said.

I glanced down at my jeans and my clunky utility belt, hung with dual flashlight holsters. "Is this not what A-list celebrities wear to dinner?"

"I'm just going to change real quick." Stacey removed a black cocktail dress from her luggage.

"Why did you bring evening wear for a case?"

"I thought we might want to blend in with the guests at some point. And I was totally right. Do you have anything?"

"I guess I have some black slacks..."

"Here." Stacey brought out a pink top and pitched it to me. It was light and soft in my hands, made of thin cashmere. "Toss that on."

I sighed. I wasn't a big fan of pink or other extremely bright colors—they're like waving a flag asking for attention in public, when I would rather stay somewhere close to invisible, especially while on a case. Still, it was much nicer than anything I'd stuffed into my suitcase on my way out the door. A bit nicer than anything I owned, really.

Stacey called ahead to make reservations, then we headed downstairs. The front portion of the restaurant was a bar and lounge area where a finely dressed woman who looked about ninety years old played softly at a grand piano, filling the room with a peaceful sound.

We ordered drinks at the bar—sweet tea for me, mainly for the caffeine—then sat on a paisley sofa with arms thicker than my whole body, waiting for our table. We listened to the pianist and people-watched. The crowd was well-dressed, in a conservative and muted way, mostly couples.

Paintings and photographs of the hotel, particularly black and white pictures of the lounge itself, decorated one wall. The pictures included fedora-clad men in suits, uniformed soldiers and sailors from the world wars, a very young Ray Charles, and yellowed images of people in nineteenth-century garb. More recent pictures showed crowds in tuxedos, gowns, and masks at the hotel's famous annual Halloween ball, something to capitalize on all the ghost-curious tourists in town for the season.

An oil painting of a plump, red-cheeked woman in a big antebellum hoop skirt, standing by the fireplace in the big first-floor ballroom, presided above all of them. A plate identified her as MABEL LATHROP, who'd founded the hotel along with her doctor husband.

"What else should we expect from the fourth floor?" Stacey whispered. "I don't remember reading anything about it. I saw the Destination America show a year or so ago, but I'm pretty iffy about the details now..."

"I haven't seen the fourth floor mentioned much, either," I said. "I think they let the tourists and the ghost-hunter shows focus on the lower floors."

"Like whatever is on four is too awful to tell people about..."

"Or they just don't want images of that floor getting out because it's hideous and in bad shape. People might think the whole hotel is outdated and falling apart."

The hostess fetched us from the lounge and led us to our table. Candles flickered above white tablecloth.

"You should find an excuse to bring Michael in on this case," Stacey said. "This place is romantic as all get-out."

"I told you my policy on that," I said. "I don't want to put him in danger."

"Wouldn't want to put your big, strong firefighter in harm's way."

"Exactly. He's in harm's way enough without me dragging him to meet all of the most dangerous and restless spirits in town."

"Well, it's a missed opportunity," Stacey said. "This place is so nice. Can we call Jacob yet? *Somebody* needs to get some romance out of this situation."

The restaurant's blue-crab sushi sounded interesting, so I decided to try it. Stacey ordered a pad thai dish with Southern vegetables and organic free-range chicken. The menu had no prices on it. I was glad I wasn't buying.

"So you think Ithaca Galloway and her psychic friends network are the problem here?" Stacey asked. "I wonder why all the stories focus on Abigail, then?"

"Pretty girl kills seventeen soldier boys with a scalpel," I said. "It's a flashy story."

"There must have been a lot of problems on the fourth floor, if nobody ever renovated it in the past century."

"It would be an expensive job, too. Those bedroom chambers we saw didn't have any bathrooms attached."

"Not exactly five-star accommodations."

"So you'd have to add a lot of plumbing, just to begin with. Madeline's company will need to throw a lot of money up there to make it as nice as the rest of the hotel."

Our food arrived, and it looked fantastic. The crab meat in my sushi was fresh and sweet. I tried a tiny blot of the Tabasco wasabi and found it spicy and weird.

"We can't rule out other ghosts yet," I said. "This place has a long history."

"But why did they suddenly turn violent?"

"It's hard to guess the ghosts' motives when we don't know who they are. I bet the Historical Association has a thick file on this place. I'll call Grant Patterson."

"Excuse me," a woman's voice said, just after clearing her throat. I turned to see Big Hairspray Lady in droopy ripped jeans and a Judas Priest shirt, looking at me through big black wraparound sunglasses, even though we were indoors and it was night time. Her husband sat two tables away, gray ponytail coiled around his shoulder. I wondered if that was the formal way for a man to wear his ponytail. A girl of eleven or twelve sulked at the table beside him, dressed in a bright tie-dyed shirt as if thumbing her nose at her darkly clad heavy-metal-loving parents. She tapped furiously at her phone, seemingly oblivious to the physical world around her.

"Yes?" I said.

"I couldn't help but overhear you discussing the ghosts in the hotel," she said. "Are you here with the paranormal adventure package?"

Uh-oh. Madeline had asked for discretion, and we'd just totally failed at it.

"Sorry, um, no," I said. "What's that?"

"Oh, we book them through our travel agent back home in Seattle. Ted Leibowicz?" She said it like she expected me to know her travel agent personally. I nodded. "They come bundled with reservations at a haunted hotel and haunted restaurants, several ghost tours..."

"Sounds fun," I said.

"Are you here to see Abigail, too?" she asked, but continued talking without leaving me time to answer. "Maurice—that's my husband, Maurice—Maurice and I, we've been all over. The Winchester House in California, the Magnolia Hotel in Texas, the Congress Plaza in Chicago, you name it. I think I'm a little psychic, but Maurice disagrees."

I nodded along like a bobble-headed doll. Across the restaurant, by the brick corridor to the kitchen, Madeline stood talking with an elderly Japanese chef in a white coat. Madeline kept glancing our way with a tight, nervous smile and a cold look in her eyes.

"My name's Carla," Big Hairspray Lady told me. "It's so nice to meet a few fellow spirit seekers. Should we team up?"

"Uh..." I began. "We're not really—"

"Are you the lucky ones renting 208?" she asked, breathless and excited, and I gathered this might be the real point of her approaching us.

"Sorry, no," I said. "We just happened to hear this place was haunted a few minutes ago."

"Are you sure?" She removed her shades and narrowed her eyes. "It sounded like you were speaking in-depth about it. Determining the ghosts' motives? Research at some historical society? That doesn't sound casual at all."

"You must have overheard wrong," I said.

"It's not nice to eavesdrop," Stacey added.

Carla gaped at her for a second, then scowled.

"Excuse me for existing and following my path of enlightenment," Carla said. "I hope you'll find your way to that path one day." Then she stalked back to sit with her grinning husband and totally disengaged daughter.

"We'd better wrap this up," I told Stacey, explaining about Madeline's unfriendly stare. "I think we've just annoyed the client by being out among the hotel guests."

"Why? Don't we look fabulous enough?"

"We also have information she wants to keep contained...and here she comes."

Madeline strode toward us, her shoulders squared up, not exactly jogging but not exactly strolling, either. Her smile was far from generous.

"How are your entrees this evening?" she asked us.

"Pretty amazing," Stacey said.

"We weren't planning to charge it to our rooms," I added.

Madeline waved a hand. "I'm sure you weren't. I'd be happy to arrange a discount on room service. I know you're busy, and coming all the way down here to eat must be an inconvenience."

"Oh, we don't mind!" Stacey said. "It's a lovely restaurant. So historic."

Madeline kept her eyes on me, and I nodded to indicate I'd

caught her meaning.

"Thanks so much," I said. "We'll be sure to take advantage of that."

"I know you have a lot to do. Please let me know if you have any questions at all." She turned and departed quickly, making it clear that any such questions weren't meant to be asked out here, in front of hotel guests.

"We'd better ask for a doggie bag and skedaddle," I said to Stacey.

Five minutes later, Stacey and I slipped through a jib door in the first-floor hallway between the hotel's small library and the main ballroom. I wanted to explore the first floor a bit more, but if Madeline wanted us scarce, I supposed it could wait until the dead of night when most of the guests would be asleep.

Stacey's room on the third floor now looked like a weird mix of an antiques shop and a low-budget TV studio, with little black and white monitors removed from our van and placed on every piece of furniture so we could watch feeds from the hotel's security cameras as well as our own. We didn't have nearly enough monitors to watch all the security cameras at once, so the displays had to rotate between cameras every few seconds to keep up with everything.

It was nearly 10 p.m.—we'd gone to the restaurant just before it officially closed, but a number of guests had still been there.

Now we could feel the hotel winding down as guests settled in. The occasional footsteps in the hall became rarer the later the hour grew. Madeline had tucked us at the back of the third floor, away from as many paying guests as possible.

I crossed into my room and changed back to my work clothes—jeans, thin turtleneck, thick black leather jacket.

"I think I'll stick around here for a while," I said when I returned to Stacey's room. I dropped into the armchair next to the one she already occupied. "It would be kind of a shame if I got killed on the first night."

"That could slow down our investigation," Stacey agreed. "Well, then again, once you became a ghost, maybe you could accomplish something from the Other Side."

"I'd rather not test that out," I said. "I'll make some coffee."

We sat and watched, looking into empty hallways where guests and staff passed occasionally. I kept most of my attention on the thermals and night vision cameras.

Activity started to heat up as midnight approached. Occasional cold spots formed and disappeared on the fourth floor. They were mostly centered in the strange "temple" room up there, but they also showed up in the fourth-floor hallway. One of our night vision cameras caught a mist passing through the temple area, which vanished after eight seconds. None of the shapes we saw looked particularly human, and they faded rather than form into clearer apparitions.

A creak sounded over one of our audio monitors. It took us a moment to notice that one of the fourth-floor doors had opened.

"Maybe I should go up there and try an EVP session," I said. This involves walking around with a handheld recorder, asking questions. Typically, you can't hear the ghosts while you're there, unless it's an extremely strong apparition or you've got a poltergeist situation with things being thrown all over the house. It's more common to hear nothing until you play back the audio. This makes it pretty difficult to really have a back-and-forth conversation with the ghost.

"I thought we were playing it safe tonight," Stacey said.

"I won't go out of camera range," I said. "If anything happens—"

"Look!" Stacey said. She pointed to the thermal feed from the second floor, where two red-orange blobs had appeared in the hall outside Room 208, famously haunted by Abigail Bowen's ghost. The shapes looked like just another pair of living people, but they were running at high speed toward the elevator.

"Where's the security camera feed for that hall?"

"Here. I'll lock it so the view doesn't shift." Stacey tapped at her laptop keyboard and pointed to a black and white monitor on the dresser. On the screen, a man and woman who might have been in their late thirties dashed down the hall, looking back over their shoulders. There was no audio, but their mouths were wide open as if screaming. They were barefoot, the man wearing boxers and a t-shirt, the woman wearing a nightgown. They didn't exactly appear to be heading out for a leisurely stroll in the garden.

The door to 208 stood open behind them, but I couldn't see anything inside the room.

"You think they saw the ghost?" Stacey asked.

"Either that or they just found the world's biggest cockroach in their hotel room." I jumped to my feet, double-checking that I had two tactical flashlights holstered at my utility belt. "I'm going to have a peek while they're out."

"Are you sure that's a good idea? Stabby Abby might be the killer ghost."

"So stay in touch and get ready to rescue me," I said. I double-checked my headset on the way out to make sure we could hear each other.

I opened the door to the guest stairwell. Unlike the steep, narrow stairwells in the hidden service area, this one was wide and warmly lit from sconces, with brick walls trimmed in dark wood.

Above me, the stairs continued up into the darkness of the fourth floor, where the lights either didn't work or had been extinguished to discourage guests from going up there. A heavy brass floor-to-ceiling security gate across the stairs added further discouragement. The gate looked like an expensive antique itself, the bars embellished with tiny sculptures of ostriches and lions.

I dashed down to the second floor, rounded a corner, and slowed as I approached 208. The fleeing guests had left their lights off. As I drew closer to the dark room, I shivered at the ice-cold air spilling out, as if someone had left open a door to a freezer instead of a luxury hotel room.

The door was only partially ajar. I nudged it open, gaining a view of a large canopied bed, the sheets and blankets in disarray as if the couple had kicked and struggled their way out. Suitcases sat open on the floor.

I moved into the cold, dim space with my hand on my flashlight, ready to draw if I needed it. A powerful blast of light can sometimes discourage ghosts or even make them leave you alone, but of course I was trying to *find* the ghost, so I kept it turned off.

The room was as nice as any of the others, including a brick fireplace and a bay window looking out onto the night. The flowers in the vases had all wilted and shriveled, though the flowers throughout the rest of the hotel were still fresh and bright.

"Hello?" I whispered, stepping inside. The air was frosty, and I probably would have seen my breath if it hadn't been so dark. "Is anyone here?"

Nobody answered. A bronze plate was screwed onto the wall just inside the door, and I turned my flashlight on to read it, keeping the light to its dimmest setting.

## NOTICE

**Room 208 is inhabited by the Lathrop Grand's famous ghost, Abigail Bowen. Guests have reported seeing apparitions of a woman in white, hearing voices, and being physically touched by the ghost.**

**The desk clerk should have informed you of this ghost's presence. If you were not informed, you may request a different room. The Lathrop Grand is unable to offer refunds due to ghost activity in Room 208.**

"Wow," I said, after reading it aloud to Stacey over the headset. "Imagine if you got this room and didn't know about the ghost. That sign alone would freak you out."

"So the power of suggestion could play a role here?" she asked.

"When people have been told an area is haunted, they're more likely to attribute unexplained...." I fell silent.

"Ellie?"

I'd happened to look at the ornate mirror above the room's dresser, trimmed in a wooden frame carved with wildflower shapes. In the mirror, I could see a portion of the bed, a portion of the bay window, and an armchair parked at the room's polished spinet desk, which is a deceptively simple piece of furniture that looks like a small table with a single drawer but actually unfolds into a more complicated arrangement with pigeonholes and a pull-out writing platform. Like a lot of our haunting cases, it's much more complex than it first appears.

In the space between the spinet desk and the bay window stood a misty white shape, suggesting a woman about my height. There was no clear face, only the hint of long white hair around the head and shoulder areas. I could also faintly see the wrought-iron stiles of the bay window behind her. Definitely an apparition, not a live person.

From her stance, she appeared to be watching me in the mirror, her blank, misty face angled directly toward me.

My breath seemed to freeze inside my throat as the room grew colder. My heart accelerated to triple-time. When encountering a ghost, you'll likely find that every cell in your body, motivated by basic survival instinct, will scream at you to run away as fast as possible. Animals have the same negative reactions to restless spirits. Only humans are stupid enough to stick around and try to have a conversation with an unfriendly dead person.

"Abigail?" I whispered, summoning all my courage just to speak aloud.

"Ellie?" Stacey replied, but her voice sounded distant and full of static. "Ellie? I'm flying blind—can't see—you okay?"

I tapped my microphone three times with my fingertip, our usual sign for *Yes, I'm still alive, now please be quiet.*

The figure in the mirror didn't react to the word "Abigail," but it was possible I'd said it too quietly to be heard. I couldn't quite force myself to speak again, so instead I turned around slowly, not taking my eyes off the apparition in the mirror until I was fully facing the window.

I drew my flashlight as I turned, but resisted the urge to lance the ghost with three thousand lumens of white light.

She wasn't there. I looked at where she'd been, then spun back around to look at the mirror, worried she might use it as a doorway from which to attack me.

The woman had vanished in the mirror, too. I did see some movement in the darkness outside the window. I ran to the window and looked out.

She was hanging from the thick oak branch outside. She was clearer now, her clothes torn, her face and long blond hair filthy. A hemp rope was tight around her neck, and her eyes were closed, her face as limp and lifeless as the rest of her body.

When Abigail Bowen's crimes had been discovered by the Union army, she'd been arrested and executed on the same day, in the manner of military occupations everywhere. She'd been hanged from an oak tree on the hotel grounds. *This* oak tree, I was guessing.

A hand touched my shoulder, and I screamed, letting out all the pent-up fear and tension in my body. I turned and clicked on my flashlight, illuminating a very pale white face framed in blond hair.

It was Conrad, the beefy security guard who'd questioned us while we'd hung the cameras. His thin eyebrows rose as I screamed into his face, and he squinted and raised a hand to shield his eyes from the searing white light.

"You shouldn't be here," he said.

"I was just...there was a woman..." My brain was scrambled, leaving me momentarily unable to speak. I pointed to the oak tree outside, but the gently swaying corpse was gone. "She disappeared."

Conrad grunted and pointed to the big wall-mounted plate that explained about the ghost.

"Yeah, I know, I just..." I tried to shake it off. "Have you ever seen her?"

The security officer grunted, a completely uninformative response. Behind him, an older bellhop gathered the guests' belongings and zipped up their suitcases.

"If they're not coming back, I'll need this room tonight," I said, forcing myself to sound calm.

"I would need Madeline's permission to do that, and she's gone home," Conrad said.

"Okay...but if nobody *else* is going to be in here tonight—"

"There are other guests requesting this room as soon as it becomes available. Even if it's the middle of the night. People travel from all over the country to try to see that ghost."

"But surely housekeeping needs to come through—" I began.

"We have policies in place," Conrad said, cutting me off. "Do I have to escort you out of here? You're not a paying guest, so we don't need to play nice."

"Okay, okay, just asking." I started for the door. It wasn't going to take much to convince me to stay out of the room for the rest of that particular night, anyway, no matter how valuable it was for our investigation.

"Can I give you a hand with anything?" the bellhop asked with a forced smile. He was loading the suitcases onto a luggage cart as I passed him.

I shook my head and continued into the hall and around the corner.

The stairwell was silent when I entered it, but as I ascended, I could hear the echoes of footsteps above me. They sounded as if they were descending from the fourth floor.

I paused, but the footsteps continued, approaching me from above.

"Hello?" I pointed my light up, but I couldn't see much beyond the undersides of the flights above me. Some living person could easily be up there, choosing not to answer me, but I didn't feel like waiting around for the details.

I ran as fast as I could to the third floor landing. The footsteps were louder and closer, but I didn't see anything through the ornate brass security gate that blocked the way to the fourth floor.

Shoving the stairwell door aside, I dashed around to Stacey's room. She jumped up as I burst into the door.

"What happened?" she asked.

"I saw her. Stabby Abby."

"What did she do? Did she hurt you?"

"No, I'm fine," I said, but then I winced as I dropped into a chair. My back was stinging as if something nasty had bitten me back there.

"You sure?"

"Not so sure anymore." I stood and shrugged off my jacket, then turned my back to the room's biggest mirror and lifted my shirt.

A long, thin slash ran between my shoulder blades, weeping blood. I hadn't felt it happen. Some of these ghosts are as sneaky as piranhas with their attacks—you don't even know they got you until you see the blood.

"Ellie, that looks awful!" Stacey grabbed our first-aid kit from the heap of gear.

"Take a picture for our records." I sat on the bed while she snapped a few shots of the wound, then swabbed it with antibiotic ointment.

"What do you think caused it?" I asked Stacey.

"Um, a mean ghost?" Stacey guessed.

"More specifically. Does it look like a claw mark to you, or what?"

"Maybe a really sharp knife?"

"Like the scalpel Abigail used to kill those hospitalized soldiers?"

In the mirror above the dresser, I saw Stacey's eyes widen.

"Like a scalpel," she agreed. "Well, congratulations, Ellie. You finally met one of Savannah's most famous ghosts."

I nodded, but I couldn't say I was thrilled about it. If Stabby Abby could cut me across the back, she could do the same across my throat. Stacey and I would have to be extremely careful for the rest of the investigation.

## Chapter Five

We spent the rest of the night holed up in the hotel room, watching the monitors. Occasional cold spots appeared in the hall around Room 208, but the most active area still appeared to be the fourth floor. In the "temple" room, spots of extreme cold as well as extreme heat repeatedly formed up and vanished, about one every fifteen or twenty minutes.

The strangest thing that happened in those early-morning hours, though, had to do with the living and not the dead.

After Conrad the Amazing Albino Security Giant escorted me out of 208, he lingered in the door of the room while a housekeeper arrived to clean the place and switch out linens. After that, Conrad left and returned with the bellhop and three hotel guests. Though it was close to two in the morning by then, the hotel staff had apparently woken them and transferred them to 208 the moment it became available. I assumed the guests had requested this treatment.

I recognized them as the Seattle family we'd encountered earlier, Carla and Maurice and their tween daughter. Carla and Maurice wore giant smiles as they approached 208, but the girl looked pretty annoyed at being awake, her rumpled hair framing a scowling face. Carla had bothered me a bit at dinner, but now I worried for the safety of all three of them. Abigail Bowen might have been a benign ghost for decades, but it looked as if she was back to her old slice-and-dice tricks again. I had to wonder what had triggered her, what had made her turn to violence.

We called the front desk and asked to be put in touch with Conrad.

"Yeah, what?" he finally answered.

"I think Abigail's ghost cut me," I said. "You might want to warn the guests in 208."

"They know about the ghost. They want to see the thing."

"But the ghost has turned to attacking people—"

"It's covered by hotel policy. I know my job." Conrad hung up, leaving me shaking my head.

"Well?" Stacey asked.

"He's not going to help. He doesn't seem to understand that things have changed."

"So what do we do? Camp out by 208 all night?"

"I doubt Madeline would appreciate that. Just keep a monitor locked on that hall for the rest of the night. Watch for white apparitions or screaming tourists."

We watched until sunrise. Signs of paranormal activity continued throughout the night, including bubbling hot as well as cold spots on the fourth floor, accompanied by more of the low whispering voices. On the third-floor hall outside our door, our microphone caught a few faint footsteps accompanied by a strange, rusty squeaking sound I couldn't begin to identify.

At about seven in the morning, when the sun was just beginning to rise, a room service cart arrived with breakfast for both of us. Good stuff, too—little cheese omelets, grits, cut melons and strawberries, French toast, orange and tomato juice, coffee. We avoided the coffee, since daylight meant bedtime was approaching, but we took the rest out onto the veranda and ate at a small table.

"This is great," Stacey said. "We should live here full-time."

"Ha. Madeline probably just sent us breakfast to keep us hidden away up here. She didn't like us going to the restaurant."

"Suits me fine. If we make her mad again, do we get cake?"

"Let's not push it."

Other hotel guests stepped out onto the veranda a few doors down, so we had to keep our conversation low-key.

"So what's the plan today?" she asked.

"I want to have a look at the fourth floor again before we go," I said. "And I want Madeline to put me in touch with that last contractor, the one whose worker...you know. I want a firsthand account of what happened."

"You think she'll arrange that for us?"

"She will if she wants this case solved quickly. Grant Patterson answered my text a minute ago. He says it'll take a couple of days to gather what he can about the Lathrop Grand's history. You should probably sift through audio and video data today. Find out what we picked up last night."

"I can do that here!" Stacey said, beaming. "Hanging out on my awesome five-star bed. I don't care if this case lasts a month. Do you think we can attend their Halloween ball if we drag it out that long?"

"I'm sure the tickets are very pricey. Probably sold out."

"Yeah, but we have the inside connection."

"Not at the moment, we don't. Maybe after we get back on Madeline's good side."

After breakfast, I called Madeline's office from the phone in Stacey's room.

"How's it going?" she asked, her voice all sunshine, practically glowing out of the telephone receiver. "Did you enjoy breakfast?"

"It was really the best thing ever. Seriously, I can never eat anywhere else ever again. Listen, I think you'll need to close down Room 208. I tried to tell your security guy, but he wasn't cooperative."

"We charge a premium for that room," she said. "Guests request it months in advance."

"Right. Well, I checked it out when last night's guests ran off, and I came back with a pretty nasty cut across my shoulder blades. It looks like somebody got me with a scalpel."

Madeline was silent on the other end of the line, clearly reluctant to close off such a highly overpriced room.

"The family that replaced them has a kid," I said. "If it was just the ghost-tourist adults, I'd say let them proceed at their own risk, but once there's a child in danger, that changes things for me."

Madeline sighed. "I'll see what I can do."

She wasn't thrilled when I asked about meeting with the contractor, either. But finally she agreed. She would have to arrange the meeting herself, since he was also bound by a nondisclosure agreement and wasn't supposed to tell anyone about his experiences at the Lathrop Grand.

Then I went into my room, closing the connecting door behind me. It was a little smaller than Stacey's room but decorated in similar fashion, pastoral paintings on the walls, sunny French doors opening onto the veranda, fresh flowers and polished antique furniture.

My bathroom had a clawfoot tub like the one in Stacey's room, with little dragon-like feet. It was charming and cute, but I opted for the glass phone booth of a shower stall in the corner. The hotel seemed to have high standards of cleanliness—if you ignored the forbidden fourth floor—but I can't help getting a little icked out at the thought of lying in a tub where thousands of strangers have bathed before me.

The hot water hit me, and I hissed a little bit when I turned my back. I lathered a tiny complimentary glass bottle's worth of shampoo into my hair, and of course the phone in my room rang at just that moment, while the suds were just starting to run down over my closed eyes.

Normally I would have ignored it, but I didn't want to miss Madeline's call and possibly delay my chance to speak to the witness.

Wrapping a towel around my head, I dashed to the phone.

"His name is Javier Morales, Morales Construction," she said. "He's agreed to meet you at five p.m. at La Comarca on Ogeechee Road."

I jotted this down on the pad of official Lathrop Grand stationery by the phone. The paper felt like silk.

"Okay, thanks," I said.

"My pleasure," she said, her voice a flat monotone. "If there's nothing else..."

"The doors on the fourth floor have some very old locks on them," I said. "Our staff keycards can't open them. Do you have the keys?"

"Oh..." She sighed. "I'll ask the custodian about it."

That didn't sound promising. "Thanks for all your help," I said.

"Are we much closer to getting rid of the ghost?" she asked.

"We have to identify her before we can trap her. Yes, I think things will move quickly," I added, mostly to make her feel better. I certainly hoped it was true, as long as "moving quickly" didn't involve me getting cut to pieces by Stabby Abby. That would be a less than satisfactory ending to the case.

After the call, I debated driving home to rest, then decided to stay in my hotel room instead. I'd left my cat plenty of food and water. Also, my room had a very attractive-looking sleigh bed made of beautiful blond wood, with a soft mattress. I was exhausted from a night of frights, and I couldn't see the point in driving anywhere at all. The hotel might have been haunted, but not our floor, in particular. I've slept in much worse places.

Just as I closed my eyes, my phone rang again—the cell this time, not my room phone. It was Michael.

"Just calling to say goodnight," he greeted me when I answered.

"You know me so well." I approached the curtain across the French doors and adjusted it slightly to cut off some unwelcome sunlight leaking into my room. "Aren't you just starting your day?"

"I've been on shift since six a.m. I guess I know you better than you know me."

"Ugh. How do you handle those hours?" I lay down and pulled a pillow over my eyes.

"How was your first night? Did Stabby Abby grab you in your sleep?"

"I wasn't asleep when it happened."

"Seriously? What did she look like?"

"Creepy. Like a woman-shaped fog." I decided against telling him about the scalpel slash on my back. I didn't want to worry him. "This place is pretty ghost-infested. It's going to take a while to narrow it down to the dangerous ones."

"How dangerous are we talking about?" The concern was clear in his voice. Michael had seen some of the worst nasties I've dealt with. One used to haunt his apartment building.

"It'll be fine."

"You're still coming with me tomorrow?" he asked.

"Sure, as long as I can get back to work by sunset, and nothing urgent comes up..."

"You don't sound very excited for a girl whose boyfriend is taking her antique shopping."

"It doesn't get more romantic than browsing for gears and springs from old clocks."

"I'm sure they'll have plenty of lace and frills for you to squeal over," he said.

"I squeal for nothing."

"Maybe we'll find some haunted knickknacks for you to exorcise."

"Let's hope not. Seriously, I can't wait to see you, Michael. Thanks for the call. Stay safe." As a firefighter, Michael has to face all kinds of dangerous situations. I try not to worry about it—I'm not exactly a stranger to danger myself—but it creeps into my thoughts.

I slept deeply, but my dreams were rough and frightening, full of shadowy figures lying in the dark, moaning in a slow, endless agony. I saw children walking up a dim hallway. When they turned to look at me, their faces were yellow, and dark blood seeped from their eyes and nostrils. One scrawny girl of six or seven with ratty blond hair opened her mouth as if to speak to me. More blood drooled from her lips, but no sound came out. She mouthed words, possibly *"Help me."*

When I awoke in my hotel bed, I was drenched in sweat and my skin was scalding hot, as if someone had cranked up the heat in my room. I felt achy and sick to my stomach, and the thin line of sunlight seeping around the window curtain seemed like a painful, blinding glare.

I groaned as I pushed myself up and out of my damp bed. The thermostat was set to a perfectly pleasant seventy-six degrees. The burning heat was from my own skin, not the air in the room. I turned the thermostat down several notches anyway.

It wasn't quite noon, so I'd only had about four good hours of sleep. Well, not *good* hours, but complete ones, anyway. I wasn't in a rush to return to the land of nightmares.

A voice mail from Madeline told me the head custodian had been instructed to loan me the old keys for the fourth-floor rooms, but his shift ended at three-thirty and the night staff didn't have access to those keys.

I got dressed and pulled my bed-headed hair back into a ponytail so I'd look partly civilized. Stacey was still asleep in her room, her knees up to her chest like a little kid, and I decided not to wake her. At least one of us ought to be well-rested.

Ten minutes later, I was enjoying the gray-metal, rubber-floor ambience of the freight elevator as it chugged downward into the basement.

The doors clanked open, and I stepped out into a dusty, brick-walled underground space. Brick archways helped support the heavy, marble-trimmed four-story structure above. Chain-link gates blocked some of these archways, which stored heavy equipment like a floor polisher and pressure washer. Others store large unidentifiable objects draped in white sheets that looked like the ghosts of old furniture.

The door to the head custodian's office stood open. An elderly man sat at a fire-scarred desk in one corner, filling out paperwork. The wall immediately above his desk featured thumbtacked pictures of sun-drenched tropical islands and rickety sailing ships, like some kind of shrine to Jimmy Buffett. The rest of the office was cluttered with a rusty file cabinet, a couple of broken chairs, and shelves of cleaning fluids and supplies all the way to the ceiling.

I knocked on the open door. "Excuse me. Are you Earl Brinkman?"

The man's rolling office chair creaked as he turned to face me. He was tall and rail-thin, his gray hair sparse, his eyes rheumy and watery. He was wiping at his eyes and nose with a handkerchief, as though they wouldn't stop leaking, something he would continue to do throughout our conversation. He wore starched, ironed khaki coveralls with the Lathrop Grand's curlicue logo, probably meant to imitate the swirling wrought-iron railings of the trademark veranda.

"What can I do for you?" he finally asked.

"I'm Ellie Jordan. Madeline said you had some keys for me." I offered the best smile I could manage, but the dark basement was creeping me out a little.

Earl looked me over like he was trying to assess me somehow. He seemed to be in his middle or late sixties. He finally gave his tooth a long suck and looked me in the eyes.

"You want to go up to four?" he asked.

"Yes, sir."

"You shouldn't. Nothing good comes from up there."

"I know it's haunted."

"Haunted?" He leaned back in his chair. "My granny's house was haunted. Ghost of my great-gramps used to smoke his pipe out back by the woodpile. You could see the red glow some nights. *That's* haunted. But this here?" He pointed up to the dusty ceiling joists. "They don't have words for it. It's more'n just haunted. Bad things could happen to a little girl like you up there."

Resisting the urge to get defensive, I widened my smile and tried to butter him up for information. "You sound like you know a lot about it. Have you worked here long?"

"Seventeen years," he said, with a shake of his head. He glanced longingly at one of the Caribbean posters on the wall. We had some nice beaches of our own nearby—Tybee Island, for example—but clearly he dreamed of getting a little farther away from home.

"Have you ever encountered anything strange in that time?" I asked.

He snorted, then let out a barking laugh. He opened a drawer in his desk. "I've seen it all, heard it all. The soldiers missing their arms or their heads. The children with yellow fever. The whispers, all the whispers...they're really bad on the fourth floor."

"Then why do you keep working here?"

"It's a job, ain't it? Besides, they just about can't fire me." He brought out a bottle of Caribbean rum from his desk and poured it into a mug featuring the cartoon-insect logo of the Savannah Sand Gnats, which was our local minor-league baseball team until they moved across the border to Columbia, South Carolina. He took a long sip of rum and closed his eyes. "Dang near everybody quits after a year or two. There just aren't many of us willing to hang in there. Without me, they'd have to hire a new head custodian every three or four months, and they know it."

I nodded. I could see why that might appeal to a man who drank hard liquor for lunch.

"Did you ever encounter the ghost of Abigail Bowen?" I asked.

"All the time. Usually she's kind of a cloudy mist, sometimes she's clearer. Sometimes she touches your wrist or your neck, like she's looking for a pulse. I tell you, I might work here, but I wouldn't sleep here." He glanced at a folded-up cot against the wall. "Not in *her* room, anyway."

"Has she ever attacked you?"

"Not me personally, cause I know to steer clear, but I've heard of her scratching people just lately. Especially up on four. She's still got that scalpel. People come all over hoping to see her, but they better hope they don't get too close. She might be a pretty one, but she killed all them soldiers. Cut their throats in their sleep. It's best to remember that before you go banging around upstairs. It's best you stay away from four altogether."

"I appreciate your concern, but I have to do my job."

"And what exactly is that?"

"I'm a private investigator, here as a security consultant. I have to check the fourth floor, there's no way around it."

"It's secure enough up there, if it's burglars you're worried about," he said. "Unless you know how to get rid of ghosts."

"I'll see what I can do," I said. "Mr. Brinkman—"

"Call me Earl, honey." He dropped a wink, his voice beginning to slur.

"Okay. Do you believe the ghost of Abigail Bowen killed that workman on the fourth floor?"

"Oh, I believe it. It was one of them, anyway. One of them..." He gestured with his hand, as if to indicate that he couldn't quite remember the word *ghosts*. He took another sip. I could see the conversation going south from here. When his gaze dropped from my face to my shirt and lingered there for an uncomfortable amount of time, I held out my hand and gave him my coldest look.

"I need those keys," I said. "Now."

"Just trying to look out for you." He sighed, put down his mug, and eased himself to his feet. He unlocked a drawer in the file cabinet and took his time rummaging through some loud, clanking objects in there. He finally fished out a fat ring of long metal keys and held them out to me.

I reached for them, but he held tight, almost as if trying to tug me toward him. I tensed, ready to give him a hard kick if he tried anything inappropriate.

"You gotta be careful," he said, the rum strong on his breath now. I couldn't have been less comfortable being alone in the basement with this man. "I mean it. And I'll tell you what I told the others. If something happens to you up there, if something gets you, don't go blaming Earl for it. It ain't Earl's fault. I done told you stay away now. Right?"

"I got you," I said. "It ain't Earl's fault."

"But you going anyway, ain't you?" His voice was even more slurred now, his eyes unfocused. "I can tell."

"I'll be fine." I gave the keys a tug, trying to pull them away. "Thank you."

"Uh-huh." He released the keys, then stumbled back and dropped into his office chair. "You think I'm crazy. That's how the other lady looked at me, too. Crazy stupid Earl. But I guess they figured it out when they saw for themselves."

I nodded. I was very interested to hear what Javier Morales had to say about what he and his workers had seen.

Keys in hand, I backed up to the door, thanking him again. He nodded and waved me away.

"It ain't Earl's fault," I heard him mutter as I dashed away to the nearest staircase, since I didn't particularly feel like waiting around for the elevator. "It ain't Earl's fault..."

I took Earl's advice seriously. I wanted to get in and out of the fourth floor before sunset, which meant we had to do it this afternoon. I hurried up the stairs.

## Chapter Six

"Wake up, Sleeping Beauty," I said, nudging Stacey's shoulder where she lay curled in bed. "Your prince has arrived. He's a custodian named Earl. You'll love him."

"Huh?" Stacey lifted her head from the pillow, short blond hair puffed out on one side. "Who's Earl?"

"I've got the keys to upstairs," I said, jingling them in front of her. "Want to go look for dead people? Set up the rest of our gear?" I'd loaded a luggage cart with equipment to carry up to the fourth floor.

"Want to hit the spa first? Get a massage?"

"There's no time. I have to meet with Javier this afternoon."

"Who's Javier?" Stacey pulled on a pair of jeans. "A friend of Earl's?"

"Javier's the contractor who lost a man up on the fourth floor."

"Sheesh. Makes it sound like a war zone. We're putting the REM pods up there?" she asked, lifting one of the black hockey-puck-sized devices from the cart. These are radiating electromagnetic sensors that create a little electric field that, if you're lucky, can be interfered with by ghosts. Then the little thing lets off a kind of spooky digital "woo" tone and the lights on top flash. Occasionally people manage to have yes-or-no conversations with spirits using the pods.

"There seem to be a number of entities up there," I said. "I want to scatter those like tripwires so nothing can sneak up on us."

"Sounds good to me. Then we hit the spa, get that massage—"

"Then you start sifting video and audio. Professional massages are overrated, anyway."

"Wow. Is there, like, *any* room for joy in your life, Ellie?"

"You know there isn't. Now let's get to work."

The freight elevator did that thing again—creaking and rattling as it approached the fourth floor. The overhead lights flickered as the metal doors opened.

We rolled the cart out into the work area. Plastic sheeting, loosely attached to vertical wooden studs in the partially demolished walls, swayed like heavy sails in a gentle breeze, though I couldn't say I heard any air conditioners running up there.

"Let's go this way," I said, pointing in the opposite direction from the jib door that led into the wacko dark-temple room. I wasn't in a hurry to return there.

"What's this way? Do we have a map?" Stacey asked.

"I think we can manage without a map." I walked along the aged brick wall housing the elevator shaft. An open doorway led into a kitchen with a brick fireplace and a massive wood-burning stove flecked with rust. Cobwebs hung everywhere.

We opened one creaky pantry door after another, finding mostly dead bugs, though Stacey let out a little hiss when she found a row of sealed mason jars in one high cabinet. They were filled with unidentifiable black gunk.

"Ugh, what do you think this is?" she asked me.

"Dip your finger and have a taste," I said. "Maybe it's blackberry preserves."

"I think they passed 'preserved' a long time ago." Stacey curled her lip a little as she closed the cabinet. "They really haven't updated this place in a hundred years."

"Just too haunted," I said. "I've seen it before. Somebody could make a fortune flipping these old buildings and mansions all over town, if they knew how to get the ghosts out. A lot of places are left abandoned or underused because of them."

"Hey, *we* know how to get the ghosts out—" Stacey began, and then a loud crash sounded from the next room, like dishes and glassware shattering on the floor.

Without a word, we dashed toward the strange sound in the dark room, like a couple of teenagers running to their doom in any horror movie.

Tall batwing doors led us into a spacious dining room with a vaulted ceiling. The windows were shuttered from the outside, sealing out most of the light while protecting the antique glass in the tall panes against hail and hurricane winds.

The table at the center could seat a dozen people, and the matching chairs were still there, too, intricately carved wood with a grapes-and-nymphs design, the red upholstery at their arms and seats thick with years of dust. The chair at the head was noticeably taller than the others, its high back engraved with goat-headed men. It sat in front of a giant ship-stone fireplace, built from big round ballast stones used in the eighteenth and early nineteenth centuries to weigh down ships from Europe.

Enormous pictures adorned the wall. One was a painting depicting a heavyset, lantern-jawed woman in a long white dress dripping with black lace, her hair braided up, her eyes big and dark. She held a thick, crooked branch in one hand, with little green leaves sprouting out of it here and there, and posed in front of the big oak tree in the courtyard, the same one from which Abigail Bowen had been hanged in 1864. With the staff and the funky dress, plus the little stars and moons on her jewelry, she gave me the overall impression of some kind of 19th-century Druid or Wiccan. Or maybe somebody who got their jewelry from a box of Lucky Charms cereal.

The little brass plate on the portrait frame confirmed my suspicion that this was Ithaca Galloway, the wealthy Boston widow who'd purchased and renovated the hotel at the end of the nineteenth century. We were standing in her private apartment, which had been preserved like a time capsule since then. Well, a poorly sealed time capsule that let in tons of dust and spiders.

Ithaca had shared the apartment with a gang of supposed psychics and other hangers-on. They were depicted in a large, framed black and white photograph that hung on the wall, an assortment of about twenty men and women, most of whom appeared to be in their twenties or early thirties, a fairly young crowd. They wore funky attire even for the day, the women's dresses hung with lace, dark stones, and more jewelry featuring stars and moons in imitation of Ithaca's attire. The men looked thrift-store fabulous in their assortment of top hats, vests, ascots, and so on—again, funky dressers even for the Victorian era. There were more women than men, I noted.

Ithaca sat at the center of the picture, in the same monster-sized dining chair that occupied the head of the table in front of me. She looked to be in her late forties in the photograph. A man about ten years younger sat just beside her, an intense gaze in his eyes. He looked like a barbarian, with a long, thick, unkempt beard that didn't quite fit with his neatly tailored white seersucker suit. Something about the look on his face and his position next to the throne made me think of Rasputin, the mesmerizing faith healer to the last imperial family of Russia. I hoped Grant Patterson's research would turn up some information about him, since the photograph was not labeled to identify the people it depicted.

"So, what crashed in here?" Stacey examined the hardwood floor with her flashlight. "It sounded like a ton of breaking glass."

"I can't find anything broken," I told her. "It might have been an auditory apparition, or an energy echo of some past event."

"It sounds a little scary when you get all sciencey about it." Her light went to the goat-men decorating the big chair at the head of the table. "I think I saw this same chair in a Marilyn Manson video when I was a kid. Or maybe a horror movie."

"Satyrs. Looks like old Ithaca was into ancient mythology."

"Or Satan."

"Yeah, or Satan," I agreed. "But that's not your typical Spiritualist area of interest. Neoclassicism was more of a hot topic among the upper-class types in the nineteenth century. I'm going with satyrs until further notice."

We set up a night vision camera and a microphone, then unlocked the high, ornate dining-room doors and moved on into another dusty, arched hallway. There was a big sitting-room type area with large but tightly shuttered windows. Antique, heavily padded chairs and couches were here in a cobwebbed jumble, as well as an old piano in the corner, and a massive black grandfather clock against one wall opposite the fireplace.

"This must have been where Ithaca and her psychics hung out, probably chatting about contacting the dead or whatever," Stacey said.

We took a few readings, but there was nothing unusual about the temperature or electromagnetic fields in the room, so we didn't set up any of our dwindling supply of gear. We moved on, leaving REM pods along the hallway behind us like a trail of bread crumbs so they could alert us if some entity showed up.

Stacey and I unlocked a door across the hall from the kitchen and dining area. We stood in the doorway for a moment, trying to process what we saw.

"That's...interesting," Stacey said.

Her comment was an understatement. We'd apparently discovered the fourth-floor bathroom, outfitted with several clawfoot tubs around the perimeter—I counted seven of them—and a luxuriously deep black-marble bath at the center. I could have spread-eagled in the center of that big tub without my fingers or toes touching any of the marble edges.

"More Greco-Roman stuff?" Stacey asked, shining the light along the walls. Peeling frescoes depicted more satyrs and nymphs, along with columns, fountains, and a cave full of fiery lava. "They bathed together because the Romans did?"

"Maybe. It seems pretty culty to me. Breaking down personal barriers to make people submissive to the group. There were a lot of little attempts to create utopian societies in America in the late 19th century. The Oneida community required all property to be held in common, and everybody was married to everybody else at the same time. That didn't work out. The Shakers, on the other hand, required celibacy even within marriage."

"So...how did they have kids?"

"I have no idea, but they've managed to outlast the Oneida commune for more than a century. Anyway, it's possible Ithaca Galloway was trying for some kind of planned community up here. A utopia devoted to communication with the dead."

"Call me a negative Nancy, but wouldn't the people of Savannah have a major problem with that? This is a pretty religious city, even now. Back then...I can just imagine the scandal."

"I hope there *was* a scandal. Grant is especially gifted at discovering those. It's possible they managed to keep their activities secret at the time. She might have just been seen as an eccentric wealthy Yankee lady with a large entourage. We'll learn more soon."

In the next room, we found sinks, marble counters, and a row of private water closets outfitted with the sort of old-timey chain-box where Michael Corleone hid his gun in *The Godfather*.

"You'd have to redo this whole floor to make it into hotel rooms or suites," I said. "Knock down walls, add a new plumbing system, new electrical, the works. No wonder every owner has kept putting it off."

"Well, that and the killer ghosts," Stacey said.

My equipment didn't indicate any activity in the bathroom area, so we moved on down the hall, leaving another activated REM pod on the floor behind us.

The next room we unlocked was like a dark oven, the air thick and hot as it rolled out into the cool hallway where we stood. A smell permeated the place—acrid and sour, like somebody had broiled a rotten possum in there. It was bigger than the other bedroom-cells, the windows shuttered tight like all the rest. Our flashlights revealed a bare bedframe and other bedroom furniture jammed into one corner.

"There's no cobwebs," Stacey whispered. "All the other rooms had cobwebs. This place must be hot enough to deep-fry spiders."

"Well, thanks for making me think of deep-fried spider legs," I said. "Yeah, something's discouraging the living critters from coming in here."

"Thermal camera?"

"Yep. And pass me a REM pod while you're busy with that."

I activated the hefty plastic saucer-shaped device and set it on the dusty hardwood floor. Almost the instant I let go of it, the lights began flashing, and the speakers let out a *woo-woo* alert like the sound when you blow across a glass Coke bottle, only digitized. The manufacturer could have gone with a less eerie sound, if you ask me.

"Is someone here?" I asked. The REM pod immediately fell silent. I took a shot in the dark: "Ithaca Galloway? Am I speaking to Ithaca? Or maybe one of her friends?"

The pod stayed dark and silent.

"Thermal goggles." I held out my hand to Stacey, since she was between me and the luggage cart.

"Your thermal enhancement spectacles, Master Eleanor," Stacey replied in a weak attempt at a posh English accent.

I strapped the heavy, boxy thermals onto my head, then looked around the room. It was all red, giving the space a hellish appearance, and it was a stark contrast from the relatively cool atmosphere in the hall. I could not find a source of the ambient heat, or any shape or apparition to indicate the presence of a specific entity. If Ithaca was here, she was keeping herself well-hidden.

"Can you tell us about the man who just recently died in the other room? Someone pushed him off a ladder. Was that you?" I asked.

No obvious response came for a moment. Then the room cooled slightly, just a few degrees, all at once, as if the presence had retreated just a bit.

"I'm not seeing anybody," Stacey said. I glanced over at her orange-red form leaning over the room-temperature shape of the thermal camera on its tripod. "You?"

"No, nobody's coming out to play." I removed my thermals and looked around with my own eyes again. "You'd better not hurt anybody else," I said to the unseen presence.

"Ooh, threatening," Stacey whispered, and I scowled just a little.

"Let's see what's in here." I crossed to a heavy, closed door near the bed and heaved it open. A sizable walk-in closet lay on the other side, with only a few old garments on its shelves and hooks.

It grew more interesting when we realized it was a walk-*through* closet, with another door at the far end. In fact, we'd just emerged from a wall of empty shoe racks that closed automatically behind us, becoming almost invisible like any of the jib doors throughout the hotel.

I had to test several keys before I managed to unlock the door at the end of the closet.

It opened onto a much larger room. A monster of a bed occupied the center, some of its dark curtains pulled back and tied to the thick columns of the posters, others left in place to create a lightless cave inside. Spiderwebs shrouded the entire thing.

Deeply upholstered chairs sat near a huge arched window—shuttered, of course—and more were placed by the cold marble fireplace. Built-in bookshelves flanked the fireplace, running all the way to the corners. A couple of large rugs on the floor had been eaten to thread by moths.

"Another bedroom," Stacey said. "Connecting bedrooms! Scandal!"

"*Our* rooms connect," I pointed out. I approached the dresser, made of the same heavy black wood as the bookshelves. The mirror above was a huge circle, squared off by a heavy wooden frame that surrounded the mirror with little shelves. Long-dried drips of yellowed candle wax protruded downward from a few of the shelves like rows of sharp yellow teeth.

"Mirror, mirror, on the wall..." Stacey intoned, shining the flashlight toward me.

"Don't try it," I said. "It might answer you."

"You think it's cursed?"

"Judging by the scale of this room, I'm guessing this was where the rich widow slept. Who knows what kind of black magic she might have practiced in here?"

"But you don't believe in that stuff."

"These days, I take everything on a case-by-case basis. Anyway, an obsession with dark things can give rise to a very wicked ghost." I opened one little drawer and tiny cabinet after another, searching the dresser, but found them all empty.

"My Mel-Meter's kicking up a little," Stacey said. "One to two milligaus right here by the bed."

I found similar readings near the mirror, but zilch in the rest of the room. "Worth a night vision camera," I said, and Stacey set one up quickly, encompassing both the bed and the mirror in its frame.

"So who do you think had the connecting bedroom?" Stacey asked. "Beardy Rasputin Guy?"

"You got the same impression, huh?"

"Don't cut me out of the historical research on this one," she said. "I want to know what kind of weird stuff was happening up here."

"I'll get you your own box of dusty documents." I took a few more readings and double-checked Stacey's camera on its tripod. Then we passed through a narrow room, possibly once a private sitting room or office, and out through a pair of huge double doors into the main hall. We were around the corner from the door where we'd entered.

We found a short sort of receiving room, with the fancier guest elevator at one end and double doors at the other, small padded benches along the sides under mirrors and old paintings. The main purpose of the room seemed to be added security for the people on the fourth floor, keeping out stray hotel guests. The doors opposite the elevator had little glass lenses installed, giving a view of any visitors who might arrive before they could be admitted deeper into the fourth floor.

After that, we continued along the main hall, laying a few REM pods behind us, and finally reached the more familiar area with the row of small bedrooms and the weirdo black-temple room. Stacey sighed as I pushed open one of the double doors to the temple area, which were ornate on this side, with more occult symbols and hieroglyphs, even though they were a virtually invisible pair of jib doors on the other side.

"I guess we need to change out the batteries..." She shook her head and went to work with the cameras and microphone we'd set up the previous day.

The air in the room felt heavy and cold. I set out our last few REM pods around the circle of empty sockets built into the floor. They flickered, just slightly.

When we were done, Stacey began rolling the luggage cart toward the hidden jib door in the side wall, the quickest path to the freight elevator. I followed, my boots clicking on hardwood.

All four of the REM pods around the center of the room let out their digital *woo-woo* sounds, making us turn back. The rows of lights on top of each pod flickered and pulsed, which indicated something was interacting with their electromagnetic fields.

"Who's there?" I asked, shining my flashlight around the room.

The temple room seemed to be growing darker, moment by moment, as if black clouds were seeping out of the walls and corners, absorbing our flashlight beams until they were too weak to reveal anything. This kind of total darkness means a very heavy presence haunts the area.

My Mel-Meter detected sudden falling temperatures, and so did the goosebump-o-meter all over my skin.

Then the whispering began. The low voices spilled out all around us, filling up the room, as if a crowd of spirits emerged from the walls, floor, and ceiling and moved toward us from every direction. All our gear went wild, the REM pods chiming ceaselessly, my meter showing surges of eight to ten milligaus.

Stacey and I looked at each other. Her face was bleach-white, and I'm sure mine was the same. The hotel was infested with ghosts. It was like an eruption of them, drawn to our presence, bringing darkness with them.

"Should we run?" Stacey whispered.

"Did one of you kill a man?" I asked the whispering darkness as it closed in around us.

The voices seemed to grow louder and more agitated.

One of our REM pods, flashing and chiming as fast and loud as it possibly could, slowly rose several inches from the marble-tile floor and hovered. It turned in place, like a flying saucer, all the while flashing and beeping.

I felt a chill pass through me. This was some very focused psychokinetic energy, pointing to an active, conscious presence in the room with us.

"We just want to ask some questions," I said.

The hovering REM pod flew at me at high speed, fast enough to make a whooshing sound as it passed through the air. I barely managed to dodge aside. It cracked into the jib door behind me, then tumbled to the floor, dark and silent.

The three other pods rose from the floor, spinning and flashing.

"Out out out!" I yelled at Stacey, and we shoved the luggage rack with our remaining gear through the jib door in the wall. We slammed it shut behind us, and three loud bangs sounded on the other side, as the other pods smashed against the door.

"That's going to make a dent in the tech budget," Stacey whispered. She was still pale, catching her breath, but she pounded the closed door with one fist. "Hey, you'd better leave my cameras alone!"

The freight elevator took its time coming up to fetch us. Distant sounds, like low voices and footsteps, echoed from the dark rooms nearby.

Downstairs, the big, bright windows filled the third-floor hallway with sunlight. It was a jarring sight after the shadowy fourth floor, like emerging from a dark horror movie at the theater into a sunny Saturday afternoon.

## Chapter Seven

We spent the afternoon in the hotel room, Stacey sifting through audio and video footage. As far as we could tell, the ghosts hadn't damaged any of the other gear in the temple room upstairs.

I checked the internet for any more information about the Lathrop Grand hotel, especially any ghost-enthusiast footage I could find. One tourist had caught a suggestion of a reflection in the mirror of Room 208, a glimpse of a woman in white, her facial features blurred. Another YouTube video showed a hallway on the second or third floor. The sounds of boots were captured, along with a shadowy figure that blinked across the hall. Any of these could have been easily faked, but my experiences in the hotel so far didn't exactly lead me to doubt them.

Little information was available about the fourth floor, though. Nobody was ever allowed up there, not even the ghost shows from television. A few ghost-lore websites mentioned Ithaca Galloway's séances and occult interests, describing how she bought the hotel in 1895 because it was already so haunted.

There was much more information about Dr. and Mrs. Lathrop, who'd founded the hotel back in 1851. Dr. Uriah Lathrop had died during the yellow fever epidemic of 1876, while working night and day to treat patients. His wife Mabel lived until 1885, and then the hotel was closed for a decade until Ithaca Galloway's purchase and renovation. Ithaca herself died in 1921, and the hotel passed through a succession of owners over the following century, often sitting vacant for years.

Unable to find much new information, I soon found myself looking up Paranormal Solutions, Inc. yet again. This was the organization attempting to buy our detective agency from my boss, Calvin Eckhart, who was looking to retire and move to Florida to be close to his newborn grandchild. My future felt pretty shaky.

Paranormal Solutions seemed to have its strongest presence in New England, including Boston, a city that I'm sure has its own large ghost population. They investigated and removed unwanted entities, just like we did, and also manufactured high-end ghost-hunting gear for investigators and hobbyists with lots of money to burn. Their "Higher Self Metaphysical Centers" offered everything from psychic tests and ESP classes to relatively traditional activities like yoga and meditation.

They had offices in Baltimore, but no locations south of Maryland. It was obvious why they wanted to move into our market, with heavily haunted cities like Savannah and Charleston.

Calvin had made it clear that we really had only two options— sell out to the bigger company, or refuse and lose lots of business when they inevitably set up a competing shop in our town. I couldn't say either possibility really appealed to me. I liked being an independent scrapper and didn't want to get absorbed into a larger corporate situation, assuming they chose not to fire me and replace me with their own people. Stacey could get fired just as easily.

I hoped to find some dirt, something that would make Calvin reject their offer, but I couldn't come up with much. I slammed my laptop in frustration.

"What's wrong?" Stacey asked from the video editing station she'd rigged up with a laptop and two tablets. "Did you find out they're going to remake and totally ruin another one of your favorite childhood movies?"

"Something like that." I stood up from the armchair and stretched. "I should probably get ready to go meet Javier."

"Hey, check this out." Stacey removed her headphones and turned up the volume on her speakers. "It's from that weird temple room."

I listened.

"Who's there?" my voice asked on the recording.

*"We are."*

*"Always."*

*"He's coming."*

"Who's coming?" I asked, and Stacey shrugged.

On the recording, my voice asked whether someone present had killed a man. The response was a loud, overlapping chorus of voices, but Stacey couldn't sharpen them enough for us to hear the actual words.

"I wonder if *he* refers to the entity that threw the REM pods at us," I said. "Maybe that bearded Rasputin-y guy. We need to find out more about the individuals who lived up there. Grant emailed and said we could meet tomorrow."

"Aw, email," Stacey said. "He's so old-fashioned."

"I'd be ready for Jacob's walk-through after that. Do you think he's available tomorrow night?"

"He'd better not have any major nighttime plans I don't know about." Stacey narrowed her eyes and glowered, then broke character and laughed.

"You know, there's truth in humor," I said. "If you're joking about being insanely suspicious and jealous, then at *some* level, maybe you really are."

"At some level, we're all just fish wondering how the heck we stumbled onto dry land. That's science."

"Sure it is," I said. "You make arrangements with Jacob. I'll go talk to that construction guy at the Mexican restaurant. Want me to bring you anything for supper?"

Stacey nodded. "Yeah, bring me anything for supper. You sure you don't want me to come?"

"I'd really prefer if you could, but I probably won't be back until after dark. Someone has to monitor the monitors." I gestured toward the array of little TV screens we'd transplanted from the van, and I indicated the video feeds from the second floor. "Keep a special eye around Room 208. I feel like that family doesn't get how much danger they're in, or they would have moved out by now."

"Should we approach the family ourselves?" Stacey asked.

I took a deep breath. "I'm pretty sure Madeline would fire us if we tried that—she doesn't want us interacting with guests, much less telling them their lives could be in danger."

"I'm liking Madeline less and less as we go," Stacey said. "She should've made them leave the room. She shouldn't let anyone stay there until we're done."

"I agree. But if she fires us, there will be nobody looking out for that family, and nobody to stop Abigail from cutting anyone else. Nobody to get rid of whatever's on the fourth floor, either."

"Maybe they could call Paranormal Solutions, Inc. instead."

"Not funny, Stacey."

I changed into fresh jeans and a black blouse, which is about as colorful as my wardrobe gets. I wore short sleeves for a change, since I doubted I'd get jumped by a vicious spirit over at La Comarca. I still wore my leather jacket just in case. You never know in this town.

La Comarca turned out to be an unexpectedly authentic place tucked into a low brick building with a flea market and a granite-supply yard for neighbors. Definitely not one of those faux-Spanish-mission places with a cartoon donkey on the sign. Inside, the staff and crowd spoke Spanish, and the air was rich with spices and beans.

I glanced from the menu to the crowded tables. I had no idea what Javier looked like. Fortunately, he found me pretty quickly. I don't know if he'd stalked me on Facebook or what, but probably I just didn't fit in with the crowd.

He was a man in his forties, balding, handlebar mustache, broad-shouldered and muscular at the arms, quite a bit softer at the belly. He wore a pressed white shirt, tie, and jeans over polished leather boots.

"Are you Ms. Jordan?" he asked.

"Ellie. Are you Mr. Morales?"

"Javier," he said. "Madeline Colt told me to speak to you. I want to be honest—I don't like the idea of talking about it at all. But she said you're some kind of expert on these things?"

"I have some experience with...these things," I said.

"You aren't a priest, it's obvious." He led me toward a table in one corner, already occupied by three other young men. "Are you a nun?"

I laughed. "Nothing so exalted."

"A *curandera*?"

"Just a regular, workaday ghost hunter." I gave an uncertain smile as I sat with Javier and the three younger men. "Are you sure you don't want to speak privately?"

"These men all worked on the Lathrop Grand job with me," he

said. "Hector, Mateo, Luis."

The young men nodded, and I shook their hands. They all had strong grips and thickly calloused fingers. They smiled but didn't speak.

At Javier's insistence, I tried some of the food from the buffet, and it put my allegedly five-star breakfast to shame, even though all I had was simple tamales and some rice and beans.

"I want to hear all about your experiences," I told them, when Javier was finally satisfied that I was eating. "Everything unusual you saw while working in that hotel."

They spoke among themselves in hushed Spanish, and whatever they said drew curious looks from nearby tables. Finally, Javier said, "First, there were voices. Like whispering. Like the building wanted to tell you something, or..." He shook his head. "More like the hotel was whispering to itself. Like a crazy person. Then, on day two or three, the footsteps, the slamming doors. You'd go to look and there would be nobody. We started to lose guys right away."

"They must have been scared."

He nodded. "I promised these guys extra pay if they stay and finish the job. They agreed, and Valentino agreed, too." He fell silent for a moment, and so did the others, as if to momentarily honor the dead. I realized I hadn't heard the dead man's name before. Madeline certainly hadn't mentioned it.

I waited, sympathizing with the loss of their friend. I've lost people close to me, too.

"It got worse," Javier finally said. "Crashing sounds. Screaming. Our tools moved around when we were out of the room. Destruction. Then Valentino's death."

"Can you tell me about that?"

"He was up on the ladder. And he just squashed against it, like some giant had pushed him. The ladder folded up like that." Javier clapped his hands. "It was over before any of us could move. He landed the wrong way, broke his neck."

"Did you see any specific apparition before or after that happened? Hear any specific voices?"

They spoke among themselves again, and then Javier nodded. "Luis saw a thing like a white shadow. I saw something like this myself, the day before that."

"Where was it?"

"The jib door leading to the elevator was propped open," Javier said. "I saw it pass by there. When I went to look, nobody was in the hall. And Luis saw it in that doorway just before Valentino's ladder fell."

"A white shadow?" I asked, just to make sure I had that right.

Javier glanced at his workers, then back at me. "It cut me."

"Cut you?"

He nodded, then unbuttoned his shirt cuff and rolled up his sleeve. A long, thin scar was visible across his bicep, very reminiscent of the injury on my back.

"Ouch," I said.

"It cut us all." He spoke in rapid Spanish to the other men. One of them pulled his shirt collar out to show me a mark across his shoulder, and another lifted his shirt to show a long, narrow mark across his abdominal muscles. "Luis was cut on his thigh," Javier added. "But if you want him to take off his pants—"

"No, that's okay, I get it," I said. "When did these happen?"

"It's hard to say," Javier replied. "We all noticed them later. We were so busy with Valentino's accident, trying to help him, calling for the ambulance. I didn't feel it right when it happened, but sometime later I looked down and saw red on my shirt."

That was just how it had happened for me, too.

"Can you remember anything else unusual from that day?" I asked.

They spoke among themselves yet again, then Javier shook his head. "Some footsteps, some voices, the usual. Valentino's death was my fault. We should have quit as soon as we saw the fourth floor was haunted. I convinced these men to stay and work, I saw only the money...I will never make that mistake again."

"You would never work in the Lathrop Grand again?"

"Never. Nowhere like that, I don't care what it pays."

The group fell silent, and I wasn't sure what else to say. They didn't seem to have much more to tell me.

Then something that the head custodian had mentioned clicked, and I thought of one more question.

"Is there a female on your crew?" I asked. "Or was there, when you started at the hotel, before the workers started quitting?"

"No, there never was."

"Then I wonder who Earl was talking about. He mentioned a lady in the 'last group' that went up to the fourth floor. He said he warned her not to go up there."

"Who is Earl?" Javier asked.

"The head custodian at the Lathrop. Kind of an older, skinny guy."

"Oh, I know who you're talking about. He never said a thing to us. Definitely no warning. I did not really believe in ghosts before this, so I probably would not have listened. I thought the ghost was supposed to be on the second floor, anyway. Nobody warned us."

"Huh." I had to wonder who Earl was talking about, then. A previous contractor? I wasn't filled with joy at the idea of going down to see him in the basement again. "You don't have any idea who he might have been talking about?"

"Sorry."

I passed out business cards to all of them. "I really appreciate your help. If you think of anything else, please let me know."

"Call me if you need any work done at your house," Javier said. "As long as it's not haunted."

I doubted that would happen, since I'm a renter, but I just nodded and smiled. "Thanks again."

Driving back to the hotel, I sifted through what I'd learned. I felt like the family in 208 was definitely in danger now, but there was no clear way to deal with that except to keep an eye on them. I'd already informed the hotel's management, and that was all I was allowed to do. If things grew too dangerous, though, I would have to act to save the kid, even at the risk of losing the client and getting sued over the nondisclosure nonsense.

I stepped on the gas, wondering whether Stacey had discovered anything new while I was away.

# Chapter Eight

I arrived at the hotel around sundown, and Stacey did have some things to show me. She'd edited them away from the massive amount of raw footage, creating a kind of video summary for me.

Her instruments had detected cold spots all over the second and third floors, shadowy figures in the guest stairwell, and the usual array of craziness on the fourth floor. The camera had picked up something from outside 208 just before the previous occupants ran out screaming. It was a pale partial apparition, only visible for a second, suggesting the outline of a female. Given the location and the events, it looked like we'd caught a glimpse of Stabby Abby on her way to terrorize the guests in her room.

The live night and thermal feeds from inside the temple room abruptly turned black on the monitors. I pointed it out to Stacey.

"They're not broadcasting," she said, after checking her laptop. "Could be a shutdown, battery drainage, destruction of the cameras....You're not going to say we should go up there."

"It seems too dangerous at night. Though after what Javier and his workers told me, it's easily as dangerous during the day."

"So let's just avoid it altogether."

"I wish we could. Let's wait and see before heading up there again. Make sure they're not going to get even more active and destructive tonight."

"I like the wait and see part," Stacey said. "What's in the box?"

"Empanadas." I handed her the takeout box from the restaurant. "I'll eat the leftovers if you have any."

"That's a pretty big endorsement. Better than three thumbs up." She began picking open the deep-fried yellow shell with her plastic fork.

The early night hours were relatively calm. I paid extra attention to the hot room that we suspected to be Mr. Rasputin's bedroom, with its secret connection to the widow Galloway's private quarters. The temperature rose and fell in slow pulses lasting several minutes each, as if some enormous presence, big enough to fill the room, were breathing very, very slowly.

I was surprised by the complete lack of activity in Ithaca Galloway's bedroom. Stacey said she hadn't noticed anything while I was gone, either, though she still needed to review the footage.

"It's like the ghosts are hiding from us," Stacey said.

"They might be. Maybe they're just lying low, hoping we'll leave. Or lying in ambush, hoping we'll come back." I looked at the hallway outside 208. The aging metalhead couple and their daughter were returning to their room. I sighed.

Ghost hunting might sound glamorous, what with the poltergeists throwing you down the stairs and such, but sometimes it moves slowly, like a police stakeout. Watching and waiting. Listening. Lulling you into face state of calm just before something grabs you from the shadows.

Around midnight, I left our room and took a walk around the third floor. I found a few cold spots and elevated EMF readings that were uncomfortably close to our rooms, located right on the same hall.

Down on the second floor, I found spikes just where I expected them, clustered around the door to 208 like invisible electrical arrows pointed right at the famously haunted room. I loitered there for a minute, listening for any activity within, but I didn't hear much.

"Stacey, I'm heading down to the first floor," I told her through my headset. "The place is dead quiet. Madeline shouldn't mind me poking around this late, if she finds out."

"Ten-four," Stacey said. "Copy that. Aye-aye."

I rolled my eyes just a little as I returned to the stairwell.

With help from my staff keycard, I checked out the major rooms on the lobby level. One had a long conference or dining table and paintings depicting Dr. and Mrs. Lathrop and the hotel's nineteenth-century glory. An immense fireplace sat opposite a huge bay window that looked out onto the street between light blue curtains the size of frigate sails, currently drawn tight against any curious pedestrians on the sidewalk.

I moved to the library, stocked with old leather volumes that I would bet nobody had touched in decades, other than to dust them. Framed maps of colonial and antebellum Georgia adorned the wall, and one pedestal held a globe manufactured in 1899.

Activity seemed elevated here—it was sporadic all over the hotel, as if I were constantly passing ghosts who drew back from me and didn't want to be seen. Better than constantly running into ghosts who want to attack, I suppose.

The first-floor ballroom was an expansive and open space, the exact opposite of the dim, column-cluttered room that Madeline had called "the fourth-floor ballroom" and Stacey and I called "that weird temple place." Floor-to-ceiling mirrors were embedded along one of the long walls, opposite windows of the same size on the far side of the room, reminding me of pictures I'd seen of the Palace of Versailles. Again, the drapes were pulled tight.

I clicked on my flashlight as I entered, since I didn't want to draw attention to myself by turning on the giant chandeliers overhead. My boots sounded too loud on the floor as I passed the stacked tables and chairs, then the long marble bar. I could imagine years and years of parties and events here, all the memories and emotions piled up like geological strata under the calm, silent surface. Built to accommodate crowds, live music, and dancing, the room was eerie when it sat dark and deserted. This was where the hotel held its glamorous Halloween ball each year.

I exited through glass double doors into the courtyard, where tall heaps of fall flowers bloomed inside raised brick planter islands. Benches and covered swings were nestled here and there among the gardens. The high brick wall offered complete privacy from the outside world. I was a little worried about accidentally stumbling into vacationing couples who might have retreated to the hidden nooks of the courtyard for a little romance, tucked behind arching tree limbs thick with purple wisteria.

My main interest was the massive, centuries-old oak tree at the corner of the yard, whose gnarled, curling limbs were each as large as a sizable tree trunk. Massive old oaks always look as if they're full of secrets, and maybe dark magic hidden somewhere in their twisted, ancient bodies.

Abigail Bowen had been hanged here after a very speedy arrest and trial. I'd glimpsed her apparition here the night before. On top of that, Ithaca Galloway had featured this tree in her own portrait on the fourth floor, holding a branch—possibly from this tree itself—as her walking staff.

I reached out and touched the rough, mottled old bark, thinking of the woman who'd died here. I wondered if Abigail really deserved her nickname, Stabby Abby, or if she'd been a scapegoat, blamed and executed for a crime committed by someone else. The occupying army would have been eager for revenge against a local who murdered their wounded soldiers, possibly too eager to do a thorough investigation. I had no specific reason to believe her innocent, but no real evidence to prove her guilt, either. Maybe Grant could clarify things.

I looked up at the thick branch where I'd seen her from the second floor. I wondered what it had felt like, being strung up in front of a curious crowd like that. I wondered what had gone through her mind at that moment, her last moment of life. I supposed it depended a lot on whether she was guilty or innocent.

"Hello," a female voice spoke right behind me, startlingly close, almost too low to hear. My fight-or-flight instincts went into high response, and I spun around, drawing my flashlight. My other hand went to the iPod on my belt, ready to blast some potent gospel music if the entity threatened me.

The girl who stood behind me looked solid enough. She wore a black felt hat that looked like it had been stolen from Boy George somewhere around 1983. It hid her face in shadows. Her purple t-shirt depicted, perhaps ironically, a cutesy flying unicorn, trailing a rainbow like a comet tail, and all kinds of glittery junk was glued to her jeans. Brightly colored plastic bracelets decorated her wrists. Overall, nothing about her really said "murderous ghost from centuries past."

She tilted her head to look at me, a startled expression on her face. A thin, sallow girl with a bad overbite—she was the one staying in Room 208 with the ghost-enthusiast parents from Seattle.

"You scared me," she said.

"I could've sworn you were the one sneaking up and scaring me." I looked around for her parents, but they were nowhere in sight. "You aren't out here alone, are you?"

"I didn't leave the hotel!" she said in a rushed, automatic way that told me she'd used this defense before. "I'm still inside the walls."

"Your parents don't mind you wandering around at night?"

"I'll just tell them some stupid ghost made me do it. They'll believe that. I had to get out of our room."

"You don't like it in there?"

"Feels like someone's watching. I don't know how they can sleep in there. Makes my skin go crawly."

"Have you told them that?"

"They just want to *see* the stupid ghosts," she said. "All the time."

"But you don't want to."

"They never ask me if I want to go all these scary places."

"Shouldn't you be in school right now?"

"I *am*. My parents transferred me to Emerald City Free School, where 'the world is your classroom.' So we flew all the way from Seattle just to come *here*. Why couldn't we just go to Wild Waves and do roller coasters? Or Bellevue Botanical Garden. That's where I want to go, and it's not far from the apartment, so why can't we go there?"

"You like flowers?"

"I like *all* the plants, not just the angiosperms." She said the last word carefully and slowly, as though she'd learned it recently. "Um, do you think the hotel would care if I took a couple of these flowers?"

"Probably not, if you just take a few."

"Good. Because I, um, already did." The girl stepped back into a nook under an arching tree branch and emerged with a book-sized wooden box painted with nail-polish flowers and decorated with butterfly stickers. She opened the hinged top to show me a few bright blossoms and red leaves taken from around the garden, now flattened under a sheet of clear paper. She pointed to a pink blossom. "This comes from an azalea, I think an Encore azalea. I'm not sure about this one..." She looked up at me.

"If you're asking me, you're barking up the wrong tree," I said. "I think you know more about flowers than I do."

"Oh." She seemed a little saddened by this. "My mom doesn't

know about them, either."

"That's why we have the internet," I said. "I do know about ghosts, though. Did you see anything in your room? Hear anything?"

"Oh, great. Another kookaburra." She circled her ear in the gesture for *crazy*. "You should hang out with my parents. You can all talk about ghosts together."

"You don't believe in ghosts?"

She shrugged. "I believe in tarantulas, but I don't go *looking* for them."

I laughed at that. "I see what you mean."

"It touched me," she said, her voice lower. "I woke up and my arm was way out from the bed, like someone was holding it, and I could feel fingers."

"The ghost in your room was a nurse. They say she sometimes checks people's pulses."

"It was creepy." The girl shivered, wrapping her arms around herself.

"Did you tell your parents?"

"They were already asleep. And they'd probably just be *happy* about it."

"Maybe they should get you a separate room," I said. "I've been in 208. There's a connecting door to the next room."

"Yeah, like they'd pay for *that*. Can we stop talking about the ghosts now?"

"Sure. My name's Ellie. We didn't actually meet before."

"Lemmy," she said with a wrinkled nose. "It's not short for anything. Just Lemmy."

"Did they name you after that guy from Motörhead?"

Her only response was an *ugh* sound.

"You collect a lot of flowers?" I asked, trying to get her back to a subject that neither frightened nor annoyed her.

"Yes. I have six albums of them at home. And I make greeting cards. Want to see one?"

"Sure."

She handed me a card made of bristol board. A cluster of tiny blue, yellow, and red pressed flowers covered about half of the front flap, and the words "HAPPY BIRTHDAY!" had been carefully written in curling, floral letters.

"That's birthday – general," she said, and it took me a second to realize she was referring to the section where you'd find it at a retail store.

"It's very pretty."

"It's two dollars if you want one."

"I do, thanks." I scrounged out a couple of dollars from my pocket, my change from dinner. I was lucky to have it since I'd left my purse in the hotel room.

"All sales are final," she added as she passed me the birthday card.

"Ellie?" Stacey's voice crackled over my headset. "I've got...activity."

"Where?" I asked.

"Right up here," Stacey's voice whispered. "They're on our floor. Near our room. Cold spots...and *footsteps*, Ellie. I can hear them through the wall. Coming and going...then coming back again. Wouldn't be so bad if they would just go and *not* come back. They're heavy, like boots, but I don't see anybody on camera..."

"I'm coming." I looked at Lemmy, thinking I should tell her to go back to her room with her parents. Then I decided she was probably safer wandering the first floor of the hotel, where ghostly activity seemed minimal. "I have to go. Will you be okay?"

"I was okay before you got here."

"Good point. Promise me you won't leave the hotel, okay?"

"Duh." She turned and walked back to the flower garden, resuming her search for blooms to swipe.

I returned through the quiet, empty lobby. The night clerk was nowhere in sight as I passed the front desk and continued on to the ornate brass doors of the guest elevator.

The third floor was chilly, like someone had decided to try for a deep-winter outdoorsy feel. My Mel-Meter indicated it was about forty degrees, not far above freezing.

The hallway was deserted, and the lights seemed dimmer than usual, though they were always on the subtle side. I drew my tactical flashlight to be safe, keeping it off for now.

I passed paintings of people in antebellum garb standing around what looked like luxuriously appointed garden parties. They'd seemed innocuous enough at a glance, but in the current atmosphere they took an oddly sinister aspect. Little knots of wealthy planters and their wives, speaking in whispers to each other. In one picture, they seemed to be watching a young slave man clad in livery and serving drinks. There was something hungry and cannibalistic in their faces.

Voices echoed ahead, from around the corner I was approaching as I headed toward the back of the third floor to meet up with Stacey. They were not the voices of the living, I was almost sure of it from the strange, elongated tones. Not whispers like on the fourth floor, either, but moans and groans, overlapping expressions of human agony, like a classic haunted house is supposed to sound, minus the heavy chains dragging in the attic.

I rounded the corner, ready to face whatever apparitions the house was about to show me.

I saw nothing—primarily because the lights had gone out all the way down the hallway, creating a long, dark tunnel for me to traverse, filled with those agonizing moans.

My flashlight managed to push back the darkness for a moment. Then it faded as if the batteries had abruptly died, though I'd added new ones just the previous day.

"Stacey, what are you seeing?" I whispered. Our room was ahead, just around the next corner. All I had to do was cross through the inexplicably dark hallway that echoed softly with tormented cries.

No answer came. My headset battery was drained, too, which probably meant all my electrical gear had been sucked dry. My flesh crawled with the cold and the certainty of being surrounded by the dead. Not the grateful kind, either, but the definitely-unhappy kind.

They'd sucked all the heat out of the hallway, and now they'd drained the power from my gear. It meant my primary go-away-ghost defensive weapons, my high-powered flashlight and my iPod loaded with holy music, would not function, and also that I was cut off from Stacey.

What worried me more, though, was the question of what exactly the spirits were planning to *do* with all that energy they'd just gathered.

"Okay." I took a deep breath, feeling very alone. The doors on either side of the hall remained shut, as if the hotel guests within could not hear these frosty, aching voices—or maybe they could, and wisely chose to stay inside their rooms. Or maybe they were all just sleeping like the dead.

"Stay back," I whispered to the unseen presences in the hallway. I took one step forward into the darkness, wondering why there wasn't any light from the big window at the far end. The curtains might have been pulled for the night, or the place might have just been thick with dark ghosts.

I took another step, then another, the light from the previous hallway fading much too fast as I walked away from it. The air grew colder and thicker as I went, the moans clearer as if they were already surrounding me. There was another sound, a faint buzzing like....bees? No, flies.

The smell struck me almost immediately after I heard the flies. Rotten meat. Blood. The rancid stink of sweaty, diseased flesh was unmistakable. My stomach clenched in revulsion, and I clutched it, fought down my immediate urge to run and empty its contents, and forced myself to continue walking into the thick of it. The situation was clearly dangerous, but it also might give me some idea of exactly what kind of entity I was up against, as long as I didn't get killed along the way.

"Who's there?" I asked, reluctantly breathing in the rank air in order to do so. "You can speak to me. Or show yourself."

The moans rose like a chorus of the damned.

Then I heard the footsteps, like heavy boots approaching from behind me.

I spun, ready to face it, whatever it might be. A dark, empty hallway stretched away behind me, the red carpet runner still neatly positioned along the center of the polished floorboards. The spillover light from the first hall kept it partially lit, revealing nothing at all. The boot steps had ceased, too. Just a creeper, I hoped, trying to scare me but too timid to actually face me. Making sounds, then running away, the ghostly equivalent of a ding-dong-dash.

I let out a sigh of relief, then turned back to continue walking.

He was *there*, just in front of me, standing so close it would have been rude had the man actually been alive. Since he was clearly dead, it wasn't just rude, it also sent a jolt of terror screaming right into my heart. I'm surprised I didn't flop over from cardiac arrest right there. I heard myself draw in cold, rotten air with a gasp.

He was only inches away, a dark but solid apparition, much taller than me, definitely more than six feet high. Pale metallic buttons glimmered down the front of his blue-black wool jacket, the edges of which were completely indistinct from the shadows around him.

He stood close enough that I had to tilt to my head up to see his face, and I quickly wished I hadn't. His skin was translucent. His eyes were vacant sockets, seeming to look deep into me despite the complete lack of eyes. I hate when they do that. It's just deeply horrifying to have black sockets boring into you from a pale dead face.

A black slash ran all the way across his throat. As my brain began to slowly function again after the initial shock of seeing him, I thought of the infamous throat-slasher, Abigail Bowen.

My mouth opened as if I had any idea what to say to the dead soldier. I couldn't make a sound. If I could have, I probably would have screamed.

*Okay, get it together, Ellie,* a part of me whispered, making its bid to be the get-tough and get-moving voice in my head. I took a deep breath and held my ground, letting the dead guy make the next move.

He raised his left arm from his side, and something long and sharp slashed through the air by my head. I gasped and dodged away, then turned to see what kind of weapon I was dealing with here.

He swung a pale, rust-dotted bayonet in his left hand, and it continued its upward arc until it pointed directly to the ceiling. The cuff of his Union Army coat slid back just a bit, and then I realized he *had* no left hand at all, just the bayonet in place of it. If there was a rifle attached below the bayonet, it was still concealed in the heavy coat sleeve...but, rifle or not, the guy definitely had a bayonet for a left hand.

Okay. I've seen things like this before. A ghost's apparition is often a projection of its self-image, which can grow extremely distorted from what the person actually looked like in life. It's particularly true if the person was mentally disturbed or traumatized in life, or became that way after existing as a ghost for years and years. So the bayonet-arm showed something about how far he identified his life with his weapon, or maybe that he identified himself as a weapon, as a killing machine who wasn't entirely human. Totally understandable, really, given the relentless industrial-scale brutality of the Civil War.

I couldn't say that understanding this on an intellectual level offered much comfort. Here was a spirit with a long, sharp weapon for a limb. It might also represent concentrated aggressive psychokinetic energy that could slice and dice me. I'd already been cut once in this supposedly luxurious hotel.

So I wanted to keep my distance.

He didn't come leaping at me with that bayonet, very fortunately for me, but continued its swing until it came to rest on his shoulder, as though he were carrying the weapon in formation rather than being biologically attached to it.

Maybe I should have questioned him, asked him if he knew anything about the workman who'd died upstairs. Maybe I should have whipped out my little Lois Lane notepad and pencil to really give him the investigative what-for. It's easy to say that, but much harder to pull off when you're looking into the black eye sockets of a man who's been dead and gone for more than a century and a half.

What I didn't do was break and run, screaming my head off, and I'm going to say I'm proud of that.

He swiveled on his heel—giving me a moment's relief from that hollow, unblinking death gaze—faced the darkness ahead, and began to march, one foot a little limp and dragging, which added a rasping sound to the heavy boot-clomps. I was willing to bet those were the same clomping sounds Stacey had called about.

The moaning voices and the unpleasant smells grew sharper. A few candles sputtered to life, scattered at irregular intervals down the hallway. They didn't give much light, but after a moment, I was grateful that they didn't.

The visuals had arrived, accompanying the other sensory apparitions. I walked down another version of this hallway, the luxurious carpet runner missing, the walls decorated with peeling floral wallpaper.

Men lay on makeshift wooden cots jammed against the walls on either side, leaving only a narrow aisle along the middle for me to attempt to pass. The bayonet-armed soldier marched on ahead of me, between the cots, but he was taking his time about it. Why not? He had years and years to pass.

These were clearly the war wounded, missing arms, legs, and eyes, their amputated stumps swaddled in blood-stained cloth rags. They writhed on their wooden-plank beds, seeming to grow more excited as I walked between them. Mixed with my fear was sorrow at the sight of their obvious and extreme pain.

One man reached out and grabbed at my hip as I passed, and I jerked away. The man's right leg was a stump below the knee, the wet black bandaging peeling away from it. Half his head was swaddled in dirty cloth. His visible eye was pale shades of white, no hint of color at all.

Others began to grab at me, their moans becoming more intense, like maximum-security prisoners who hadn't seen a woman in decades. They were probably just desperate to establish some contact with the living, to reach out from their private hell in search of compassion, but I didn't want to wait around to see how things developed.

This was something between a cluster of apparitions and a full-on time slip. A time slip is when a location's past suddenly bleeds through into the present, usually recreating some moment of peak emotional intensity. This wasn't just a recording of the past, though—the souls of those soldiers, or at least fragments of their souls (theories differ) were trapped here, continuing to suffer. I could tell because they were trying to interact with me. I wondered what kept them in the hotel all these years.

I wanted to dash down the hall, past the horribly wounded souls and their desperate grabs for attention, but Ol' Bayonet Arm marched at half-time. I did not want to push past him and have him walking behind me. If we were going to be in the same room, I wanted him right where I could see him, thanks.

So I had to move slowly, avoiding reaching hands and amputated stumps, feeling a mix of fear and pity for the wounded men on their cots.

Another detail I couldn't help noticing: every single one of them had a black slash mark across his throat, not unlike the thin line drawn on my back by what I'd assumed to be a ghostly scalpel.

Doing my best to keep my distance, I followed the soldier apparition to the far end of the hall, and I managed not to get my soul sucked out or my jacket sleeve torn along the way. The window showed nothing but pure black outside.

The soldier turned and began to march down the next hall, also lit by candles and smelling of death. I wondered where he was going, and whether he intended for me to follow or if he was going to turn back at any moment and attack me for riding his tail.

One sagging wooden door creaked open beside me, and Stacey stood in the doorway, looking out from her completely modern hotel room. Strange alien sounds, which I strongly suspected to be a Katy Perry song, drifted out from behind her.

"Ellie?" she asked.

Just like that, everything was back to normal, a softly illuminated hotel room corridor appointed with antique knickknacks and fresh flowers, nothing more. It was as if the whole nightmarish scene had been a bubble of illusion, vanishing all at once with a single pinprick.

Stuff like that will make you question your sanity.

Stacey repeated my name again, and I stumbled inside, closing the door behind me. I was shaking and, I realized, freezing cold, a fact which did not stop me from sweating profusely.

"What happened?" she asked, while I collapsed onto her bed. "Ellie? What did you see?"

I took a deep breath, really trying to pull my brains back together so I could form rational sentences again.

"Well," I said. "Either there's a convention in town of the most hardcore Civil War reenactors ever, or I just saw the ghosts of those men Abigail Bowen killed."

"Did they have anything interesting to say?"

"Mostly a lot of groaning in pain." I detailed what I'd seen, pausing to drink some hot green tea she was thoughtful enough to brew. She also wrapped a blanket around me, since I was freezing cold.

"All that, right out here?" Stacey reached toward the closed door. "They're hanging out in the hall outside our room? What are they doing?"

"Lying there bleeding, for the most part. Except that one bayonet-armed guy. He's marching up and down. I don't know if he's the commanding officer or he's guarding the others or what. But he's pretty scary."

"Huh." Stacey opened the door and peered out into the hall. "Hard to believe. My cameras cut out—I was trying to get them back online, and re-establish contact with you...Ellie?"

I'd lain back on her bed, my eyes drifting closed. The spirits hadn't just drained my gear to pull off that big appearance, they'd drained the energy from my body. I felt vulnerable and weak, and I didn't like it one bit. I didn't like the idea of operating in a house where the entities could do this to me.

"Gotta get back to work," I mumbled. "After I rest my eyes for a second."

Then I zonked out into a deep sleep.

## Chapter Nine

I awoke groggy and still sweaty a couple hours later, washed in the light of a score of black and white monitors. It took me a moment to get my bearings.

Stacey sat a few feet away in one of the deeply upholstered armchairs, watching the video array, her headset on.

"Ugh." I sat up, smearing away a mat of my long black hair that had stuck to my face. I didn't exactly feel rejuvenated and refreshed after my nap. More like I wanted to go soak my throbbing head in a tub full of ice for an hour or so, then hop right back into bed.

I rubbed my eyes and tapped Stacey on the shoulder. She jumped—she'd been staring at a complex line graph of audio data displayed on her screen.

"Hey, you spooked me," she said, removing her headset. "I'm trying to decipher these crazy inhuman voices from the fourth floor. Not a good time to sneak up on me."

"I wasn't sneaking." I glanced at the clock. Almost three a.m. "Why'd you let me sleep so long?"

"I didn't have much choice, did I? Does this sound like Latin to you?" She placed her headset around my ears. I heard static, interspersed with a flat, chanting voice or ten.

"Could be. Sounds like a lot of *-us* endings. *Dominus, spiritus*...uh, *octopus*, maybe?"

"That's from the fourth floor. Now look at the third floor. I managed to get the cameras outside our room online again." She gestured to a pair of monitors. The regular camera showed nothing, but the thermal revealed lumpy cold spots alongside both walls where I'd seen the suffering war amputees. "Doesn't look like they plan on going anywhere. I think this one's your eyeless boyfriend." She pointed to a cold spot drifting slowly down the middle of the hall. "It's like he's pacing out there. Maybe waiting for you to come back, huh?"

"Maybe it has nothing to do with me."

"They weren't out there last night. Not according to the thermal camera."

"The cameras don't always capture everything," I said. "They might have spent the last hundred years hanging out in that same hallway, and now they're getting stirred up..." I blinked away a flashback of the agonized faces and grasping hands.

"Because of you? Or us?"

"More likely because of whatever has *all* the spirits getting active and destructive around here," I said. "Madeline's renovations, maybe."

"Do you think Ol' Bayonet Arm is the one who's been cutting people? Maybe the murderer we're looking for?"

"I'd say he makes the suspect list."

"Then maybe he's trying to stop us," Stacey said. "Maybe he's waiting out there to attack—"

"Maybe we'll be shut-ins tonight." I stretched my legs and crossed to our heap of gear. I checked the battery in the ghost cannon, the ridiculously intense heavy portable light that can help run off truly stubborn or difficult spirits.

"Think we'll need that?" Stacey asked.

"If they do try to come in, let's blast them fast, before they get a chance to drain the battery." As I returned to the bed, I noticed a roughly Ellie-shaped sweat imprint on the blanket where I'd been lying. Gross. I pulled it off and rolled it up for housekeeping, keeping the sweat imprint on the inside to hide my shame. "Anybody run screaming out of 208 yet?"

"Not tonight. Kid's wandering the halls, though, like she wants to be anywhere but there. No parents with her."

"I think she's more sensitive to ghosts than they are. She's not up here on three, is she?" I didn't want to think about her stumbling into all those mangled, unpredictable soldiers with their hungry eyes and hands.

"Sticking to one, mostly. And the lounge on two."

"All right." I settled in for the long watch, but I also tried and failed to learn more about the history of the hotel's fourth floor.

Some general biographical information was available about Ithaca Galloway. According to some of the sketchy details I found, including very old archived articles of the *International Journal of Psychical Studies,* Ithaca had been born on a struggling family farm in Pennsylvania and had run away as a teenager, then established a reputation as a gifted medium during the Spiritualist heyday. It was not clear whether "Ithaca" was really her given name or an assumed one.

Her acquaintance with the minor iron magnate from Boston, Archibald Samuel Galloway, began when she purported to speak for his beloved deceased wife and children. All five of his children had died, three of them very young, two as young men in the Civil War. Galloway had made his fortune supplying railroads and factories at the dawn of the industrial age. At the time of their marriage in 1890, Ithaca was thirty-four and Archibald was sixty-three.

After Archibald's death in 1895, Ithaca wasted no time selling the remnants of the flagging ironworks to Andrew Carnegie's steel conglomerate and moving herself and her coterie of servants and psychic friends down to the haunted Lathrop Grand in Savannah.

The portion of her life that connected her to the iron and steel industry up north was relatively easy to find. Once she moved to Savannah, the available information plummeted. I could read all about how she'd renovated and modernized the hotel, but nothing about what her life was like there.

According to one source, she'd died in relative poverty in 1921, her wealth lost, squandered, or embezzled by her accountants and lawyers. The hotel had been sold and went into a period of criminal activity and disrepair before its next restoration decades later.

I already knew that, though. I was going in circles, getting nowhere.

On the monitors, Stacey caught some odd things—a decorative dish leaping from the mantel of a second-floor fireplace, splintering when it reached the hardwood floor. A chair in a hallway window nook turned slightly while unoccupied. A cupboard door in the third-floor service area opened for no reason. Just little events, many of them things that would have gone altogether unnoticed by the living if the cameras hadn't been there to capture them.

The cold spots just outside our rooms cycled between periods of intense frostiness and periods of fading away almost completely, according to the thermal imaging. We remained alert and on edge all night, but nobody tried breaking down our door with ghostly bayonets or cannons.

In the morning, I met with a very tired-looking Madeline in her office to summarize our progress so far. I'd showered off the cold-sweat residue and changed into fresh clothes.

Our investigation had raised a number of questions without resolving any, so the meeting was a bit tense. Madeline pulled up a list of complaints from guests and showed them to me on her desktop.

"Broken flower vase...room disorderly, clothes thrown all over..." Madeline shook her head. "We keep seeing more and more people check out early. Most of these guests like the idea of a ghost, but they don't want to feel threatened."

"Anything from 208?" I asked.

She shook her head. "People who reserve that room usually want to see something supernatural happen. That doesn't always stop them from running away once it does, but the current guests haven't complained so far." She gave me a hard look. "I can't keep losing guests like this."

"We should learn a lot today," I said, telling her about our scheduled visit to the Historical Association and how Jacob was coming to pick up any psychic readings. I didn't mention that I'd be meeting Michael for antiquing and a late lunch before any of that happened. I'm entitled to a sliver of personal time here and there. "In the meantime, have you done anything about the situation in 208?"

"What situation?" She looked genuinely puzzled. I tried not to gape at her.

"I told you Abigail's ghost might be getting violent. I've been cut. Several of Javier's people got cut. You didn't mention that when you first told me what happened up there."

"I was a little more concerned about that poor dead worker."

"Valentino?"

"Was that his name?"

I held back a sigh. "Listen, it's clear that the parents in 208 want to stay near the ghost, but the kid is scared. She wandered around the hotel all night to avoid that room."

"Conrad told me he saw a kid out alone, but he just told her to return to her room."

"I think you should offer them the connecting room. It might help keep the girl safe."

"Have you been talking to them about your investigation?" Madeline's smile, very slight to begin with, vanished from her face.

"The girl chatterboxed me," I said, shrugging, as if I couldn't have helped talking to her. "She was desperate for someone to talk to, I guess. I didn't reveal anything, but she told me something was in her room. Watching her, then touching her arm."

"That's just Abigail." Madeline waved a hand. "The parents wanted the most haunted room. If they wish to change, they can ask the front desk—"

"They aren't aware of the current risks," I said. "What are you going to do if that kid gets seriously hurt by the ghost?"

"I could do with a few less kids around the hotel, honestly." Madeline shook her head. "That was a joke. All right, I'll see about making arrangements."

"Thank you," I said, feeling a little relieved. "I do have one more question. The head custodian mentioned he'd warned a woman about going up to the fourth floor, that she was part of some group. Javier said he didn't have a female on his crew. Any idea who Earl was talking about?"

Madeline thought it over, looking annoyed by the question. "I don't think the other contractor had any female workers, either. I believe I would have noticed."

"Could you give me their contact information?"

"Why don't you just go back and ask Earl himself?"

I opened my mouth to answer, then closed it again. I couldn't just say that the basement was creepy, not without calling my professional ghost-exterminator credentials into question. I didn't want to say out loud that Earl unsettled me, either, because then I'd just sound mean. He was just a sickly old man.

"I suppose I could," I had to admit. "Just trying to save an extra trip downstairs."

After meeting with her, I passed by the front desk in the lobby. Steve, the guy from St. Croix, was on duty. I waited until a couple of guests left and he was completely alone before I approached.

"Hi again," I said, approaching Steve, who gave me a warm smile.

"Hi again. What can I do for you?"

"I just have a question. How long have you worked here, Steve?"

"About three months."

"Okay." I quickly summarized my question about female workers in the crews Madeline had hired to renovate the fourth floor.

"I don't think so," he said.

"Any idea who Earl was talking about?"

"Not..." He shook his head, then his eyes widened. "Unless he means the camera crew, because there were a couple of women with them."

"What camera crew?"

"One of those TV shows, you know. *Ghost Finders, Ghost Seekers*, something like that. They filmed upstairs a month ago. It was the last week Gary managed the hotel, just before Madeline and the new owners took over. I remember the old-timers talking about it, because *nobody* was supposed to go to the fourth floor, especially not the media. Strict rules from the old owner. Some people said...I don't know if it's true, but maybe Gary took a bribe from the TV producers to do it. He was about to lose his job. We were all worried about losing our jobs when Mrs. Colt came, but Gary knew he would be fired to make room for the new general manager."

"Do you have any contact information for the ghost-show people?"

"I can check...." Steve worked at his keyboard for a minute, frowned, clicked the mouse, and shook his head. "I don't even see a record of their reservation. It was definitely that final week. Maybe Gary did take a bribe...oh, yes." He finally smiled and looked up at me.

"You found it?"

"Yes. A little bit."

"What does that mean?"

"The Red Suite was comped on Gary's authority that week. No record of the guests. I think that's where the ghost people were staying."

"So...do you have a name or phone number or anything for these people?"

"No." His smile faltered. "I don't have any of that."

"Can you remember the exact name of the TV show?"

"Ah...sorry. *Ghost* something. Or *Haunted* something. How many can there be?"

"You'd be surprised." I took a deep breath. "Okay. What about Gary? Can you get me in touch with him?"

"I...shouldn't do that."

"He can't fire you now," I said. "Remember I'm here as a security consultant for Madeline. You can hand over any information I need."

"If you say so." Steve called up the former hotel manager's information and gave it to me—telephone, address, email. "Don't tell him it came from me. Gary was the one who hired me. He was all right, for a boss."

"Thank you."

Back in my room, I looked up every ghost-hunting or true-haunted-house show I could find—nineteen of them, I was surprised to discover, if you counted the ones from Canada. Then I tracked down phone numbers for their production companies and called each one of them, asking whether they'd recently filmed at the Lathrop Grand in Savannah. Nobody said yes. A few said they would have to get back to me.

After another nap to finish recharging, I met up with Michael in front of the hotel.

"Any luck catching Stabby Abby?" he asked with a grin as I climbed into the passenger seat.

"I may have run into her once or twice." I'd taken care to select a top that covered my shoulders and upper back so he wouldn't see the long cut in my back, which was starting to heal but still felt tender. As an EMT, he would probably insist on taking my shirt off and having a closer look—though that only made me think that maybe I *should* mention it to him.

We hit some of the major antique and salvage shops downtown, including Universe Trading Company, mostly stocked with outlandishly large items, like carousel horses, jumbo-sized toys, and dragon and pirate statues that might have once adorned a kitschy miniature golf course.

I dared Michael to try on an oversized antebellum ball gown that was currently worn by a gigantic fuzzy gorilla statue, possibly one of the Kongs. It looked more Donkey than King. He said he would if I tried on a clunky suit of medieval armor that stood in one corner, but I declined.

We walked through the cultural flotsam and jetsam that had washed up in the booths at the Wright Square Antique Mall, everything from old china and pottery to jewels, records, dog-eared books, and endless jewelry boxes, old bottles, and glassware of every kind. Michael had no trouble finding broken clocks—he never took parts from machines that were still working—but he needed some specific gear or spring that was only made by a particular clan of Bavarian tree elves in the nineteenth century or something, so it took a while.

When he could, he would surreptitiously open an old clock to check its innards. Michael usually focuses on the elaborate antique automaton clocks, the kind with lots of moving parts that animate little mechanized spring-driven characters, like cuckoo clocks. It could take months to restore a single one, which he would then reluctantly sell at a profit to wealthy collectors.

Meanwhile, I browsed among the old knickknacks and decorations. Part of me was always looking for things that reminded me of my childhood, before I'd lost my house and my parents to the fire. Even random objects, like the little pastel owl salt and pepper shakers that had perched on the kitchen counter, or the poster of Linda Carter as Wonder Woman that my dad hung in the garage, just between his tool bench and his worn-out armchair, much of it chewed to bits by my dog when he was a puppy. My poor golden retriever, Frank, dead from smoke inhalation after saving my life.

I went back to watching Michael. I didn't care about the wheels and gears inside the delicate old machines, but I liked the intense focus on his face when the wheels inside his head were spinning.

When the proprietor of one place allowed him to open up a big, non-functioning clock taller than I was, he stared at the inner workings for a full minute without moving or saying anything. The exterior of the clock was made of heavy cracked walnut, with a cluster of doors and curved pathways around the clock face, the whole exterior shape of the clock suggesting a castle tower, with little curtain walls and narrow arrow-slit windows.

"Is it sucking out your soul through your eyes?" I whispered to Michael, after the silence had begun to seem awkward.

"I'm just trying to see where it's broken," he said. "I might be able to fix it. Look at those characters." He pointed to the compartment hiding the little figures that would come out at different times of the day. Several were missing, but I saw a snarling black horse in black armor—a knight. There was a dirty white bishop with a dead-solemn look carved into his face, a black king with no face at all. "Chess pieces. There are people out there who would go totally ape for this."

"You're still thinking about wearing that giant hoop gown from the gorilla mannequin," I said. "Admit it."

"I'm serious. I really have to get this."

"Weren't we looking for just a couple of tiny little gears?" I was trying to keep it light, but the old clock made me a little uncomfortable. The black king seemed to stare at me with his nonexistent face, reminding me of the dark, eyeless sockets of the soldier I'd encountered the night before. "This clock is kind of spooky."

"I thought you liked spooky things."

"Just because I deal with them, it doesn't mean I like them. I get enough creepy at work, thanks." I tore my eyes away from the dusty, disturbing little figurines and tried to ignore the spider-crawl feeling up my back. "Can we get lunch yet?"

"I really think I should..." His fingers were already working at the little mechanisms within, tightening, coiling. His voice trailed off. The elderly gentleman who'd opened the clock squinted at Michael from behind the counter, as if annoyed. I'm sure he was.

"Repairing creepy old clocks. I guess it passes the time," I said, attempting to lighten the suddenly dreadful mood.

"Clocks can teach you a lot about life," he said, still mesmerized by the gearworks inside.

"Okay. Elaborate, guru," I said.

"At first, when you wind it up..." He turned a crank, raising weights until they reached as high as they would go. "The weight is far off the ground. Gravity's pulling on it, so it's loaded with potential energy. That's like when you're born, you have the highest potential. And then..."

One of the weights dropped, very slightly, and I heard a tick as the second hand advanced a notch.

"I see where you're going with this," I said. "Over time, you fall down, you lose your potential and your energy, until you finally stop moving and you're dead."

"I was going to take the comparison in a less depressing direction..."

"How else could it go? We're all mechanisms that run down,

wear out, and finally break down. That's where your analogy leads."

The clerk finally cleared his throat. "Sir? I'm afraid I can't allow that unless you purchase the item."

"How much?" Michael still didn't look up.

"Michael, come on—" I said.

"Eight seventy-five," the clerk said. I don't think he meant eight dollars, seventy-five cents.

"See, that's way too much." I tugged on Michael's arm.

"It's a good investment," Michael said, reaching for his wallet. "I'll make a lot more than that after I restore it. Do you take Visa?"

I stood glumly aside while he bought the thing and made arrangements to pick it up later, when I wasn't around to complain about it, I guess.

I felt better once we were outside in the early afternoon sunlight, the dim antique shop and the weird old clock behind us. I hoped he would change his mind about the clock, but I didn't think pressuring and nagging would get me there.

I'd also hoped to eat over at Ruan Thai, a gorgeous place with delicious food over on Broughton, but Michael pretty much had his heart set on the Soda Pop Shoppe, an intensely 1950's-themed place where the outdoor tables, if you could get one, had a pretty great view of the leafy green park at Wright Square. He seemed to think it would go out of business if he didn't personally eat there.

"Then He Kissed Me" by The Crystals played over the jukebox, but I can't say that watching my boyfriend order a chili cheese dog with added slaw really compared to that scene in *Goodfellas* where Ray Liotta shows Lorraine Bracco around the exciting world of mafia nightclubs. I had a chicken salad.

"Where would you want to go?" Michael asked, finally getting more talkative. He'd seemed withdrawn for a minute. Probably thinking about that stupid clock.

"Well, I wanted to go to Ruan Thai..."

"I mean, if you were going to live somewhere else," he said.

"I guess I could use a bigger apartment." I didn't get where he was going with this.

"If you could move anywhere in the country. I've been thinking out west, you know, the huge national forests and everything. A lot of places are still wild out there, untouched by civilization."

"Sounds like somewhere Stacey would like to go," I said. "I like air conditioning."

"But you've lived here most of your life. Haven't you ever wanted to move?"

"Not really. I belong here."

"How do you know? Ever tried belonging anywhere else?"

"What are we talking about, Michael?"

"My sister's going off to college in the fall. I was thinking about it while she was working on her applications—she'll move out, and I won't need to stay here anymore. I can go anywhere now. Ever since my mom...you know, my whole life's been about taking care of Melissa. Soon I'll be free of all that."

"And you want to leave town?"

"What do you think? Do you plan to stay here your whole life?"

"My life is here. My work is here."

"I'm sure there are ghosts in other cities," he said.

"Yeah. But this is *my* city. And it's not like it would be easy to get established somewhere else, even if I wanted to. Which, I should add, I don't."

He nodded. "I was thinking it might be nice to try life somewhere else for once. Even just to get out of town for a while."

"Yeah, I could use a vacation or something. But not, ideally, sitting around in the woods the whole time. I want to visit cities. San Francisco, maybe. New York. Europe, if I could afford it."

"Sounds cool." He didn't say it like he was ready to sit down and make plans. Not when there were woods and mosquitoes out there waiting to be enjoyed.

"And I'm not ready to leave Savannah. I don't feel like I ever will be."

"Even if Calvin sells the agency to that other company? What's it called, Supernatural Services?"

"Paranormal Solutions." I thought about it. "You know, you might be right. I might just want to get out of town if that happens."

"You can hunt ghosts out west! On horseback."

"I'm not saying I want it to happen, though."

"Yeah, I understand. Want a bite of my dog?" He held out a mess of yellow, brown, and green that was very poorly contained by the bun.

"No, thanks."

"Let's go for a walk down River Street after this," he said. "That always puts you in a good mood."

"I actually have to get back to work soon," I told him, which maybe sounded like a blow-off, but it was also true.

"A walk around the park, then?" He pointed to the little one about twenty feet away from us.

"Maybe halfway around. I'm in a hurry."

We moved back to easier subjects as we strolled under the brightly colored autumn canopy—music, movies, anything people talk about when they want to keep their deeper thoughts and concerns to themselves. The brick walkway led us to benches by the fountain, where we sat, and we might have spent a few minutes kissing while we were there. I was confused, uncertain whether to pull him close and hold tight, or to push him away if he was so eager to get out of town.

I told myself it didn't matter, at least not today. Today I could bury myself in work, my usual response to any situation where I came dangerously close to exposing my feelings for someone else to crush.

So much for the world of the living. Back to the world of the dead, where things make much more sense.

## Chapter Ten

The three-story federal-style mansion housing the Savannah Historical Association looked lovely surrounded by trees glowing with autumn colors in the afternoon sunlight.

"We have an exciting day ahead, don't we?" Grant asked when he greeted Stacey and me at the front door.

"If you say so, it must be true," I said. "I'm guessing you found some juicy dirt on the Lathrop Grand."

"The juiciest and the dirtiest," he assured me while ushering us into the front hall. He glanced around as though preparing to share a deep, dark secret—though he's in his late fifties and going gray, he still moves with a kind of childlike enthusiasm. "We'll have to step down to *the vault*."

"What's the vault?" I asked, following him to the wide, polished stairs surrounded by bright windows.

"*The vault.* It must be whispered, never spoken of aloud."

"Now I'm excited," Stacey said.

We followed him into the softly carpeted, well-lit basement, past the archives and storage rooms of to-be-sorted materials, past the book restoration room, and to a very normal-looking interior door near the end of the basement hallway.

He pulled the door open to reveal *another* door immediately behind it, this one made of steel, with a digital combination lock at one side.

"This is where we keep the valuables," Grant explained. "Don't take offense, but standard security measures require you to look away while I enter the combination."

"How mysterious and dramatic." I turned my back on Grant, and so did Stacey.

"That is what we're known for here at the Historical Association," Grant said. "Mystery, drama, and intrigue. We somehow fit it all in, just between the touring senior citizen centers and tea on Friday afternoons. You may turn back now."

Grant was opening the door as I turned around. Actually, the door was silently swinging inward under its own power, which was probably a good thing since the Association is made up mostly of genteel ladies between the ages of sixty and a hundred.

The climate within the vault was cool and dry, a dehumidifier humming quietly in the background somewhere. Sealed glass cases displayed a number of items, including paintings and antique jewelry, as well as crumbling leather remnants of a very old pair of boots that, Grant confided, was believed to have belonged to James Oglethorpe, founder of our city and state.

Grant opened one of a row of steel cabinets and removed an old book sealed in thick plastic, its title too faded for me to read.

"This has not yet been digitized," Grant said. "Miss Tolbert, you may take images of the pages within for your research—provided you share copies with me."

"Of course!" Stacey said. "What's the book about?"

"The Lathrop Grand Hotel," Grant said. "If you wish to learn more, follow me."

He led us out of the vault, carrying the book as if it were a lost treasure from a lost civilization from a lost age of history on a lost planet.

We followed him to an archive room where stacks of papers and photographs sat in the center of one rectangular work table. He eased the book down alongside these.

"At times, I struggle to find details for the properties about which you inquire," he told me, while gesturing for us to sit across from him. "In this particular case, it was a matter of sifting, sorting, and weighing to determine which details might be useful to you.

"The Lathrop Grand," he began, sliding the first stack apart to reveal paper copies of old drawings and paintings. One showed a wood engraving of the hotel, with its wrought-iron veranda, overlooking a dirt road crowded with horses and carriages. Ladies in huge flounced skirts and bonnets adorned with lace and flowers accompanied men in dark long-tailed coats and white cravats, strolling outside the hotel or passing in and out of the front doors. All around, it was a super-fancy scene.

"The Lathrop Grand was a center of high society for some time, or at least that portion of high society that enjoyed Caribbean rum, gambling, and dancing. For a decade or so, it was *the* place to stay when one visited Savannah and wished enjoy comfort and luxury.

"By all accounts, Mabel Lathrop, the wife, was instrumental in the conception and construction of the hotel, and could be found carousing in the hotel's lounge and restaurant nearly every evening. Her husband Uriah was not so social, preferring the company of his books and a cat or two in his library. There was more than one scandalous rumor of affairs on the wife's part, in fact."

Grant showed us images of the doctor—a small, pinched-looking man with thick glasses whose muttonchops nearly swallowed his face—as well as his wife, including the painting of pudgy, red-cheeked Mabel Lathrop that now hung in the restaurant bearing her name. That restaurant was the latest incarnation of the downstairs saloon where she'd drank, danced, and flirted while her husband studied his books.

"The war forced the doctor out of his little retreat as the hotel became a hospital for Confederate troops," Grant continued. Yellowed photographs showed the hotel's lobby crowded with men on makeshift cots. I shuddered, thinking of the vision I'd seen the night before, during the slip backwards in time. "By all accounts, the doctor worked quietly and diligently, day and night, hardly resting until the war was over. When General Sherman took the city, he worked just as hard to help Union troops. That, of course, brings us to the hotel's most famous resident—Abigail Bowen."

"Stabby Abby," I said.

"A flip nickname for a woman who murdered seventeen wounded Union soldiers. The occupying army hanged her from an oak tree on the property. I found no images of her, but she was described as quite comely. At times, she's been treated as just a tiny bit of a folk hero among the Daughters of the Confederacy crowd.

"In any event, she was a local girl, eighteen years old when she was executed. She'd been working as a nurse for two years. Her body was tossed into an unmarked grave in the Potter's Field area of the Colonial Park cemetery, but her spirit is rumored to haunt her old room at the hotel, which she likely shared with other hospital workers."

"I've seen her there," I said.

"I would be disappointed if you had not," Grant said. "Guests in that room frequently report an apparition of a young woman. Sometimes they awaken to find themselves being touched, their arms extended as though she were checking their pulse. I'm sure you're familiar with the popular legends."

"Very much."

"After the war, the hotel continued in operation, though its glory days were past. The city and the entire region were war-torn and dominated by Reconstruction policies that hampered what remained of the economy. High times were not to be so easily had, and of course most of the wealthy patrons had lost their fortunes to war and emancipation.

"The hotel limped along until the yellow fever epidemic erupted in the summer of 1876, killing thousands." Grant also had sad pictures of this, including sick children bleeding and dying on wooden cots, probably the same cots where soldiers had squirmed in agony about a decade earlier. "The hotel again became a hospital, with Dr. Lathrop attempting to cope with the flood of victims. Thousands died, and thousands more fled the city, but the Lathrops remained, giving what comfort and treatment they could. Dr. Lathrop fashioned an early surgical mask meant to guard against yellow fever, though it was more of a latter-day plague-doctor mask from the medieval period, with air filtered by herbs and such. Lathrop dabbled in inventions beyond his capability, indeed beyond the capability of the technology available to him. He filed patents for the mask, as well as crude attempts at medical prosthetics during a time when the U.S. government was doling out large postwar contracts for them, but none of these inventions took off in any commercial sense. In those days, it was widely believed that the yellow fever arose from 'bad air,' from miasmas of infection spread from trash dumps and the river.

"Unfortunately, the yellow fever mask did nothing to block the mosquitoes that actually spread the disease. Dr. Lathrop himself contracted yellow fever and died during the epidemic. His wife Mabel kept the hotel open until her death in 1884, and then it closed down and remained in that state for another ten years. Locals avoided the place, reporting strange sounds and visions when they passed near—bloody-faced children or soldiers with missing arms, for instance, looking out the windows."

"Then Ithaca Galloway moved from Boston and bought the place," I said.

"After hearing of the haunted hotel and visiting, yes," Grant said. He went over what I already knew—that she'd gained a reputation as a medium and traveled the circuit that existed at the time, giving demonstrations and allegedly helping audience members speak to their dead relatives. He offered a picture of her in her younger years, a square-jawed woman with dark eyes standing on a wood-plank stage in front of a crowd in Hartford, Connecticut. Then Grant recounted her marriage to the much older industrialist Archibald Galloway, finally catching up to her purchase of the hotel in 1895. "She remodeled the entire fourth floor as a private apartment for herself and her entourage. I can tell you very little about what happened up there during her tenure...and that is where this particular book comes into play. Shall we have a look?" Grant touched the plastic-wrapped book and raised his fluffy white-sheep eyebrows in a questioning fashion, as if there were any chance I would decline.

"Let's see what you've got," I said.

Grant opened a drawer in the work table and pulled on a pair of white cotton gloves, moving like a surgeon preparing for a delicate procedure. Then he slowly removed the layers of plastic.

The book's leather binding had crumbled significantly, and the spine was cracked. Grant used great care in lifting the front cover.

"This item was published by a company in Dublin, Georgia, now long out of business," he said. "The author was a young woman named Katherine Moore. Apparently, she worked at the Lathrop Grand for some time...this book was an attempt to reveal to the world what occurred there."

"*The Forbidden Secrets of the Lathrop Grand Hotel: Recollections of One Woman's Journey into the Mysteries of the Spirit* by Katherine Croghan Moore," I read. "They weren't into punchy titles in those days."

"Certainly not," Grant agreed.

"So why was this book locked inside the treasure vault?" Stacey asked.

"Because, as far as can be determined, this is the only remaining copy in existence," he said. "The others, we believe, were deliberately tracked down and destroyed, possibly by one or more of the people named within or their descendants, most likely to avoid scandal. I have been eager to read it myself, but have not taken the time to do more than examine it briefly, because it has not yet been scanned and digitized. We have the necessary planetary scanner, if someone skilled in photography wished to provide the labor..."

Grant and I both looked at Stacey.

"Fine," she sighed. "Let's do it."

We brought the book to another room adjacent to the bookbinding area. The scanner occupied a large section of one wall, and Grant demonstrated how to line the delicate old book inside the V-shaped cradle. An overhead camera took images of the open pages, and a digital monitor on the back displayed the camera's viewpoint so the book could be properly aligned. Stacey nodded and got to work.

Grant and I sat at a nearby table, and he continued his story.

"The Lathrop Grand faced another decline in 1921, with the death of Ithaca Galloway. According to court documents, she appears to have been fairly destitute by then, owing back taxes and leaving very little in the way of an estate, aside from the luxurious furnishings and art inside the hotel. It was sold at auction and changed hands. The front entrance to the old saloon area was walled off and the saloon officially closed, but apparently it remained in business as a speakeasy, accessible from a hidden doorway."

"There are plenty of those in the hotel," I said.

"Unfortunately, the new owners had little interest in maintaining the hotel, much less renovating or modernizing it. The top two floors of the hotel were closed off and left in disuse. The crowd became rough, and eventually the hotel fell out of business amid the Depression.

"In 1959, amid a general fervor for preserving and restoring the historical areas of the city, a group of local businessmen purchased and partially restored the hotel. The top floor was never opened to the public. The hotel experienced a resurgence for a decade, but closed again. A group of vagrants—flower children, by their descriptions—was arrested in 1971 for squatting inside the old hotel.

"Attempts were made to re-open the hotel, but it wasn't until 1993 that a local company, Warren Real Holdings, made the investment to bring it up to modern codes so that it could operate once again, though again the fourth floor was apparently left alone. The Halloween balls began a few years later under the management of Gary Schultz, capitalizing on the hotel's haunted reputation. Very recently, it was sold to Black Diamond Properties, and here we are."

"Here we are." I checked Stacey's tablet, where she was sending the pages as she scanned them. "Should we look into Katherine Moore's book of secrets? Find out what Ithaca and her psychic friends were up to on the fourth floor?"

"Please," Grant said, leaning forward a little, eager as a kid preparing to dig into his candy basket after trick-or-treating.

The book began with Katherine's declaration *"before the Almighty Powers That Be"* that each word in the text was true, and that she presented her account *"for the Enlightenment of the World."*

We soon read of her difficult childhood in Ireland, her mother a maid, her father an apparent lowlife who died in a gambling dispute. Katherine had departed on a ship for America, along with her mother and her little brother Gilby, largely to escape her deceased father's gambling debts. Her mother and brother both died of illness on the way. Katherine arrived in Savannah in 1899, fourteen years old in a strange land with no family and no money.

"That's a nineteenth-century story for you," I said, shaking my head.

The book recounted how she'd worked whatever jobs she could find, cleaning and cooking, before she finally landed a position in the Lathrop Grand kitchen.

*It was there I saw shadows about the corners, and often a strange woman in a large skirt. One of the cooks told me it was the Spirit of Mabel Lathrop, the hotel's founder, who made appearances in the kitchen and the dining room from time to time. She was many years deceased but had not left the hotel.*

*Mabel gave a kindly and gentle presence, but in time I saw more and more figures, horrible shapes of children bleeding from the eyes and of men missing arms and legs. Each man or woman employed by the Lathrop Grand saw spirits on occasion, but I saw them always, ceaselessly, everywhere. It was for this reason that the lady and master of the house, the Widow Galloway, gained an interest in me.*

The text recounted how she was transferred to service on the forbidden fourth floor, serving and cleaning in the apartments of Ithaca Galloway and her entourage.

*Madame Galloway sought for me to serve, but also wished for my education, and to this end assigned a young Scottish gentleman, Edward Fletcher, to tutor me. He was an established part of the household, knowledgeable in the arts of divination and medieval sorcery. A devoted and attentive teacher was Edward, his eyes brighter than any I'd ever seen, and in our hours together we became close. He taught me well, and in time I could read the books in the hotel's two libraries. On the first floor I came to know Homer and Virgil, Plato and Emerson. On the fourth, I read rare and forbidden texts by Johannes Trithemius, Collin de Plancy, Zosimos of Panopolis, and other scientists of the occult and dark arts.*

*I grew fond of Edward, thinking of him in a husbandly way and of marriage and children, but Gregor Zagan, in his role as Madame Galloway's intimate companion and chief adviser, warned me that any such involvement could dispel our developing powers, and urged chastity.*

"Gregor Zagan?" I said. "Sounds like a fake name to me."

"Perhaps a magician's stage name," Grant said.

The author's further description of Zagan made me realize this was our guy, the long-bearded one seated next to Ithaca Galloway in the group portrait on the fourth floor. Apparently he was always at her side, whispering into the woman's ear. He was about a decade younger than Ithaca but sounded fairly dominant in their relationship.

"We found Rasputin," I told Stacey.

"Sounds like some great reading," Stacey said, gently turning a delicate yellow page to prepare for the next scan. "Wish I were involved."

"I'll give you the Cliff's Notes later," I told her. "Right now she's in love with a cute young Scottish guy, but the Rasputin guy is warning her to stay chaste."

"Ugh, and I'm missing it?"

"Shh," I said. "We're trying to read over here."

Katherine recounted her integration into the cult-like atmosphere of the fourth floor. She shared a room with an older Frenchwoman who could allegedly channel spirits. She described how *"all things were done in common, our meals, our bathing, and various rituals meant to strengthen our spiritual capacities. Mme. Galloway and Mister Zagan insisted such practices constructed an 'Over-Mind' that was powerful for our magical purposes."*

Séances were frequent, sometimes trying to reach people that had been known to those present, other times trying to contact long-spirits of occult masters. Automatic writing, spirit boards, and crystallomancy were also among the group's activities. All of this was done in the dark temple room on the fourth floor, decorated with hieroglyphs and occult symbols. Ithaca and her psychics referred to it as "the necromantium" after the oracle of the dead in ancient Greece.

*"The chief concern of Ithaca and Gregor was the construction of the Mortis Ocularum, a machine for summoning and speaking with the spirits. To this end were hired metalsmiths, glassmakers, and men knowledgeable in electricity, magnets, kinetoscopes, and so on. One monstrous machine after another was constructed at great expense in the necromantium, each one destroyed in turn when it proved a failure."*

I thought of the deep holes in the floor of the temple. Maybe they'd anchored the experimental machine. I couldn't be sure, because Katherine seemed to have little interest in it and quickly moved on, giving no description beyond "monstrous."

"All done over here!" Stacey asked. "Did she hook up with Cute Scottish Boy yet?"

"No hook-ups so far." I checked the time. "We'd better get going soon. We need to make an extra stop before we go back to the hotel."

"No time for a game of cribbage?" Grant asked.

"I'm afraid not. Thanks for your help, Grant. This should help us identify which ghost is the dangerous one, once our psychic has a look at the house. Any chance you could find out more on Gregor Zagan?"

"I will do my best," he said, standing to escort us out. "Does this mean our city will be losing one of our most famous resident ghosts?"

"I don't know that Abigail is our target. There are a few possibilities," I said.

"Will you let me know the results?"

"We're kind of under a nondisclosure agreement," I said. When he frowned, I added, "I'll let you know if we learn anything of purely *historical* value."

"That is the tune I wanted to hear."

Stacey and I left the Association mansion and climbed back into the van before she asked about our extra stop.

"We just need to do a little detective work," I said, starting up the engine and pulling out into the road.

Then I actually explained where we were going and why, because me being vague and mysterious wasn't going to help Stacey prepare.

## Chapter Eleven

Gary Schultz lived in The Landings, a gated community on Skidaway Island, in a two-story cubic house with steeply slanted roofs that screamed 1970's. A red Chevrolet convertible sat in the driveway. It looked as though the Lathrop Grand had paid him well, though not extravagantly, during his tenure as general manager.

I approached his front door alone, dressed in my stupid black pantsuit, glasses on, hefty briefcase in one hand. He came a minute or so after I rang the bell, a balding, frowning man in his fifties, unshaven in recent days, his outfit a hodgepodge of crumpled dress-suit pants and a shirt depicting Big Al, the elephant mascot of the University of Alabama.

He was very guarded as he opened the door, giving me a quick look-over and a gruff "Hello?"

"Mr. Gary Schultz?" I asked.

He nodded, glancing at my briefcase. "Who are you?"

"My name is Ellie Jordan. I'm a private investigator looking into Black Diamond Properties, the new owners of the Lathrop Grand, in preparation for a legal action."

"Are you working for Black Diamond or against them?" he asked, narrowing his eyes.

"Against them."

"Those pig-kissers that fired me? Someone's suing them?" He stepped aside, smiling now, and gestured into his bright, square-shaped foyer. "Best news I've heard all month. Come right in, and don't spare any gory details. Who's after them?"

"I'm bound by a nondisclosure agreement, so I can only say it's a wrongful death lawsuit by a contract employee. Well, his family."

"Get you a beer?"

"No, thank you." I followed him to a boxy living room with a pair of skylights in the ceiling. He paused an old James Bond movie on the big flatscreen that dominated one wall, then picked up a bottle of Heineken. Several empty bottles were scattered on the coffee table, as if he didn't know what to do with himself besides drink and watch television. I wondered if it was a coincidence that the two longest-term employees of the hotel I'd met, Earl and now Gary, both seemed to have drinking problems.

A framed, autographed picture of legendary Alabama coach Bear Bryant hung on one wall, surrounded by commemorative posters of the stadium in Tuscaloosa and team pictures from various championship seasons.

"I'm guessing you went to Alabama?" I said, thinking that maybe I should have let Alabama native Stacey do the interrogation while I sat out in the van as backup.

"Florida State, actually, but I've always been an Alabama man. I grew up in Philadelphia, you see." He dropped onto his couch and motioned toward a recliner. I dusted what looked like Funyuns crumbs off the cushion and sat down to face him.

"Philadelphia?" I asked, unable to summon the connection I was obviously supposed to make.

"The one in Mississippi. Just over the fence from Tuscaloosa. So what can I do to help you with those piles of trash bags full of horse manure that call themselves Black Diamond Properties?" he asked. "Are you gonna bleed them dry?"

"If possible. They do have deep pockets."

"Good."

"I'd like to start by reviewing the basic security and safety procedures that were in force under your management," I said. "That will help us find any area where Black Diamond's new policies varied from yours, creating hazards for hotel workers and guests."

I put him at ease with very dull and easy questions that could have been answered by the hotel's operations manual, like the existence of emergency escape routes and a disaster plan, very standard things. He was chatty, as if he'd hadn't spoken with anyone in weeks and was desperate for human contact.

Finally, we reached the nub of the matter.

"Did you ever hire contract workers for any kind of work on the fourth floor?" I asked.

"Oh, the owners tried that in the early days. By the time I got there, they'd just about given up. The policy was that nobody was allowed upstairs except for critical maintenance like roof and sprinkler system work."

"Why had they given up on restoring the fourth floor?"

His smile grew, and he shook his head. "You wouldn't believe me if I told you."

"If you're referring to the alleged ghosts in the hotel, I've been hearing these stories all along," I said. "You won't shock me."

"All right. They couldn't get any good contractors to stay up there for more than a week. Because of the haunting." He took a sip of beer, looking a bit morose and philosophical, and a bit unsteady. "I never believed in ghosts before I worked at the Lathrop, except for the Holy Ghost. My church doesn't recognize ghosts as real. I know, because I've spoken with my pastor about it at least a dozen times over the years.

"That place, though. Whew. I saw more than one in my years there. Mabel Lathrop shows up in the kitchen and restaurant. Most of the staff have seen her. She seems harmless, and sometimes she'll even close doors and cabinets in a helpful way. Even tidy up the kitchen a little."

"The world could use more ghosts like that," I said, and he laughed.

"Don't I know it? There were worse things, though. The yellow fever kids, they show up here and there, always quick to hide. Just blurry shapes, usually. Once I saw a soldier crawling on the second floor, a Union soldier I'm pretty sure, one of his legs stiff and dragging behind him. Heard a rusty scraping or squeaking sound. He didn't look at me or act like he knew I was there, and an eyeblink later, he's gone."

"Did you ever see the famous one? Abigail Bowen?"

"I believe so. Young woman in a bonnet walking down the hall. Wouldn't have thought a thing of it at first, except for her old-fashioned clothes. Had this kind of short cape that buttoned at the neck, a simple brown dress. As she got closer, her clothes somehow got covered in blood, and I saw she was holding a knife. Or a scalpel, I suppose, but it was primitive. The handle looked like it was made out of deer antler. The blade was dripping blood. And she looked at me and smiled, so sweetly, pretty girl covered in blood. My heart just about stopped. Her eyes looked unnatural, no real color. I'll never forget how she looked.

"Then she was gone like she'd never been there at all. No drops of blood on the floor, either. That was her, I figured out later, once I managed to calm down. Abigail." He'd been talking toward the ceiling, but now looked at me liked he'd forgotten I was in the room. "Oh. You must think I'm crazy."

"Only if every other person who's stepped inside that hotel is also crazy," I said. "If you ask me, it must be haunted. There are so many witnesses who've reported ghosts. Anyway, what about the fourth floor?"

"That's no joke," he said. "We could only do quick little jobs, like I said. There are voices on the fourth floor, whispers that come up all around you. The air turns cold. I stayed out of there, made sure everyone else did, too."

"What about camera crews? I understand the hotel has been featured on several ghost shows on television."

"Sure, the ghost shows," he said, but he spoke a little more cautiously. "Or the local news wanting to do a spooky story around Halloween, that kind of thing. The owners encouraged all of that. Why wouldn't they? It was free publicity on a national level. International, even."

"Were the films crews allowed on the fourth floor?"

"Oh, no. They were mostly interested in two and three—Stabby Abby, you know, and the soldiers and fever victims who haunt those levels. The owners forbid any access to the fourth floor, though, and I agreed with them. It would have been bad publicity in the first place. You don't want people thinking the hotel is just an old wreck inside. In the second place, there's the liability. No matter how many waivers people sign, they can turn around and sue you anyway. That's going back on your word, if you ask me."

"The liability? Because the fourth floor was more dangerous than the others?"

"Absolutely. The lower floors, a guest stays for a week, they might glimpse a ghost, or they might see nothing at all, but that's it. Child's play. That fourth floor, though. The things up there are terrifying."

"Did anyone sustain injuries on the fourth floor while you managed the hotel?"

"No, but I saw more than one worker—for those occasional critical repairs I was talking about—more than one worker run out of that fourth floor paler than a dead trout's underside, never to return to the hotel. Place had the same effect on me, those few times I went up there. I saw the shadows and heard the voices and avoided the fourth floor as much as I could after that."

"What did the voices say to you?"

"Like I said, just whispering, like a dozen people whispering up and down all around you. Like they're real close and have you surrounded." He shuddered. "People talk about the ghost of Abigail Bowen, but she's harmless to the living, always has been. There's something truly horrible up on four. I don't know what it is or what you'd call it, but it's a little slice of Hell up there."

"This didn't deter you from working at the hotel?"

"It made me think twice—three, four, a hundred times, really—but there's something about the place that keeps drawing me back. I miss it now. Like I belong there and nowhere else."

"So you never allowed any camera crews up on the fourth floor?" I said, trying to bring us back to the point.

"No, ma'am. That was right against hotel policy."

"Not during the last week of your employment there? Even then?"

His face hardened into an unpleasant stare. "What are you getting at?"

"From what I understand, a camera crew was allowed on the fourth floor during that time. They stayed in the Red Suite on the third floor, and their entire visit was complimentary, on your authority."

"Who told you that?" Gary was looking much less friendly by the second. "Who?"

"Multiple sources," I said. "It may have slipped your mind. Do you remember now?"

"I don't know what you're talking about."

"To whom did you comp the Red Suite, then?"

"I don't have to answer this." He sat up. "Maybe you should get going."

"Did they pay you a location fee?" I asked. "Would a quick check of your bank records show a mysterious extra deposit around the end of your employment? Or did you credit the fee to the hotel's general account, as you should have?"

"There was no—"

"So far, this information has not been released to your former employer, nor the current ownership of the hotel," I said. "Should I share it with them or keep it to myself?"

"I don't see how it matters. They already fired me, so what else can they do?"

"Your former employers could sue you to recover the sum you embezzled," I said. "The new owners will be even more furious. They don't want any footage of the fourth floor released to the public any more than the old owners did. They could file a legal injunction, and then the production company might sue you to recover what they paid you. There's a whole mess of things that could be thrown at you, Gary."

"Well, thanks for stopping by," Gary said. He swigged his beer and pointed toward the front door. "The way out's just the same as the way in, only backwards."

"On the other hand, I'd be happy to not mention this to anyone. All I want is the contact information for that production company. You're not my concern here, Gary, unless you make yourself into an obstacle."

Gary looked back at me, not saying anything.

"Everyone's going to figure it out when that footage airs on television, anyway," I said. "Why don't you just put me in touch with them now and help us build this lawsuit against Black Diamond? Then they'll be too busy to worry about any silly TV shows. I thought we were on the same team here, Gary."

"Team Bleed Black Diamond Dry," he said.

"Exactly."

"It's obviously not the best-kept secret in the world, anyway." He shook his head, looking disappointed more than anything else, as if it hadn't occurred to him that his authority over his former employees had ended along with his job. He left the room and returned with a business card. "You can copy that down, I guess. It's not as if a business card is private information."

"Thank you." I arranged it on the end table beside me and took a few snapshots with my phone. It read METASCIENCE PRODUCTIONS, LLC with a simple clip-art logo of a camera, a phone number with an 828 area code, and the name KARA SMITH, PRODUCER. "Who's Kara Smith?"

"The lady who contacted me and made the arrangements."

"Can you describe her?"

"Blue eyes. So thin she almost looked sick. Like a fashion model. She was charming, could probably talk a turtle right out of its shell."

"All right. I'm sure I'll be talking to her soon. Thanks for your help, Mr. Schultz."

"You're not going to mention the, uh, anything to do with me and that production company to anybody, are you?"

"I'll keep a tight lid on it. Maybe it won't air for a long time."

"Maybe." He swallowed, looking worried.

Stacey had been listening the whole time, so I didn't have to update her when I climbed into the car. I'd worn a hidden microphone under my shirt, so she could record whatever he told us, and so she could come help if he turned threatening. You get the best results from a one-on-one interrogation, according to Calvin. People are more likely to open up in front of one person than a group of them.

"So we don't have to burglarize his house later?" Stacey asked, frowning.

"I thought you hated plan B."

"Yeah, but I got kind of excited thinking about it. It would have been fun."

"And illegal. Good thing plan A worked out."

"I guess." She looked at my phone while I started up the van. Then she did a quick search with her phone. "828. That's North Carolina."

"Metascience Productions?"

Stacey thumbed it in, then scrolled slowly, frowning. "Nothing on Google. Kind of weird for a media company. Maybe they only produce industrial films or something."

"Industrial films about haunted hotels?"

"Yeah, I admit that's kind of reaching," Stacey said. "But I thought we were at the brainstorming stage. I didn't realize we'd skipped ahead to the telling-Stacey-her-ideas-are-silly stage. I'm not finding anything, not even an address."

"Can you narrow it to just North Carolina?"

"Yeah, of course. I just add the word 'North Carolina' to the search bar. I bet detective work used to be a lot harder. Okay...and nothing. I'm finding multiple video production studios in Asheville, but nothing even vaguely like 'Metascience Productions.' Want me to call old Kara and see what she has to say?"

"Call old Calvin instead, pass the information to him. Maybe he can find something, or one of his buddies on the police force."

"We're callin' in the coppers, see?" Stacey said, squinting with one eye and doing a cheesy 1930's gangster-movie voice.

"Yeah. And then make sure Jacob's still planning to come see us."

"Then he can finger our button man, see," Stacey said, really doubling down on that voice. "Make our killer ghost sing like a canary."

I hoped she was right. I also hoped she'd stop with the bad movie-gangster imitation, like right away, but mainly I hoped she was right.

## Chapter Twelve

We had some time before Jacob arrived. We'd scheduled him later than usual, since Madeline was so concerned about keeping our investigation secret. In the later hours, it would be easier to walk the hotel without encountering too many guests.

In the meantime, I headed downstairs and spoke to a few more of the hotel staff. The workers in the kitchen all seemed to have a story about Mabel Lathrop's plump, red-cheeked ghost, either encountering her or seeing objects move on their own. She was generally considered a benign presence, and the kitchen staff had far less turnover than other areas of the hotel. I didn't encounter her myself while I was there, but I lingered at her portrait out in the restaurant, the merry-faced woman depicted in a giant hoop skirt, standing by the giant ballroom fireplace. A great fire roared within, and evergreen branches decorated the mantel, making me think of Christmas.

"Want to give me a hand?" I whispered. "Surely you want this place safe for guests. You must want the dangerous ghosts out of here. Can you help?"

Mabel's painted face didn't reply. Her eyes had a laughing look, and she was smiling just slightly, though people usually tried to look very serious, even grim, in their portraits back in those days.

Upstairs, Stacey had something interesting to show me on her laptop.

"This is the second floor," she told me, pointing to grainy black-and-white footage from a security camera, timestamped at just past four in the morning. "It's the opposite side from Abigail Bowen's room, near the fitness center and the art gallery. Check it out."

She clicked the play button on the video-editing app. For a long moment, nothing happened except for the timestamp changing once per second. The hallway lay empty and silent, the carpet runner lying still along the center of the old polished hardwood floorboards. Two wing-backed chairs occupied a niche in one wall, flanking a small table topped with an overflowing vase of flowers.

I caught a blur of movement at the corner of the hall, which vanished as quickly as it appeared. Two seconds later, the vase toppled over, spilling flowers and water across the floor.

"What was that?" I pointed to the corner of the hall where the blur had appeared.

"Exactly." Stacey reversed the footage slowly, paused it when the blur was most apparent, and zoomed in. The little apparition had appeared right where the hall turned ninety degrees, as if it had crept up and peered around the corner.

As Stacey blew up the image, I realized it was *two* apparitions, not one. They were not distinct at all, but I could make out two pale oval shapes with simple dark smudges to indicate eyes and mouths. They were stacked on top of each other in a way that made me think of small children peering around the corner together.

"Maybe those are some of the yellow-fever kids we keep hearing about," I said.

"They've got enough psychokinetic energy to pull a few pranks, obviously. Knocking over decorations."

"Kid ghosts can have a lot of energy. It makes them dangerous."

"Do you think they're our killers?" Stacey asked, maybe half-kidding.

"We have to consider it. I've seen child ghosts who think killing someone is nothing more than an amusing joke."

"At least they haven't lost their sense of humor. Jacob should be here in a few minutes. Should we wait for him downstairs?"

We arrived at the lounge portion of Mabel's a few minutes before ten. Several well-dressed people drank here, alone or in small groups, a mixture of tourists and locals.

Jacob already sat at the bar, drinking a glass of dark liquid garnished with a cherry on the rim.

"Hey, why didn't you tell us you were here?" Stacey approached him wearing a mock scowl.

"I knew you'd come down to wait for me here," Jacob said. He dropped into a goofy horror-movie mad-scientist tone and wiggled his fingers mysteriously in the air. Stacey joined in with the same voice and gestures as he said, "Because I'm *psyyyychiiic.*"

I was beginning to understand where Stacey was getting her dorky bad-movie impressions.

I waited for the obligatory kiss, which seemed to run on a bit long for a public place, before greeting Jacob with a light clap on the shoulder. "Hey there," I said. "Picking up any vibes in this place?"

"You must be joking," he said, shifting to a B-movie vampire Transylvanian accent for some reason.

Stacey sipped his drink. "Are you having a Shirley Temple, Jacob?"

"Don't insult me," he said. "It's a Roy Rogers."

Stacey and I ordered small iced coffees to help jazz us up for the night. They immediately fell into a conversation about some concert they'd attended, but I interrupted.

"So Jacob," I said. "The vibes?"

"I'm picking up a strong female presence around this restaurant. I'm going to save time and say it's that lady." He pointed to the large portrait of Mabel Lathrop on the wall. "She doesn't seem hostile. Her main concern is actually seeing that this place is run well and the patrons are happy. That's what she's indicating to me. She likes to be among the living, listening to their stories and watching them come and go. Not a powerful presence, but friendly. This whole restaurant area is her domain."

"No latent violent tendencies brewing under that surface?"

Jacob zoned out, looking off in the direction of the kitchen, then shrugged. "Not unless she's hiding something. The hostile ones tend to make their attitude known pretty fast. Unless they're intelligent and manipulative and drawing you into a trap, of course. You know, like Admiral Akbar—"

"*Star Wars*, got it," I said. "What else?"

"There's more. Let's walk." We left cash on the bar and headed out into the lobby, and from there to the main ballroom. It was silent, just a couple of lights on. Our movements echoed through the empty space. Stacey tracked alongside him with her handheld camera, recording his walk-through of the hotel.

"There are little spirits all over, but they keep hiding and scurrying away between the walls," Jacob said, his voice echoing in the empty room though he wasn't being particularly loud. "I'll call them the wally-crawleys."

"Aw, they sound cute," Stacey said.

"They look like dead children with bleeding eyes," he said. He walked to one wall and pressed his hand to the paneling between two floor-length mirrors. "Yeah. Up and down inside the walls, hiding. Because there are worse things..." He looked up at the ceiling. "Something that makes them run and hide. They aren't talking to me, but I can feel the heavy darkness up there, and they're trying to avoid it. Now they're running down, away from me. They're nervous because they know I can see them."

"Maybe we should head to the basement," I said. "Work our way from the bottom up."

"Oh, yeah, the basement," Stacey said. "We all love dark and scary basements at night. Nothing bad ever happens."

Jacob looked surprised when I pushed open a jib door and led him into the inner warren of service rooms and supply closets.

"Wow," he said, as I opened a door to the basement. "All these dark little rooms and stairways with no windows, hidden from the main hotel. It's like someone was *trying* to build a house for ghosts to haunt. And it worked. These central rooms are like a....chimney, kind of. All kinds of energy flows up and down."

Ithaca Galloway, I thought. Maybe the inner warren of service rooms hadn't been an original part of the Lathrop's design, but had been introduced during her renovations. It certainly wouldn't have made much sense in the days before electric lighting and mechanical ventilation.

We moved into the cooler basement. I drew my Mel-Meter and watched the readings tick up as we descended the stairs.

"Yeah, this is where they go," Jacob said. "The sick ones that are still here. They suffer heat, cold, aches, dizziness. Some of them are bleeding from every hole in their face. I'm guessing these are the yellow fever epidemic victims. Their clothes match the era."

"Hey, you're not supposed to research the locations first," Stacey said. "Don't feed the psychics, remember? Not information, anyway.

I think you're allowed to have snacks."

"Who did any research? This is one of the most famous haunted spots in town. I'm guessing we'll go upstairs next and I'll find Nurse Stabby Abby waving a bloody scalpel around, am I right?"

I sighed. "Okay. Anything else you can tell us about the ghosts down here?"

He paced in the dimly lit brick room, past the fenced storage areas and doorways to other basement rooms. "This is just where the sick go. Living people might feel ill down here. Spending too much time in this area could make you susceptible to disease, depression, all kinds of bad stuff. Not healthy."

"Yeah, this place does make me feel kinda sick," Stacey said.

We continued onward into the basement, the air smelling a little more foul every moment we remained. Imagine the scent of an overcrowded hospital with no cleaners or antiseptics during the hottest days of high summer.

A few machines clanked in the laundry room. Jacob glanced in there, then opened a nearby closet and nodded.

Inside was, possibly, the world's longest linen closet, shelves heaped with crisply folded white towels, sheets, blankets and bathrobes as far as my flashlight could see. It was narrow, like a deep cave.

"The younger ones like it here," he said. "There's an old staircase at the far end where they sneak upstairs. I think, of all the fever victims, the kids are the only ones brave and curious enough to travel to the upper floors. The adults seem to linger down here, lying all over the floor, focused entirely on their own misery."

"What a way to spend a century," Stacey said.

We traversed the long, long closet single file, since it was just about too narrow for us to pass any other way. The door at the far end was dusty and strung with layers of spiderwebs. It gave a rusty rasp as we opened it.

Beyond the door, the stairwell beyond was steep, narrow, and dark, and the light switch did not respond. A moldy smell hung in the stale air.

The steps creaked and sagged beneath my boots as I led the way up. I waved my flashlight from side to side to clear off spiderwebs.

Something giggled under the stairs.

"Holy cow, what was that?" Stacey asked, looking down with her camera.

I pointed my flashlight to the dark gaps between the stairs—I hate those, I'll never live in a place without solid risers between the steps—expecting some pale little hand to reach up and grab my ankle. I didn't see anything in the dusty, brick-lined darkness below.

"It was one of them," Jacob said. "A small girl, I think. Maybe she wants to come play with you. Or she wants you to go down there and play with her—"

"No sale," Stacey said. "Ellie, pick up the pace."

I double-timed it up the stairs, keeping my flashlight pointed below. I'm pretty sure a pair of eyes looked up at me, reflecting my light for half a second before vanishing.

My heart was beating fast and cold by the time I reached the top of the stairs. I shoved against the door at the top, but it wouldn't move. Then I noticed the dusty, grimy hinges were on my side of the door and pulled it open instead.

Five shelves of clean, folded cloth napkins and table linens blocked the doorway I'd just opened.

"Uh, could take a minute," I said.

I did my best not to make a mess of things, but ultimately the shelves were fully stocked and I had to remove at least two of them so we could crawl through. We finally made it, emerging into a linen closet located in the back of the restaurant.

The three of us, covered in dust and cobwebs, drew puzzled looks from the kitchen staff as we strolled past them. They were scrubbing the food prep surfaces, shutting down for the night. Stacey waved and smiled, as if it were perfectly normal for three filthy people to inexplicably emerge from a linen closet like it was the gateway to Narnia.

"Busy night, huh?" she asked them. They ignored her and went back to work.

On the second floor, Jacob stood outside 208, since we didn't have access to the room. I was pretty sure that Lemmy's parents would be happy to have two professional ghost hunters and a psychic visit their room, but then they might be a little hard to shake afterward. I certainly didn't want them inviting themselves to tag along for the rest of the night.

So Stacey and I waited down the hall a bit, taking video as Jacob wandered near the door, occasionally touching the frame.

"Yeah," he said. "She's here all right."

"Any chance she has violent tendencies?" I asked. "I'm guessing yes, based on her mass murder thing."

Jacob scowled. "You're making her angry."

"Because of our investigation?"

"No. Calling her a murderer."

"Is she saying she's innocent?"

"She's saying..." Jacob glanced at the door, then turned the other way, looking at an empty space in the hallway near him. My Mel-Meter detected a strong uptick in energy, and a temperature drop of nine degrees. "Yeah, I'm trying to keep up with her. She's saying what she did was necessary."

"Why?"

"It was an act of mercy. That's how she sees it. An act of compassion, doing the Lord's work. She says she's explained it all to the woman upstairs."

"But did she have their permission?" I asked. "To murder them?"

"Okay. I thought you were making her mad before, but now you're really making her mad."

"Is she the one who cut me?"

Jacob cringed a little, as though someone were screaming at him. "No, no, that was the man upstairs. She's really insistent on it."

"Which man?" I asked. "Gregor?"

"The man upstairs," Jacob repeated. "You know I'm not good at picking up names, dates, and numbers."

"Right, because that would be too useful," I said. "Okay. So who killed the workman up on the fourth floor?"

Jacob tilted his head, listening, and frowned. "She doesn't know what you're talking about."

"Do you believe her?"

"She's pretty stuck in her own dramas down here. Nursing, killing...men hanging her from a tree, a mob shouting at her..."

"Can she tell us anything about what's happening on the fourth floor?"

"She says to stay away from there."

"Why?"

Jacob turned his head as though watching someone walk away down the hall.

"Jacob, why should we stay away?"

"She's incommunicado now. She said it was time to make her rounds, check on the patients. Back to her own memories and obsessions."

"Well, that tells us a whole lot of nothing," Stacey said. "Shall we proceed to the art gallery and the spa? The spa's closed for the night, sadly..."

"This whole place is thick with residual hauntings," Jacob whispered as we explored the hallways of the second floor. "Imagine the floor and walls covered in transparent video screens, all of them overlapping and blurring together. I've never seen it so thick before. I'm trying to look past those, just focus on active, conscious presences...if I include all the residuals, this hotel seriously has too many ghosts to count."

"They should put that on the brochure," Stacey said.

We passed the small art gallery, which seemed composed mostly of pleasant landscapes and nature paintings depicting Georgia's variety of ecosystems—the beach at sunrise, the dark Okefenokee swamp, rivers and waterfalls, the verdant Blue Ridge mountains. Another painting showed the obligatory rustic general store made of weathered boards, a faded Coca-Cola sign out front, summoning nostalgia for a rural small-town past you may have never actually experienced.

Lemmy sat alone in the second-floor lounge, doing something that involved cutting up magazines with scissors and pasting them onto construction paper with rubber cement. She waved at me while Jacob glanced into the room and moved on down the hall. The lack of any active ghosts in the room probably put the girl at ease, even if it was only subconsciously.

Then we ducked through one of the nearly-invisible jib doors and headed up through a narrow service stairwell.

On the third floor, things started to get a little crazy.

## Chapter Thirteen

The temperature was noticeably colder in the silent hallways of the third floor, and my Mel-Meter ticked up and down between four and six milligaus, which indicated something was stirring.

"Somebody's awake," Jacob whispered. I didn't think he was talking about the hotel guests behind their doors.

He took a deep, startled breath when we entered the hall where I'd encountered the crowd of wounded soldiers. I felt it, too—a thick, undeniable presence so strong it made my bones shiver in their sockets. I had to fight the urge to turn and run. Stacey looked like she was experiencing the same thing, her eyes huge and her face pale.

I would have liked to warn Jacob about this part of the hotel, but that could have interfered with his work.

"There's a lot of dead men all around us," Jacob said quietly. "They're missing limbs, they're wounded and scarred. They radiate pain. They're kind of lying all over, on cots, on the floor...and now they're starting to notice me."

The voices I'd heard before began to return, groans and moans of pain. Jacob jumped.

Ice-cold invisible hands clutched at me, and something narrow and sharp brushed against my hip. I dodged away from it, but didn't get far. I felt the unseen fingers digging into my arm, my calf, my ribs.

Stacey was squirming, too, as if trying to escape the grasp of more hands. The moaning in the air grew louder.

"They're filling me up with memories..." Jacob reached for his head as though he meant to clutch it in both hands, but then something invisible blocked his arms from moving. "Battlefields littered with bodies, so thick the ground was muddy and red. So thick you couldn't walk around them, you had to walk on top of them. Then they're lying on cots...here, I think...the long amputation knives, the bone saws...there was a hand-cranked chain saw that cut very, very slowly..." Jacob howled in pain and dropped to his knees. Stacey rushed toward him, but the invisible hands restrained her before she could touch him.

"We need to get him out of here!" Stacey snapped at me. "They're hurting him!"

"Good idea," I said. Then I shouted, "Let go of me!"

The invisible hands clutched harder, their moans going more desperate.

"Jacob," I said, "ask if they know who killed the man upstairs."

"You...don't get it." Jacob crumpled on the floor, laboring to breathe. His face was flushed dark crimson. "They aren't...rational."

I felt cold fingers on my throat now, and I still couldn't move my arms or legs very far. This was getting serious. They weren't choking me. It was almost worse than that—they were slowly stroking me, as if savoring the texture of my flesh.

"What about Abigail Bowen?" I asked. "What do they say about her?"

"They say...we...should talk to her." Jacob pushed himself up the floor, managing to regain a kneeling position.

"We already did," I said, while an invisible sharp thing slid up along my back. I thought of that soldier's rusty bayonet and wondered if you could get tetanus from a ghost's weapon. "She said it was an act of mercy. She wanted to end your pain. Is that true? Was she lying to us? Was your suffering truly so bad that you wanted to die? All of you?"

The invisible fingers shuddered against my throat...then, very fortunately, drew back. The hands gripping me all over my body relaxed or pulled away entirely.

"Looks like you said the magic word. I wonder which one it was," Stacey said. She dropped to her knees beside Jacob and put an arm around his shoulders to comfort him. He seemed to breathe easier now.

"Did they answer my question?" I asked.

"They're all lying down now," Jacob said. "On the floor, on those cots. Stretching out like corpses waiting to be buried. Wow. They're really still except for one guy." Jacob stood, pulling Stacey with him. He was looking directly behind me.

I turned, and I saw him again, the soldier with no eyes, his bayonet arm resting on his shoulder. I stepped aside, and he marched right past me. It looked like he would have gone *through* me if I haven't moved. A ghost walking through you is not a pleasant experience. Imagine chills, fever, loss of coordination, nausea, dread, panic...all at once, sometimes. No ectoplasm slime, but it's bad enough.

"Hey, guy," I said to him. "Are you the one who's been cutting people? Like me, for example? Or can you tell me who's been doing that?"

I'd really expected him to ignore me, so I was startled when he stopped in mid-march. His head turned slowly to face me, with a creak of dry tendons and muscles. His eyes remained empty, nightmare-inducing sockets that seemed to stare right through me.

Then his head turned to front again, and he resumed his march, vanishing in an eyeblink.

"I think your attempt at conversation failed to engage his attention," Jacob said.

"That happens all the time. It's why I hate going to parties," I said. "Can you still see him?"

"He's marching down this way. Not really marching, I think, but patrolling. Like he's been posted to watch the area."

"What are the other guys doing?" Stacey stayed close to Jacob's side, casting a worried look at the hallway around her.

"Just lying there," Jacob said. "Playing dead. Well, not really playing, I guess, but they've slipped into a more peaceful state of death."

"So let's get going before they turn un-peaceful again," Stacey said.

We stumbled along to the corner at the end of the hallway, where Jacob stopped.

"That soldier's keeping watch on somebody or something in this room." He pointed to a closed door.

"Uh, that's our room," Stacey said. "Is he watching us?"

Jacob nodded. "That's why he's marching out here. This might not even be the soldiers' usual area of the hotel. They're in this hall because you're here."

"Are they watching us in a good way, like trying to protect us from other, more dangerous spirits?" she asked. "Or in more of a waiting to butcher us in our sleep sort of way?"

"He's not sharing," Jacob said. "It's like it's his duty. Just carrying out orders."

"Who gave the orders?" I asked.

Jacob just shook his head.

"He might as well be a residual at this point," Jacob said. "Pacing up and down, up and down, keeping watch...waiting for more orders, I guess."

"It would be nice to know something about the intention here," I said.

"I can't help you," Jacob said. "He's all locked up now. Doesn't trust me."

"Aw, come on, you can trust Jacob!" Stacey said.

This did not seem to sway the spirit. Jacob could glean no more information from him.

We stopped off in our room to rest for just a minute. Jacob walked around and assured us that he couldn't find anything harmful in the room.

"Some of the kids have peeked in at you, though," he added. "The fever kids who sneak upstairs late at night. I think they do that to a lot of guests."

"Poor kids," Stacey said. "Probably bored out of their minds."

"And looking for ways to harass the living," I said.

We did a quick check to see that our nerve center of monitors was running well. Everything looked fine except for the temple room upstairs—the necromantium, according to the book—where our cameras refused to function at all anymore.

I made sure I had a fresh pair of flashlights and a pair of thermal goggles hooked to my belt before we started out for the fourth floor. The goggles were annoyingly heavy and slowed me down, but I didn't want to get caught off-guard up there.

We ascended through a hidden service stairwell. Stacey and I were silent, knowing that we were heading into the dark heart of the hotel. Jacob picked up on our mood, not saying a word.

At the top of the stairs, he leaned against the door and listened.

"Whispering," he says. "Lots of whispering."

"Can you make out any words?" I asked.

Jacob was silent for a while, then finally said, "I think they're talking about us. They know we're coming."

"And they're...really happy about it?" Stacey ventured. "Planning a fun surprise party for us?"

"They sound a little less friendly than that." Jacob took a breath and clicked on the tactical flashlight we'd loaned him. Stacey and I did the same, trusting him to know when danger lay ahead. The electricity on the fourth floor was hardly reliable, anyway.

We pushed open the door and emerged into lightless service catacombs, the place where Katherine Moore would have worked as a servant while being initiated into Ithaca Galloway and Gregor Zagan's inner circle. Layers of wallpaper and paint remnants clung to the walls. In one room, a table with a sewing machine that must have been a hundred years old stood against one wall, the broken remnants of a chair heaped in front of it. A mess of rotten cloth lay under a layer of dust in one corner.

From here, we passed through a jib door into the hallway outside Ithaca's old bedroom. The hall's overhead lights did not work at all when I tried the switch, so we had to rely on our flashlights, which played over moth-eaten rugs and the dusty old dining chairs that lined one side of the hall.

Jacob touched a finger to his lips, though nobody had been talking. The feeling of being surrounded and watched by an unnatural presence was strong here, and much more powerful and sinister than what I'd felt when surrounded by the soldier ghosts downstairs. Dread permeated my body and brain.

One of the REM pods we'd left in the hall was already flickering its light and letting out a soft *woo* sound, indicating something was interfering with its little electromagnetic field.

The whispering voices reached my ears a moment later, and Stacey cried out in surprise. They were whispering to all of us, I supposed.

"This...this is..." Jacob shook his head. "This is beyond me, guys. They all know we're here, they know I can see them, they don't want us here. They have something to hide, something very big."

"We'll get out of here as fast as we can," I said.

Then I pushed open the doors to Ithaca's old bedroom.

"They're following us, just so everybody's clear," Jacob said. "These are all very active, very conscious entities. They don't have that lost, confused, isolated feeling most ghosts have. They're working together. They have *intent*."

"Intent to do what?" I asked.

"Whatever it is doesn't seem to have much to do with this room." He gestured toward Ithaca's giant bed and equally large circular mirror. "There's residual energy—and I wouldn't recommend anyone spending the night here—but the real action is somewhere else."

"Maybe through here?" I led them into Ithaca's enormous walk-in closet. I fumbled around the empty shoe rack until I figured out how to push open the concealed door. Beyond it lay the dark chamber we believed to be Gregor Zagan's bedroom. It radiated heat like a furnace, just as it had before, and seemed filled with a darkness our lights couldn't penetrate.

"Okay," Jacob said, his voice small and mousy. He cleared his throat and tried again. "Okay, you can close that."

"You don't want to go in?" I asked.

"Definitely not." He made several urgent waving motions with his hand, letting me know he was serious about closing the door. I let it swing shut.

"What did you see?" Stacey asked.

"There's a guy in there. Long beard. Weird eyes. Creepy. He looked right back at me, and I could feel him daring me to come in. He's *hot*. You don't need me to tell you that. Most ghosts are cold, desperately sucking energy where they can. This one radiates. He's been charged up somehow. He brings his own energy. I think he's one of the dominant spirits around here."

I wanted to ask whether he picked up a female companion for the man, a square-jawed woman about a decade his elder, but that's too leading a question for one of these walk-throughs.

"Maybe we should go around?" Stacey suggested.

"Definitely," Jacob said. "He's got insane levels of energy. They're all—that's what's crazy about this place, a lot of these ghosts had psychic abilities in life. What this guy has is off the charts, though."

Stacey and I shared a knowing look, thinking about Gregor. Then we doubled back through Ithaca's room and into the hallway. I was surprised Jacob picked up so few signals about the queen bee of the place. Either Ithaca Galloway was elsewhere in the house or extremely talented at hiding herself.

In the hallway, the REM pods lit up and let out their tones as we passed near them, letting us know that the ghosts were walking with us.

In the cavernous dining room, Jacob paused before the group portrait of Ithaca and her twenty or so followers. This time, I tried to identify Katherine, the girl who'd written the tell-all book I was still reading. I noticed a long-haired freckled girl in her late teens or very early twenties, standing just to the side of Gregor, with his big Karl Marx beard and seersucker suit. The girl wore a lacy dress decorated with dark stones and astrological jewelry. Maybe it was her. I also identified a young man in spectacles and a brown suit, pale but attractive in a sickly, gothic way. He made me think of the poet John Keats, beautiful, gifted, and destined for an early grave. Maybe that was Katherine's sexy—I mean, um, "husbandly"—Scottish tutor, Mr. Fletcher.

"These are the ones bothering us," Jacob said. The whispering hadn't stopped as we walked, and it seemed to urge its way deep into my brain, trying to make me panic. "They don't look too much like their living selves anymore. The ghosts have evolved...not necessarily in a positive way. But they're more connected to each other and more organized than most spirits I've seen. They want us to leave now, by the way." He pointed to Gregor in the picture. "That's the hot one. I don't know how he got so charged up with power."

"What about her?" I indicated Ithaca on her dark throne capped with the goat-headed men. "Anything?"

"There are traces of a presence that might have been her." Jacob shrugged. "Like I said, I'm trying to look past the residuals to the active hauntings."

I found it hard to believe that, while Ithaca's bearded boy toy and their cultish followers were all haunting the house, Ithaca herself, who'd been so obsessed with ghosts while she was alive, had vanished altogether. Maybe we just hadn't found her yet.

I asked specifically about the people I suspected to be Katherine and her young tutor, and Jacob nodded. "They don't like me looking at this picture. It's like I'm seeing them all naked. They're trying to scare me with their appearance. They look like...well, monsters."

"Let's go into the necromantium," I said, and immediately the whispers surged around me and the temperature plummeted until I could see my breath in dense white plumes. I was sick with dread now, despite my attempts to act professional.

I swept my flashlight around and poised my finger against my iPod, ready to hit them with holy music. I couldn't be sure any of this would help—a determined and powerful ghost can brush off my basic defenses if it's intent on something, and *all* these ghosts seemed fairly determined and powerful. I just wasn't sure what their intentions might be.

"Wow, they didn't like that," Jacob said. "They're insisting we leave now and never return."

"That would make billing our client a little awkward," I said, trying to sound like I wasn't in the grip of a growing, irrational terror. Maybe not all that irrational, either, under the circumstances. "Let's go."

The air felt thick and charged, like just before a thunderstorm, as we proceeded down the hall to the big double doors. I could practically hear the energy crackling around us, even with the endless swirling rush of whispers filling my ears. I began to hear individual words now, but not pleasant ones. *Death. Die.* And my least favorite: *Ellie.*

"Are we sure this is a good idea?" Stacey whispered as we reached the doors to the necromantium. The camera trembled in her fingers. She's not easily scared, but the energy of these ghosts was eating away at us emotionally. It was probably intentional on the part of the ghosts. "I mean, they're being pretty clear about what they want. What if they...?" She didn't finish her sentence, but it was clearly going to end in *attack us*. Or maybe *kill us*.

"Jacob, do they want to tell us who's been cutting people? Who killed the worker in this room?" I tapped on the door to the necromantium, and the whispers keyed up a notch in my ears. I was really going to lose my mind if they didn't shut up soon.

"They aren't open to answering questions. Except...oh..." Jacob grabbed Stacey's arm and pulled her behind him. He was gaping at something over my shoulder.

I felt it even before I began to turn around. In the freezing hallway, the approaching wall of heat was hard to ignore. It welled up from behind us, from the direction of, among other things, Gregor Zagan's furnace-like bedroom.

"Zagan," I said. The heat seemed to hesitate in its approach for a moment, then rolled forward again, like a slow billowing cloud of roasting hot desert air. Darkness came with it.

"Okay," Jacob said. He sweated heavily, his face dripping, and he removed his glasses. His cheeks and hands were flushed, as if Zagan were scalding him from the inside out. "Can you tell us who...?" He blinked and nodded as though he'd been interrupted, then turned to me. "The bearded gentleman has indicated, very strongly, his opinion that Abigail Bowen is behind the recent problems."

"His opinion?" I asked.

"He doesn't claim to have witnessed it himself, but he thinks Stabby Abby has been up to her old scalpel-swinging tricks again."

"Okay," I said. Zagan's ghost surprised me with his apparent cooperation. I'd been expecting something closer to a sudden pyrokinetic attack that engulfed us all in flames. "Are there any, uh, witnesses among the ghost community here?"

"He says we do not need investigate this floor any longer," Jacob said. "All the answers are downstairs, with Abigail and her dead soldiers."

"All righty," I said. "Tell him we just want a quick peek in here and we'll be gone." I tapped on the door to the necromantium again.

"He forbids it," Jacob replied quickly. "Says it's off-limits to the living. For our own protection."

"How can he forbid anything? How's he going to stop me?" I asked.

"He can," Jacob said. "He can stop us all. He has more than a dozen other ghosts under his command. They're the ones who've been telling us to leave. Now they're crowding around him, and the energy level is climbing...like he's charging them up...this is not looking good, kids."

"Why doesn't he want us to go in there?" Stacey asked.

"He's a real authoritarian. Doesn't like to explain himself, or to be disobeyed." Jacob looked at me, soaked with sweat now. Stacey and I were sweating pretty hard, too. The temperature had gone from dorm-room refrigerator to funeral bonfire in a matter of seconds. "Your call, Ellie," he said.

I looked in the area where Zagan was standing—which I identified by the rippling heat waves, an extremely rare thing to see from a ghost—and then shrugged. Without announcing my decision, I shoved open the double doors to the dark temple-style room and walked inside, my flashlight playing across the fat columns with their hieroglyphs and demonic sigils and whatnot.

Jacob and Stacey followed, and Jacob immediately staggered after crossing the black granite threshold. We hurried to grab him from either side.

"What...is *that?*" Jacob was staring straight ahead at the center of the black temple room, to the place where the sunken holes in the floor might have once held the supports to Ithaca and Zagan's wacky attempts at a talk-to-the-dead machine.

The whispering rose around us to a cacophonous, chanting sound. It was almost like the opening of *2001*, the eerie sound when the chimps are checking out the black obelisk. The whole room seemed to hum and echo with the otherworldly voices, bouncing off hieroglyphic cartouches and strange serpentine figures wrought in glimmering brass on the walls.

A wave of heat began to swell in the room, signaling Zagan's approach.

"Quick, Jacob," I said. "What do you see?" My first impression was that our cameras and other gear had been shattered and strewn across the floor, roughly in a wide circle around the center of the temple, as if someone had wanted to sweep off just that particular area where the mysterious machine had once stood.

"It's all ripped open," Jacob replied, still staring at the empty space while the air grew dense and clammy around us. "Remember the well in your boyfriend's basement? This is like one of those, but bigger. Cruder. A hole torn in midair, creating a ragged doorway. Someone did this deliberately, and without much skill."

The ghosts began to appear around us, the apparitions probably fueled by Zagan's vast store of superheated psychic energy. They were, as Jacob had mentioned, not fully human in appearance. Their faces were all white, as though bled of any color, and the flesh had a wrinkled and hardened look, like weird masks.

Three of them pressed in close to me, all but their faces cloaked in dark shadows. Pinpricks of fiery light burned like tiny coals deep in their eye sockets. One raised a dry, mottled white hand and reached slowly toward my face.

"Ellie?" Stacey whispered. I forced myself to look over at her, surrounded by even more specters than me. The rest were clustered around Jacob, but at a distance. Maybe he had some psychic technique of holding them at bay.

Or, more likely, they were saving him for the hellishly hot entity that now entered the room, turning the place into a cavernous smokehouse.

He walked in amid the heat, first presenting as a twelve-foot-tall shadow that nearly reached the vaulted ceiling. Then he shrank down, slowly thickening into a large male human form covered entirely in ash, his thick beard smoldering. Glowing pinpoints of light burned in his eyes as he approached. Bootprints of ash smoked on the granite floor behind him. I wondered what would happen if he walked on one of the rugs or carpet runners downstairs.

He stopped close to me, and the other ghosts held me in place for his examination. I could smell him, a stink of burned hair and skin. Trails of smoke escaped his cracked, ash-coated flesh, as if deep fires still burned inside him.

I had the same impression when his cracked, sooty lips parted, letting out a curl of black smoke and an intense heat.

When he spoke to me, it wasn't from his cracked and smoking mouth, though. His voice whispered into my ear, intimately, and I was flooded with revulsion.

*"I forbade you,"* he said.

Then Jacob levitated from the floor, moving toward the high ceiling above. His limbs were extended out to their full lengths, as if to render him as exposed as possible. Even his fingers straightened, then spread apart forcefully, making him grunt.

"Told you so," Jacob managed to cough in my direction. Tiny curls of smoke rose all over his arms, neck, torso, and legs, as if someone had spitballed him with flecks of hot lava. He cried out as small tongues of fire appeared under the smoke, burning out through his clothes and into his flesh. It looked like his whole body would ignite.

"Let him go!" Stacey shouted, which I was just about to shout, but she was quicker. "Right now!"

"Your problem is with me," I told the ghost of Gregor Zagan. "Believe me." My gaze shifted to one of the ghosts holding me. I was fairly certain that two of my captors, based on the look of their mask-like faces, were Katherine Moore and her Scottish friend, Edward Fletcher. Maybe they'd taken an interest in me after I'd asked about their pictures in the dining room. "Katherine, I'm reading your book. I have the last copy that hasn't been destroyed. It's good."

The ghost to which I'd spoken drew back just slightly, as if I'd surprised her. I touched my iPod and charged toward her.

I wasn't taking any chances on the holy music. I filled the room with Benedictine chants at top volume, radiating a very church-like atmosphere in my immediate vicinity. I managed to pass through Katherine's ghost, feeling a weird mix of confusion and hate and loneliness, and charged on toward the apparition of Zagan.

Fire streaked all along Jacob's jeans and shirt. He struggled uselessly in the air.

The white-masked apparitions had lifted Stacey off the floor, too, and all she could do was scream.

I leaped at Zagan. I can't say I cared for the crumbling, ashy smile that crawled across his face as I launched myself toward him.

Then I felt like I was being burned alive.

I screamed, and I was conscious of being flung, and even more conscious of slamming painfully into one of those stupid columns that were in the way everywhere. My hip cracked into it, then my head an instant later.

I fell to the floor about as gracefully as a yak dropped from a helicopter. I smacked into the marble tile and nearly lost consciousness.

When I managed to look up, Zagan didn't seem to have moved at all, except that he'd turned his head to look directly at Jacob and smile as the supernatural flames spread across him. Stacey screamed at the sight of him.

My head ringing, I managed to push myself to my hands and feet. I seemed to have escaped my ghostly captors for the moment, though I doubted it would last. I'd also landed not far from the open doors through which I'd entered.

My immediate concern was pulling Jacob out of the fire. I managed to crawl out into the hall and regain my feet as I approached the fire-hose station near the servants' jib door in the hallway.

The hose was there, and looked as though it had been for decades. The big old-timey spigot handle was badly spotted with rust. I hoped the hotel had kept up its fire safety inspections over the years.

I gripped the round handle, gritting my teeth, and finally got it to shriek and to turn. The coiled-up hose began to fill with water. I grabbed the nozzle and ran, praying the old hose wasn't so rotten that it would rip or burst. I couldn't afford to move slowly. I paused only to draw the thermals from my belt and strap them onto my face.

The ghosts who'd been my recent captors met me at the door,

blue shapes through my lenses. They didn't stop me from unleashing a solid blast of water at Jacob and soaking him, the thermals helping me aim for the most serious hotspots first.

Then I turned on Zagan. The dark, purple-black mass that seemed to be his energy core wasn't in the same place as his apparition, but hovered above the central space of the temple like a black sun, not far from Jacob, radiating purple-red waves of heat as he looked down on us all. If I'd gone by Zagan's ash-skinned apparition, I would have missed the spirit's real location in the room.

I lifted the hose and hit the big superheated mass, for whatever it was worth. The cooler temperature might suck out some of his radiant heat.

Heat rushed out in all direction as I hosed Zagan down. The room turned bright red, and my view of him was obscured.

I raised my thermal goggles off my eyes and found the room filled with steam, like one of those saunas where fat old mob guys are always hanging out in movies, waiting to get assassinated.

Jacob howled, then abruptly stopped. A loud thud told me he might have dropped to the floor.

I found Stacey by her shouts and grabbed her by the sleeve, since I couldn't see her. We staggered toward where we'd last seen Jacob.

The floor quaked as though an earthquake tremor rocked the city. We stumbled and fell over each other just as we reached Jacob, and the three of us tangled momentarily in a battered, burned heap of very confused and frightened human beings.

We managed to regain our feet, and we found our way back to the double doors through the blinding steam, using the hose to guide us.

When we ran into the hallway, the double doors slammed behind us, and everything fell silent. No whispering, no white faces floating in the dark. Steam drifted out toward us, under and between the doors. I hurried to turn off the water before it flooded the hallway.

"Everybody alive?" Jacob asked, checking us out.

"You got the worst of it." Stacey touched his reddened skin through a gaping burn hole in his sleeve.

"Ow!"

"Sorry."

"How did you not realize that would hurt?"

"I said sorry." Stacey moved close and kissed him. He seemed to accept this form of apology, slipping his hands around her waist.

"Hey, I'm glad this is taking such a pleasant turn for you two, but we should probably—" I began.

The hotel shook again. It wasn't a single tremor this time, but a deep shuddering that seemed to build and build. Paint flecks and chunks of ceiling rained down around us.

"Let's go!" Stacey shouted, pulling Jacob down the hall with her. I was already on the move myself. We ran, fighting to maintain our balance as the floorboards shifted back and forth beneath our shoes as if we were running through some kind of carnival funhouse. A mirror on the wall shattered, spraying glass shards all over us.

Then the furniture began to levitate, old armchairs and end tables that had gathered cobwebs for a hundred years. These smashed against the walls, one after the other, and the broken chunks of nineteenth-century wood, glass, and nails flew at us, whirling as if carried by a cyclone.

"Take cover!" Stacey shouted.

"No, run!" I countered. "Don't stop."

The wave of psychokinetic energy was faster than we were, and within seconds we were battered by the debris as we ran. Glass shrapnel scraped across both my hands, and I couldn't help screaming in pain. And fear. Mostly fear.

As we passed the doors to the little bedroom cells, more furniture flew out at us. Antique chairs, a rolltop desk, entire beds, some of which shattered into debris as they hammered their way out the doorframes. Stacey shoved me aside at one point, trying to protect me, and took a bedpost to the elbow for it.

We passed through the next jib door we could find, into the inner service area, and I heard a tremendous crash as all the broken furniture fell to the floor.

The floor itself shook even harder, floorboards popping out of place as if trying to trip us up. The walls in the dark inner rooms cracked and bled plaster dust. I tried to open the doorway to the service stairs, but it was jammed shut. Stacey jabbed at the elevator button while the pressed-tin ceiling bulged down from above. I yanked her aside before a chunk of old copper pipe, tangled in wires, swung down and grazed her head.

An icy calm darkness filled the middle of the room, even as the walls and floor continued to shake around it. The white mask-faces faded into visibility again, their bodies as indistinct as the shades of the dead way down in pagan Hades.

They moved toward us, their voices arriving first, a cloud of voices urging, threatening, cursing us under their breath. My Benedictine chants didn't seem to deter them at all this time.

Stacey added her own music—a mingling of gentle, drowsy electric guitars and a man singing about love backed by an 80's synthesizer sound.

"What is that?" I asked her.

"Uh, Stryper?" she said.

"Seriously? That's what you picked right now?"

"I thought it might be fun to try Christian metal, you know, so I had it set—"

*"Get back!"* Jacob shouted, in a voice that was so deep, intense, and masculine that I almost developed a crush on him for maybe half an eyeblink. He stomped forward with one foot, and the mob of ghosts hesitated.

It only lasted a second, but during that second, I managed to open the door, and from there it only took a few more seconds for us to flee down the steps.

The door slammed and locked behind us. Fine with me, for the moment.

The quaking abruptly stopped as soon as the door closed. We passed Earl the custodian in the third-floor service area. He looked bored and tired, his nose leaking like before. When I asked whether he'd just felt something like an earthquake, he looked at me like I was crazy. The upstairs had shaken hard enough to crack the walls and pop floorboards loose, but the third floor looked completely unaffected. There was no visible damage, and no guests emerging from their rooms in panic and confusion.

We returned to Stacey's hotel room to lick our wounds, though I couldn't say we felt particularly safe there, either. The soldier patrolled up and down our hall, surrounded by his fallen comrades, who were once again awake and groaning in agony, according to Jacob. And maintaining their ceaseless watch over Stacey and me.

## Chapter Fourteen

We tore into our first-aid kit, a big EMT-style one Michael had given me. We were all pretty scraped up and beaten down. I mostly averted my eyes as Stacey took off Jacob's burned, soggy clothing. Even his socks had burn holes in them. The guy had definitely suffered for the cause.

We gathered on the huge and highly comfortable bed to treat each other with burn medication and bandages. I couldn't say I was completely comfortable in that bed, though. I doubted I could be comfortable anywhere in the Lathrop Grand Hotel unless the evil-spirit situation were radically revised.

"So Zagan's in charge," I said. "Jacob, you're telling me Ithaca Galloway was nowhere to be seen? That woman in the giant portrait upstairs?"

"Yeah, I read the little plate," he said. "She wasn't really a factor. It was all Captain Smokebeard."

"I kind of do the disarming nicknames around here," Stacey said. "But I'll allow it."

"Maybe she was one of the lesser ghosts?" Jacob suggested. "The face-mask people."

"I doubt it. I think if she were among them, she'd be prominent.

She'd make herself known. She doesn't strike me as a wallflower," I said.

"Sorry I couldn't help more," Jacob said.

"You helped a ton," Stacey told him, leaning against him where he sat against the headboard. "So we aren't going to trust Captain Smokebeard's testimony, are we? When he said it was Stabby Abby we're really after?"

"I'm not putting Zagan's ghost down as 'trustworthy,'" I said. "That's just not my policy with anyone who tries to kill me. Considering that Valentino died right there in the necromantium, the exact room Zagan and company seem to want to protect against outsiders, I would put Zagan and his minions at the top of the suspects list."

"I wonder what happened to Ithaca Galloway," Stacey said. "You'd think she would be involved here. She built her whole cult around ghosts."

"Maybe she already had enough of dealing with ghosts while she was alive," Jacob said. "I know I have."

"Let's see if any cameras on the fourth floor are still working." I slid off the bed and crossed to the bank of monitors. A couple of minor ones remained in the hallways. Everything looked calm and quiet now, but it was a jumbled chaos of broken furniture and loose floorboards. "I hope they have ghost insurance."

"Pretty sure you've used that joke before," Stacey told me.

"Well, maybe Jacob hadn't heard it yet."

"I have," Jacob said.

"Okay, fine," I told them. "So we haven't totally narrowed down our suspects list, but it seems pretty clear that those on four, Zagan and the dead cult of psychics, are probably the most dangerous and definitely the most powerful. It's insane how much power Zagan has. I'll ask Calvin what he thinks about it in the morning."

"Yeah, how would he get so powerful?" Stacey asked. "Usually these 'master' ghosts are people who were killers in life, and have some dominance over the ghosts of the people they killed..."

"I don't know if that's the case here. This seems like something else." I picked up Stacey's tablet, the one with the scanned pages from Katherine Moore's book. "I'll have to keep reading and see what I can find."

"We can all read it," Stacey said. "Or, better yet, I can rip the scan into a text file and then use a text-to-speech program so we can all listen together. A few of the words might be wrong, but it should mostly work."

"Sounds good to me." I grabbed a thick, soft bathrobe from the hanger in the bathroom and tossed it to Jacob, since his clothes had mostly burned away. Then I grabbed a bottle of water from the cooler we'd brought—much cheaper than the mini-bar—and sank into an armchair, watching the monitors while Stacey prepared the file.

I caught Jacob up on Katherine's story so far, as quickly as I could, hoping I wasn't leaving out any key details. Then I paged forward on Stacey's tablet until I reached the last page Grant and I had read, where Katherine had described Ithaca and Zagan's expensive, failed attempts to build the "Mortis Ocularum" for speaking with the dead. Between supporting so many people and blowing huge amounts of money on attempts at building that giant theoretical machine, it was easy to see how Ithaca's fortune could have dwindled away by the end of her life.

*"My training continued over months and years,"* the tablet recounted in a flat robot voice. *"By Mr. Zagan's advice, I restrained myself in the company of Mr. Fletcher, and would not allow him even to touch my hand, for fear I would give into my dangerous fancies of him."*

"Any chance we can use a less unsettling voice?" I asked. "A little less Robbie the Robot?"

"Sure." Stacey touched the tablet, and the narration turned to a slightly-less-robotic female voice.

*"I was initiated as a true member of the group in an elaborate rite, for which I bathed in ritual fashion and fasted for three days in preparation. I was made to swear an oath that death itself would not keep me from our work. Mrs. Galloway intended the hotel to be a bridge between the living and the dead, a place where flesh and spirit might work closely together for higher ends.*

*"In time, Mr. Zagan himself took greater and greater interest in my instruction. He would bring me to his chamber when Mrs. Galloway was away, and there unleashed life-energies from within me, of a kind I can hardly describe. Though I feared him, I found the pleasures of his attention undeniable, as though he had power of mesmerism over my body as well as my mind. He continued to forbid my interest in the young Mr. Fletcher, sadly."*

"Short version, Zagan kept her apart from the boy she liked and then had an affair with her whenever Ithaca wasn't around," Stacey said.

"Maybe he was just looking out for her best interests. You know, for the sake of her education," Jacob said, and Stacey smacked him with a pillow. He wiggled his fingers at her. "Careful! I have powers of mesmerism over your body."

"I hadn't noticed," Stacey said.

I waved for them to be quiet.

We listened as Katherine recounted the experiments and activities of the group, allegedly summoning the ghosts of notable dead men and women. She claimed to have conversed with the emperor Caligula and the czarina Catherine the Great, among others. She also seemed to distance herself from the young Scotsman as she grew closer to Gregor, taking her lessons from Gregor instead. I also noted that she took to using "Gregor" instead of "Mr. Zagan."

*"A controversy emerged between Gregor and Mrs. Galloway, leading in time to the schism between them. Mrs. Galloway thought of their work in terms of science and education, of gaining knowledge to be shared with the world, or at least 'the right sort of people.' Gregor was a more ambitious man, and read often from the Testament of Solomon and the associated Keys, and spoke of how Solomon had enslaved demons to build his Temple. He wished to learn to bind spirits in servitude and command them. Mrs. Galloway did not share in this desire and forbade him to attempt any rites concerning the enslavement of spirits.*

*"The Mortis Ocularum, a device Mrs. Galloway claimed was based on ancient designs rescued from the Library of Alexandria, was never to reach completion despite countless attempts. Perhaps the design itself was useless, but Mrs. Galloway would not hear of it. She worked on it always, sleeping little, eating little. Gregor confided to me that she would take no leisure nor pleasure until she saw the machine complete. Gregor lost faith in the machine and urged her to abandon the idea in pursuit of more fruitful aims. She would not take his counsel, wise as it was.*

*"In time Mrs. Galloway grew frustrated, and seemed to weary of us. Her luxurious apartments had been worn threadbare by use, and she did nothing to restore them. In time we no longer had servants on the fourth floor, and soon after there was less and less for us to eat. Mrs. Galloway withdrew to her own room and was rarely seen.*

*"We began to dissolve as a group, some leaving by ones and twos, some lingering but knowing the time to move on had come. Gregor proposed to take the remainder of us westward to find a new direction without Mrs. Galloway. I welcomed this move. I was then twenty-six and frustrated with playing Gregor's junior-wife."*

I listened as Katherine, by way of the text-to-speech program, described how Ithaca eventually wanted nothing more to do with the followers she'd attracted. Zagan and a dozen followers, including Katherine herself, left the hotel on a cold Saturday in January of 1912. By train and then by hiking on foot, living out of bags and tents, they reached the Appalachians. Zagan took them on a cold night hike up to a wide flat area on Blood Mountain with a sweeping view of the mountain range.

"Under starlight, Gregor led us in just the sort of rites Mrs. Galloway had forbidden. Gregor claimed that soon we would have powerful spirits under our command, and then no one could hinder us from any purpose we might hold. He told us he would construct a great Temple there on the ancient mountain, sacred to all the peoples who had ever lived near it, and proclaimed himself lord of all that could be seen from the mountain's peak.

"It was late, and I thought I would die of the painful cold, but Gregor would not be deterred from his vision. He drew circles and figures with chalk on the stony ground. He placed himself within, between the inner and outer circles, and the rest of us outside the circle, our hands extending to touch one another.

"We chanted and envisioned as he instructed. I began to think little would come of it beyond our deaths in the frozen mountain air, but the earth began to tremble beneath us, and the trees to sway and shudder with branches snapping as though blown by a great wind, though no wind touched us.

"Gregor evoked a dark and primordial entity, calling it by names I dare not attempt to recollect, nor would I set such dangerous words into writing if I did remember them exactly. He had once confided in me his belief that demonic entities were, in essence, old human souls from the earliest ages of man, spirits who have grown in power over thousands upon thousands of years and thus transformed into a different kind of Being altogether.

"I do not know whether this is true. I can relate that the entity did indeed arrive, but we were ill-prepared for it.

"A column of black smoke as wide as the outermost chalk circle appeared before us and stretched heavenward, blacking out the stars. It blinded us as it grew, and the smell was more horrid than anything I'd known, a diseased charnel-house stench of fire and flesh. I thought the poisons in the air would cause my death.

"I lost my hold on the hands to either side of me. I ran in a panic. We dispersed, all of us in fear. Most of them I have not seen again since that night, and ten years have now passed.

"Perhaps it was my particular intimacy with Gregor that prevented me from fleeing altogether. I found shelter in a shallow rocky nook, and there waited until the first light of morning. Alone, I returned to the site. The earth was charred in a great circle, the occasional weeds reduced to grains of ash.

*"I found him near the center of the circle, and it was difficult to discern him from the blackened earth and stone all around. Only his bones remained, smoke-blackened and twisted into a gruesome position that spoke of great pain. One skeletal hand held forth, as if he had been begging and supplicating before some great force burned him and crushed his bones to the earth.*

*"Years have passed, and I move restlessly, working where I can, in hotels and other places for the unsettled and unrooted. I welcome no other man into my life, for I am loyal to Gregor. Death is no thick veil, I have learned, and I believe he hears when I speak at night, and waits for my spirit to join with his.*

*"I have lately heard of Ithaca Galloway's death. Though perhaps misguided near the end, she was my teacher and benefactor, and I hold her in greatest esteem. It is for the both of them that I set out this record, that the world may learn of the great and secret things that happened in the Lathrop Grand Hotel, and the truth shall not be lost.*

*"Watch for us. Listen for us. Our work has not yet ended."*

The tablet fell silent.

"Well, okay," Stacey finally said. "Sounds like it was a real freakfest upstairs."

"It tells us something about your friend Gregor Zagan, too," Jacob said. "Like he apparently ended up as the cult leader, at least for a few days before he turned himself into toast."

"And toasting himself in demonfire could explain why his ghost is so charged up and hot. His ghost might be mingled with a much older and more powerful entity," I said. "Which can only mean fun times ahead for us."

"So what can we do?" Stacey asked.

"One possibility would be to try and figure out what happened to Zagan's body. There must be some record of a flash-fried skeleton left out in the open in 1912," I said.

"Unless Katherine buried it or something and just didn't mention it in her book," Stacey said.

"It still might have been discovered since then. We could dig into county and Forest Service records and see what comes up."

"What would you do with his body if you found it?" Jacob asked me. "Or do I not really want to know?"

"It could give us some leverage over him. Maybe lure him into a ghost trap."

"I can't wait to hike around the mountains looking for old bones," Stacey said. "Can we do it at midnight under a full moon on Friday the 13th?"

"You're the one who loves hiking so much," I said.

The hotel seemed unusually calm the rest of the night, as far as our monitors could tell. Cold spots remained in the corridor outside our room. We caught glimpses of Lemmy, roaming unsupervised, her parents either asleep or perfectly willing to treat the whole hotel like a big daycare center.

Around four in the morning, we were exhausted and decided to catch some sleep. In my room, lying in my bed, I could hear occasional strange sounds, like boots pacing outside my door. Above, on the fourth floor, crashing and banging sounds echoed every few minutes. I did the math and figured the room above me was, quite possibly, the ultra-hot chamber that had once been home to Gregor Zagan. I felt so defenseless there in the dark, I didn't even want to close my eyes.

My door banged and rattled in its frame, as if someone were trying to get inside. Then I heard a scratching sound, like a large cat trying to claw through the wood.

I got up, half-scared something would reach out and grab my feet from the space beneath the bed. I hate when they do that.

The little peephole in my door offered a fish-eye view of the hallway outside. Nobody appeared to be there, but I knew better.

I finally tiptoed back through the connecting door and slipped into bed beside Stacey, who was sleeping soundly with Jacob on the other side of her. Comforted by their presence, I finally caught a shallow, short nap, though I could still hear boots in the hall and strange noises upstairs. If I hadn't been drained to the point of collapsing, I surely wouldn't have been able to sleep at all.

I had garish dreams of ghosts, Zagan on fire, and, weirdly, I remember watching a strange, angular bird pulling the sun up over the horizon.

## Chapter Fifteen

"You're in luck. The phone number is registered to a warehouse complex near Flat Rock, North Carolina." That was how Calvin greeted me when I blearily answered the phone less than four hours later. The chirping sound of my cell had startled me awake. I'd left them in my jeans in the other room, so I'd had to do a mad dash to catch the call.

"The phone number?" I asked. My phone was almost out of power, so I fumbled to plug it into the wall charger.

"Metascience Productions? It used to be very important for me to research that phone number. Did something change overnight?"

"Uh, yeah." I looked at the hotel room's coffee maker, wondering whether I ought to brew something strong and resign myself to waking up or if there was some slim chance I'd be able to sleep again. "No, still very important. Stacey and I never found any information about them."

"Neither could I. These buildings belonged to a trucking company that flatlined during the gas crisis of the 1970's. Warehouses, a repair yard. They don't seem to have been used for much since then. They currently belong to a holding company registered in Delaware."

"So it's a fake address, then? Nobody lives or works there?"

"It's possible. It's also possible this production company has leased it. Maybe they're looking for trucker ghosts."

"Thanks, Calvin. At least it's something." I filled him in on the case so far.

"If somebody found a charred skeleton at Blood Mountain, there will be records," he said. "If not, you could spend years searching and digging."

"I don't think the client would be thrilled to pay for that," I said. "Can you hang on a sec? I'll try this number from my room phone."

I put the cell phone on speaker mode so Calvin could listen while I dialed the number from the production company's business card. I didn't see any other way to gain more information about these Metascience people and what they might have seen, or what they might have stirred up in the hotel.

I held my breath as the phone rang, then blew it right out again in frustration when I heard the voice answer.

*"The number you have reached has been disconnected or is no longer in service,"* the recording said. *"Please check your number and try your call again."*

"Well, that was anti-climactic," I said, hanging up the landline. "Disconnected, Calvin. Nobody there."

"Perhaps they've moved on."

"It doesn't make sense. If they were just there to investigate the place for ghosts, why would they put the phone number on their business cards? Why would the place even have a phone if it's been out of business for forty years?"

"All good questions," Calvin said. "I could not find any listing for a 'Kara Smith' in the area, either."

"So what do I do?"

"You may already know."

"As long as I don't have to drive all the way to North Carolina —"

"I'll follow up the Blood Mountain lead while you do," Calvin said, and I snarled silently.

"Okay," I told him. "I'll funnel some coffee down Stacey's throat and we'll go. Can you do me one other favor, Calvin?"

"What's that?"

"Don't sell the agency while I'm out of town. I'd hate to come back and be unemployed."

"You wouldn't be unemployed—"

"How much longer do you think they'll let you stall?" I asked. "And are you stalling because you really haven't made up your mind, or is this just a negotiation tactic for more money?"

"Both," he said. "Meaning I'm not sure."

"Well, when you figure out my future, let me know."

After we hung up, I truly began to wonder if Michael might have a point about just taking off and starting over somewhere new.

I returned to Stacey's room and shook her awake. Jacob was gone, probably off to work. He was an accountant by day, and nobody at his job knew about his supernatural nocturnal activities. I suppose he's constantly cooking up stories to explain the scratches, bruises, and burns dealt by the ghosts.

"Huh?" Stacey blinked, looked around, and sat upright. "I can't believe we managed to sleep here. We must have been exhausted."

"I hope that means you don't plan on going back to sleep," I said. "We might have a slight road trip today."

"Oh, no, not the road trips. Another abandoned insane asylum? Or maybe a prison that housed only serial killers and venomous clowns before being destroyed by a pack of vampire werewolves?"

"Try a trucking company warehouse."

"That doesn't sound so bad."

"It's in the mountains, and it's been abandoned for decades..."

"I knew it! Ugh. You plan the worst vacations." She hopped out of bed. "When are we leaving?"

"When can you be ready?"

"I'll need coffee," Stacey said. "And possibly a jelly-doughnut injection. I'm seriously exhausted."

"Staring at the lines along the highway for a few hours will perk you right up. And you can look forward to those mountain roads with the thousand-foot drop-offs just an inch past the guard rail."

"We should take my car," Stacey said. "It's more mountainy."

I didn't want to argue with that. It was a four-hour drive to the remote address Calvin had given me. I'd figured I could make it in three in my Camaro, but Stacey drove a hybrid Escape, an SUV that would be handy to have if the roads got rough once we left the highway, or if things went sour and we had to make a quick escape down old mountain roads. Our agency van was too sluggish and gaz-guzzling for the journey. Google Earth indicated a broken, weedy blacktop leading up to the chainlink surrounding the old warehouse complex, and I wasn't sure how the van would handle that, either.

I showered while the hotel room coffee maker gurgled. I called Madeline to check in and let her know we were following up an out-of-town lead, mainly so she wouldn't be surprised when she saw it on the expense report. She was lucky the place was close enough that we didn't have to buy airline tickets.

"We're buried in guest complaints this morning," she said. "There are broken items all over the hotel, and some of these are valuable antiques, Ellie. Monetary value is just draining right on out of this place. Guests are checking out, terrified. They're talking about dead children and mutilated soldiers."

"Those are common apparitions in this hotel," I said.

"We've never had so many complaints at once. Y'all must have really stirred things up."

"I'm pretty sure that the key to solving your problem is removing Gregor Zagan's ghost," I said. "We're working on some promising leads. In the meantime, make sure nobody goes up to the fourth floor. Zagan has all those ghosts under his control, and they're turning into a very territorial bunch."

After I hung up with her, Stacey and I packed up a few pieces of basic equipment. On the way out, I slowed as I passed the door to my room. An odd stick figure had been scratched into it, a sketchy bird grasping a half-circle in its feet. I wasn't sure what to make of it, but it reminded me of the dream I'd had earlier in the morning. Maybe it was a warning, or a threat.

We drove to Stacey's apartment building to fetch her car. We bought some spotted bananas and a few other snacks at a gas station on the way out of town. I remembered to bring music this time, so I didn't have to spend the whole trip listening to the new Britney Spears album. We spent half listening to The Clash...and half listening to Britney.

We hit open farmland pretty quickly, which eventually gave way to the tall pines of a national forest. The Appalachian mountains appeared on the horizon, looming ever larger as we approached. The road grew steeper and the drops beside it grew larger as we approached our destination. We had a few minutes to appreciate the rich autumn colors of the forested mountains.

Flat Rock was located in the foothills, near a couple of highways and just off the interstate. We didn't pull off into the village itself, but continued along a small road toward the higher peaks ahead.

As promised, the final stretch of road to the old warehouse complex was broken and weedy, bouncing us as we drove to the padlocked chainlink gate topped with rusty barbed wire.

The row of cinderblock buildings within had accumulated a fair number of vines over the years, and the gravel parking area was choked with weeds and wild shrubs. More vines had nearly buried a small guard shack just inside the gate. The gray, ugly buildings within the fence looked out of place against the background of huge old trees and ancient granite rock formations that surrounded it.

"Looks like nobody's here," Stacey said. "Oh, well. Let's turn around and head back."

"It can't hurt to look around," I told her.

"I can think of several ways it could. There's getting stabbed by vagrants, bitten by rats or snakes, run down by ghosts driving ghost trucks—"

"I've never heard of ghosts driving ghost trucks."

"Says the girl who recently jumped onboard a ghost train."

"That was a psychokinetic visual and tactile apparition pooling energy and traumatic memories from several entities—"

"Uh-huh. Ghost train," Stacey said, peering at the overgrown buildings. The sky had grown overcast above us, but the weather app hadn't mentioned rain. "So...do we go over the fence or through it?"

"Through it. I'm not dissecting rusty wire while trying to keep my balance fifteen feet in the air." I grabbed gloves and bolt cutters from the Escape and searched for a good spot to cut. About twenty feet from the gate I found a loose panel near a heavy limb that had fallen on the fence, partially crumpling it.

After cutting a gap in the fence, we strapped on backpacks with the most essential gear and ducked through into the overgrown gravel yard. This was beginning to feel like a bad idea. I briefly wished to be corpse-hunting around Blood Mountain instead.

"There's nothing here," Stacey said, kicking a bit of gravel across the lot. "I think this is going to be a dead end."

I advanced toward the largest dilapidated warehouse, wide and squat with a row of three garage doors large enough to admit eighteen-wheeler trucks. Wires hung from shattered exterior spotlights overhead. A metal door with a narrow strip of reinforced glass looked like the easiest way inside. I peered through the window.

"See anything?" Stacey whispered.

"No."

"Are we breaking into every single building?"

"If we have to." I drew my set of picks from my jacket pocket and worked for a minute to pop the rusty lock. The steel door screeched as I pulled it open to reveal a dim, cold space beyond.

We clicked on our flashlights and advanced into the spacious warehouse. The concrete floor was, not surprisingly, in poor condition, cracked into chunks that wobbled beneath our feet. The air was colder than it should have been, and I definitely felt that unpleasant sense of being watched by invisible eyes.

A battered heap of a big rig was parked along one wall, with a shattered hole over its driver-side windshield. The grill and headlights on that side were mangled, and the hood curled up in a rusty snarl above them. It looked like the truck had plowed into something serious, maybe a concrete pylon, and then been left abandoned here when the company closed. The wall mounts and the remnants of a long tool bench indicated this must have been a repair area.

"What did I tell you?" Stacey whispered. "Ghost truck. It's chilly in here."

"I'm just going to take a closer look," I said, moving toward the truck.

"Yeah, you can't go wrong doing that." Stacey swept her light around the room, over metallic debris and a couple of old tires.

I grabbed the exterior handle on the non-wrecked side and stepped up to peer into the cab. A fuzzy rabbit's foot hung from the bulging, misshapen dashboard. The driver's seat and headrest were stained with spatters of something dark.

A heavy thud echoed from somewhere deep in the warehouse, followed by a footstep.

"Ellie..." Stacey whispered.

I nodded and hopped down to join her.

We waited, expecting more, but the warehouse had fallen silent.

"Let's go check it out," I whispered.

"Admit it. You just want to get us killed, don't you?"

We made our way through the debris, toward where I thought the sound had originated. Our footsteps echoed as if to advertise our presence.

We navigated around several tall metal racks that had been shoved together in a jumble, blocking our view of the rear area of the warehouse.

On the other side of that jumble, two figures stood in the

shadows near a wall of the warehouse, not moving. They appeared to be watching us. I shouted to Stacey and turned my flashlight on them.

"Boo!" one of them said, raising his arms as if to scare me. They weren't ghosts, but obviously flesh and blood living people. I didn't recognize the husky, thin-lipped man in the black imitation-cop private security uniform, but I definitely knew the one who'd spoken. He was around my age, short black hair and sky-blue eyes, his face permanently shaped into a haughty look, his lips born to make condescending and dismissive smiles.

"Nicholas Blake," I said. "From Paranormal Solutions. You're the one who spied on Stacey and me."

"Seriously?" Stacey asked, looking from me to him. "I don't get it."

"What are you doing here?" I asked him. He seemed amused.

"I will tell you what I am not doing," he said, his Oxford accent crisp and precise. I couldn't determine if it was real or an affectation. I've never been to England. Or anywhere north of Virginia or east of the Georgia coastal islands. "I am not engaged in criminal trespass and destruction of property, which is more than either of you can claim."

"We thought it was abandoned," I said. "Isn't it?"

"Is this sort of complete disregard for the law a standard procedure for Eckhart Investigations?" he asked.

"I go where the ghosts lead me," I said. "They don't care about laws."

"While we might debate the importance of a particular law in a particular instance, surely you understand that Western society depends on a general framework of individual property rights governing our interactions with one another, without which peaceable society would be virtually impossible—"

"Okay, Encyclopedia Brown. We came here to speak with Metascience Productions, if it exists. I didn't know I'd be running into you people. I guess Metascience is one of your, what, subsidiaries? Or just a plain false front?"

"More of the latter. It does not exist beyond a few business cards."

"Which brings me right to another question—why would you go around pretending to be some nonexistent company claiming to film ghost documentaries? Why not just use your own name?"

"We like to maintain a bit of distance for special research projects," he said.

"Is that what this is?" I gestured at the mostly-empty warehouse. "What are you doing here? And what were you doing at the Lathrop Grand Hotel a month ago? It must have been after you first approached Calving about buying the agency."

"Typically I would reply that you should remove your nose from my beeswax, as you say over here," he replied.

"I've literally never heard anyone speak that combination of words before."

"If we hadn't recognized you on our security monitors, we would have simply contacted the local constabulary about the break-in," he said. I couldn't help but notice Stacey breathe the word *constabulary* under her breath beside me. "Because of the unique nature of our relationship, it was decided that discretion would be the wiser course."

"Thanks. I'm not sure we technically have a relationship, though," I said.

"You will soon be part of our family. You, as well." He nodded at Stacey.

"I feel like I'm three steps behind here," Stacey said.

"We both are," I said. "Come on, Nicky. Just tell us what's happening here. Is this a trap?"

"Yes," Nicholas said. "A cleverly laid trap in which you broke into our facility."

"You don't think 'facility' is a pretty generous word?" I gestured around at the scattered junk of the warehouse. "And this doesn't strike me as a prime location for a yoga-and-smoothie place."

"This is not intended to be a Higher Self Center," he said. "It's a facility for research that would be of great interest to you, I think. We are developing the next generation of tools for paranormal investigation, communication, capture, and containment."

"If it involves getting inside that thing, I'm out." Stacey pointed back at the ruined heap of a tractor truck I'd been investigating.

"The lorry is actually original to the building," he said. "We left it there for a touch of authentic décor."

"I assume you have more to show us?" I pointed at the pair of steel double doors just behind them.

"Does this mean you're willing to reconsider your reluctance to join our family?" Nicholas asked, with a quick smile that struck me as unnecessarily arrogant.

"Step one would be to stop calling your big corporate company a 'family,' because I hate when people do that," I said. "Step two would involve you explaining why you were at the Lathrop Grand and whether you did anything that might affect my case."

"What case is that?"

"I'm not free to disclose."

"The new owners hired you to snuff out troublesome ghosts."

"What exactly did you people do at the hotel?" I asked. I'm pretty sure I'd been asking it again and again, but you wouldn't know it by Nicholas's replies.

"We could stand out here chatting, or I could take you inside and show you," he said. "I have clearance to do that. Would you like to see?"

"Please. Make our drive worthwhile," I said.

Nicholas nodded at the silent security guy, who turned and waved toward a dark upper corner of the enormous room. There was a heavy metallic clunk, just like the one we'd heard earlier. Then the metal doors swung inward. Though they looked old and worn, they moved silently.

We passed through a short cinderblock corridor and reached another pair of doors. Stacey and I followed him inside. I had no idea what to expect.

## Chapter Sixteen

"This is the best way to gain an overview of our work here," Nicholas said, climbing a steep, narrow set of aluminum stairs up to a high catwalk. "Figuratively and literally."

"Yeah, I picked up on that," I muttered under my breath, too low for anyone to really hear. I climbed up after him, Stacey close behind me. The quiet, hulking security guy had ditched us once we were inside, which I didn't mind at all.

We looked down into rooms separated by high metal dividers, roofed with mesh, probably to create electromagnetic barriers between them. Lighting was low throughout the place. Each room centered on a large clear cube—probably made of leaded glass, I was guessing, unless they'd come up with something better—surrounded by an array of strange technical gear that might have been at home at some experimental laser-weapons lab in Los Alamos. Many of the rooms were otherwise empty, but small groups stood in a few of them, operating the gear.

I saw a flickering apparition at the center of one cube, which was followed by a murmur among the technicians around it. The entity looked tall and thin, misty and transparent, shifting in and out of visibility. A howling scream emitted from a speaker nearby, until somebody turned down the volume.

In another cube, I saw a stack of three large granite blocks, each one probably fifty or sixty pounds. The top block was moving so slowly that I barely realized it at first, but Nicholas insisted we stop and watch.

The top block slid slowly, slowly, farther and farther over the edge of the block beneath it, until gravity took over and it toppled to the padded floor with a thud.

The technicians in the room seemed happy about this, and one of them even applauded.

Then the fallen rock levitated from the floor, which seemed to take them by surprise. It hurtled toward the clear wall of the cube closest to the researchers, and they took cover just before it smashed into it. The wall shuddered but held, though a huge circle of crushed glass was visible on the inside. The outer layer of the cube must have been plastic, or something tougher than leaded glass, anyway.

"He's a bit rebellious," Nicholas said. "We found him in a defunct coal mine in Pennsylvania. Local legend, that one. Destructive and loud."

I watched the remaining stones shatter. The unseen entity flung the shards against the interior of the cube, still trying to smash its way out. I thought of the *Testament of Solomon* referenced by Katherine Moore and studied by Gregor Zagan, the idea of enslaving demons to help with major construction projects. It sounded a little quaint in the modern world, though. Would demons know how to install central heating and air? Fiber optics? A lawn sprinkler system?

"You're bringing captured ghosts here," I said. "And doing what? Trying to control them? Train them?"

"In that fellow's case, yes," he said, shaking his head. "So much psychokinetic energy at his disposal, so little intelligence or purpose with which to guide it. Our destination lies this way."

Stacey and I shared a look that told me we were both feeling the same kind of horror and apprehension about what we'd stumbled into here. Trucker ghosts might have been a more pleasant alternative.

"How do you pay for all this?" I asked as we passed over more labs. "Popping ghosts isn't really a high-margin line of work."

"Not if one insists on using a means-based sliding scale for calculating client fees," he said. "That tends to attract the low-paying riffraff."

"Are you kidding? You don't do that?" I asked. "So you only work for people who can pay big? Just let everyone else suffer?"

"I suppose we could maintain the sliding-scale philosophy at your branch, if you're so passionate about it," he said. "Provided you stay on after we complete the purchase of the agency."

"And me, too," Stacey said.

"And Miss Tolbert as well," he agreed.

"Don't add to his terms, Stacey!" I shook my head. "I'm not sure I agree with your whole philosophy there, Nick."

"I wasn't being entirely serious with you. All you see before you is funded by Bridgeport housewives paying nine dollars for a cup of pureed strawberries and yogurt."

"That's why y'all developed the wacky commercial side of your business," I said. "The Higher Self Centers are a cash cow."

"Among other things. They're also useful for identifying psychically talented individuals. Occasionally, one of those Bridgeport housewives also has precognitive dreams or similar talents."

Nicholas led us down another steep staircase, away from the catwalk and toward something that looked like a bizarre museum exhibit from the early Industrial Age.

The elements of the machine, mounted on scaffolding and wires, occupied a spherical area. Curving metal arms larger than my waist, mounted on gears, were surrounded by huge copper electrical coils that looked dangerous and primitive. A variety of glass lenses hung here and there, suspended by more thin wires, and a number of overlapping circular gears formed a kind of floor near the bottom, with more colored lenses and mirrors mounted on their surface. Most of these glass elements were cracked, and some had only a shard or two left to indicate where they'd been.

The apparatus was supported entirely by the scaffolding around it, but I could see the eight heavy steel legs on which the base had originally sat. These, too, were suspended, not bearing any weight.

"Is that...?" Stacey began, pointing at the legs. By their size and spacing, they could easily have slid into the holes in the floor at the center of the necromantium.

"The Mortis Ocularum. Seriously?" I looked at Nicholas. "Did this thing work?"

"Not nearly so reliably as desired, but progress was made," he said. "A bit of the veil was torn open, spirits were summoned, but the desired stable bridge of communication between worlds was never formed."

I moved closer to it. At the front of the machine was a viewing station that looked like a coin-operated telescope you might see at Niagara Falls. I leaned down and peered into it, and saw a heavily distended view of the center of the machine.

"The tools and technology were not available in those days," another voice said. Female.

The young woman who'd joined us was pale, with bright blue eyes, thin and incredibly pretty. Like a fashion model. Gary, the former owner of the hotel, had described his contact at Metascience Productions that way.

"Kara Smith?" I asked. "Or that wouldn't be a real name, would it?"

She looked at me, seemed to decide I was unimportant, and turned to Nicholas. "Who are these people, Nicholas? Why are they in my area without my permission?"

"We're just looking for the people who were involved in the Lathrop Grand Hotel investigation one month ago," I said. "If that isn't you, just tell us where to find them and we'll be on our way. Nicholas is being coy."

"That does not sound like Nicholas," she said. "Why are you interested in that hotel?"

"We think whatever you did on the fourth floor may have unleashed some serious problems," I said. "What were you doing?"

"That's absurd. Every spirit in that hotel knows its place, and it is well-protected against outside interference," she said.

"You might want to check your math on that, because several people have been attacked and one man was killed," I said.

"Impossible. We do not resort to violence. We have tricks of the mind. If the living interfere with us or our work, we can send them away in fear. We do not seek to harm the living."

"Why do you keep saying 'we'?" I asked.

"Eleanor Jordan, Stacey Ray Tolbert," Nicholas said, making me wince a little at the sound of my full first name. That's what my personal demon, Anton Clay, loves to call me. So did my mom, before he killed her. "I present you to Mrs. Ithaca Galloway."

Stacey gaped. I looked the girl over and shook my head.

"That would be an amazing apparition," I said. "The most detailed I've ever encountered. But I've seen Ithaca's portrait up in her old dining room on the fourth floor. She was a square-faced, mannish-looking woman—"

When the girl's hand smacked into my face, I was not the least bit prepared. It stung, too. She didn't hold back at all.

"How dare you speak that way," she hissed.

"How dare you freaking *slap* me?" I snapped back, balling my hands into fists, ready to bash my knuckles into her pert little nose.

"Uh, point of fact here, Ithaca's been dead for almost a century," Stacey said.

"Certain decision-makers in our organization took an interest in Mrs. Galloway's work," Nicholas said. "We were sent to the Lathrop Grand to find any remaining notes or designs related to the Mortis Ocularum—which is a bit of Latin-sounding nonsense, I might add."

"It's a neologism," the girl who claimed to be Ithaca said, with a little scowl.

"We did recover such information," Nicholas continued. "Along the way, we encountered the opportunity to bring back Ithaca herself. She was eager to combine her work and ideas, from both before and after her death, with the technical resources at our disposal. An agreement was made. Our investigator Kara Volkova was generous enough to lend her physical form to Mrs. Galloway."

"You're possessing this girl," I said to Ithaca.

"With permission," Nicholas reminded me.

I supposed it was possible. I've let a ghost possess me before. I can't say it's a pleasant experience.

"Shall we show them?" Nicholas asked Ithaca. "Both of these ladies will soon be part of the fam—ah, the company. We're in the process of acquiring their detective agency in Savannah."

"As long as they don't touch anything." Ithaca turned on her heel. Her voice was brassy, the voice of an imposing, even imperious woman with a strong hint of a Boston accent, which didn't quite fit the petite Eastern European frame that belted it out.

We moved into another room centered on a giant glass cube, with more of that futuristic Los Alamos machinery whirling around it. A gyroscope of concentric rings had been erected inside the cube.

Two technicians gave us curious glances as we entered, but they asked no questions. At Nicholas's urging, Stacey and I put on eyeshades. Ithaca drew on a pair of her own before activating the device.

The metal rings of the gyroscope began to rotate through each other.

"What are we looking at here?" I asked.

"Negative ion pumps, rotating electromagnetic fields..." Nicholas gestured at Ithaca as though he expected her to take it from there, but she didn't.

"You're trying to make it easier for ghosts to manifest," I guessed.

"Not just easier," Ithaca said. "We can *force* them to manifest."

A flash of light filled the room, followed by an awful cry that sounded female.

Inside the cube, within the rings, a glowing transparent form appeared. I honestly didn't know what to make of it. The figure looked like a large woman, but her hair was in pigtails and ribbons, her dress pink and little-girlish. Her rows of shark-like teeth were real attention-grabbers, and so big she couldn't possibly have closed her candy-pink lips around them.

"We found her in a rundown highway motel in Massachusetts," Nicholas said. "She would bite the hotel guests, especially babies and small boys. We call her Polly."

Inside the cube, the apparition vanished. She reappeared again at the glass, only a few feet from me, and it seemed like she wanted to attack me. She pressed her mouth against the glass in a smear of pink lipstick and shark teeth. Another angry, wordless shriek sounded from the speakers. Then she vanished again, reappearing at the far corner of the cube.

"This is all great, but we're trying to clean up the mess you left at home," I told Ithaca. It was still hard to imagine the century-old ghost of the Boston widow inhabiting the living young woman in front of me. "The ghosts on the fourth floor have turned violent."

"That's not possible. Those are my people," Ithaca said. "If anything, you should look at Abigail and her soldiers. I never trusted them."

"Interesting. That's exactly what Zagan told us."

"Zagan? You've been in consultation with the spirit of Gregor Zagan?" She looked offended, as though I'd just spat on her grave.

"You might call it a consultation," I said.

"Yeah, in a kicking-our-keesters, setting-our-boyfriends-on-fire kind of way," Stacey said.

"You should stay away from him," Ithaca advised.

"That would be much easier if he weren't throwing us like rag dolls all over your necromantium," I said. "Great job with the columns, by the way. You almost can't *not* bash your head into one."

"No. Gregor Zagan is forbidden to enter my home. I've taken every measure. He betrayed me, and led my people astray."

"I had the impression you kicked them out," I said.

"I never meant for them to leave. I may have been withdrawn for a time, but I never intended him to lead the flock into the wilderness for his abominable rites. They left me to die alone and destitute. For a time after my death, I existed in my house alone, just a sad memory of myself. Then they began to return to me, my people. They honored their oaths to join me after death. I forbade Gregor's spirit to return, and I forbade that dirty Irish maid that he chose over me. Neither of their spirits is allowed."

"I've seen them both," I said. "Zagan's ghost is powerful, maybe from dying the way he did. I think he's controlling all the spirits in the house. He's feeding them on his own energy."

"This is unacceptable." She turned to Nicholas, drawing herself up, and again seemed much larger than the waifish body she inhabited. "You assured me."

"All possible steps were taken—" he began.

"They weren't enough. More incompetence from you! I should not be surprised."

"Mrs. Galloway," I said, "We need you to come home with us and resolve this situation. We can remove Zagan from your house permanently if you can help us."

"I'm afraid she's much too busy with her research to return to Savannah with you," Nicholas said. "You'll have to do your jobs yourselves, unfortunately."

"I will go with them," she said. "I will destroy the betrayer's soul and devour it myself, if need be." Her sky-blue eyes had darkened almost to black, and fury twisted her delicate features.

"So that's settled," Stacey said. "One car or two?"

## Chapter Seventeen

We took two cars, it turned out. Ithaca Galloway, with her borrowed body, and Nicholas drove separately, mostly so they could return on their own, but also to haul some of their ghost-trapping gear with them. I couldn't complain—the ghosts in the Lathrop Grand were so numerous and dangerous that I wasn't going to turn down any help, even if it did grate on me that I'd had to ask the Paranormal Solutions people for it.

"It sounds like things went wild after they took Ithaca out of the house," Stacey said. She was riding shotgun while I drove, since she'd driven on the way up to North Carolina. "You think it'll be an easy fix when she comes back?"

"We'll see. Maybe she can convince her psychic pals to stop cooperating with Zagan, at least. If she can win them over to our side, we can all work together to push him out. That might be a temporary solution, though, if she plans to leave the hotel again."

"Sounds like she does plan to do that," Stacey said.

"Then we'll have to figure something out. I kind of hate that Nicholas and his people are helping with this," I said.

"Well, they did cause the problem by taking Ithaca away from her psychic friends, so they're just helping to clean up their own mess."

I nodded. That made me feel slightly better.

As we approached Columbia, South Carolina, we hit thick traffic caused by lane closures for road construction. Then dark clouds showed up and dumped heavy rain on us all the way back to Savannah.

Stacey and I desperately needed more sleep, after the previous night's short and unpleasant slumber, but it wasn't in the cards. We stopped by my apartment long enough to check on my cat and make some more coffee. Then we had to pick up the van from Stacey's place. Nicholas and I had traded cell numbers, but I hadn't yet received his promised text message that would let me know they'd arrived in town. I wondered if they'd made some kind of elaborate preparations before coming, or if Ithaca, who'd been attended by servants for much of her life, was not accustomed to moving quickly for anyone.

It was a good thing we arrived at the Lathrop Grand before they did, though, because Madeline was in a rage. Steve at the front desk sent us directly to her office when we arrived, even though it was approaching nine p.m.

"Whatever you're doing is making things worse," she snapped the moment the door was closed. "Guests are seeing apparitions of mutilated people all over the third floor. There's banging and crashing up on four, but I haven't sent any of my people up there to check it out. I don't want more workplace deaths on my record."

"That was the right choice," I said.

"The ballroom has been wrecked, too. Some of the tourists are checking out early because of all the activity. We're losing business."

"I thought they came because the hotel was haunted," I said.

"Haunted by a pretty blond girl in *one* room, with a few stray ghosts here and there. Nobody wants to encounter a soldier with a rotten face and a hook hand on their way to get a mud mask at the spa. You understand the difference? There's *charming* haunted, and then there's *horrifying* haunted."

"I understand, ma'am," I said.

"What progress have you made?"

I caught her up on the case, and she grew more and more incredulous as she listened. At one point, she broke in, furious. "The previous manager allowed a film crew on the fourth floor? That's a PR nightmare. When is it supposed to air?"

"As it turns out, there is no TV show. That was a cover story for a group researching Ithaca Galloway's work, and ultimately they ended up taking Ithaca's ghost with them. That allowed Ithaca's ex-boyfriend and, um, former co-cult-leader Zagan to return to the hotel. He's a powerful ghost, and he seems to have taken complete control of the fourth floor and all the ghosts up there."

"Someone *took* her ghost?" Madeline asked. "Are you yanking my boots here, Ellie?"

"No, ma'am. Ithaca wanted to go with them. She's eager to help them develop devices for paranormal communication, just like she attempted to do when she was alive. One of their investigators allowed Ithaca to possess her."

"I'm not sure I believe any of this. What can you do about it?" Madeline smiled and glared at the same time.

"The woman possessed by Ithaca is on her way here, along with one of these other paranormal researchers. Ithaca told me she can drive Zagan back out of the house. Zagan is the troublesome element, so things should return to normal once his ghost is gone."

"Will this be resolved by the end of next week?" Madeline asked. "The bigwigs are coming to have a look at the place and see how well I'm running things down here."

"If this works—"

"Yes or no."

"Uh...yes," I said.

"Good," she said. "I want to show the bigwigs a hotel full of happy guests. Not an exodus of customers caused by walking corpses in the corridors. I'm under a lot of pressure here, okay, sugar?"

"I understand," I said.

In our room, we loaded a luggage cart with assorted gear, including the fully charged ghost cannon. The intensely powerful light left no shadows anywhere, but it was heavy, sucked its batteries dry in a fairly quick way, and threw off enough heat to create a major fire hazard. Still, I wasn't going back into Zagan's lair without it.

Stacey dashed around the hotel room, gathering up her discarded socks and bath towels at the last minute before Ithaca and Nicholas arrived.

I took the service elevator and met the two of them at the loading dock in the side alley. Nicholas heaved a few hefty plastic storage cases onto the empty luggage cart I'd brought them, transferring them from the black Land Rover in which they'd arrived.

I supposed Ithaca had to travel in luxury and comfort. She waited in the sport-utility vehicle, looking bored, while he did all the heavy lifting.

When we finally reached our room, Stacey had changed into a crisp new outfit—boots, jeans, and a light turtleneck under a Patagonia peacoat jacket to protect against scratches and cuts—and had managed to freshen her hair and make-up, too. I don't know how she moved so fast. Maybe it was her version of putting up a wall against our enemies-slash-temporary-allies at Paranormal Solutions.

"I do not like that painting," Ithaca said as soon as we entered the room. She pointed to a picture of a cat playing in a patch of wildflowers. "It's childish. Unfit for my hotel."

"Feel free to complain to the management," I said. "Are we ready to move?"

"We do not need any of this." Ithaca swept her hand at the two carts full of gear, our stuff as well as Nicholas's. "I can handle Zagan myself."

"Consider it a simple show of force, then," Nicholas said. "He will see we're prepared to fight."

"It seems more like a show of weakness to me, but I won't stop you from bringing your toys if you insist on following me." Ithaca reached for the door, then hesitated. "Abigail has surrounded your room with her soldiers. You should move with caution."

"I knew about that. Any chance you could coax some of them over to our side? Seems like they could help out against aggressive ghosts," I said.

"There is no chance and no need," Ithaca said. "I told you every ghost in this hotel knows its place. The soldiers and their murderess do not go to the fourth floor."

"But you initially said Abigail might be behind the murder of that workman—" I said.

"Never mind that. I did not know Gregor was a factor here. I will take care of him now." Then she opened the door and walked out, not even glancing back to see if we were following her.

We rode the freight elevator up to four, and Stacey used a strip of duct tape and a pebble to keep the DOOR OPEN button depressed so the elevator car wouldn't leave without us.

Ithaca sighed as we entered the decrepit, half-demolished service area. "They've let it go to ruin. I would never have allowed this."

"They were actually trying to fix it up," I said. "It's hard when ghosts keep killing the workers."

"I told you, we never harmed them. Only frightened them."

"Still, if you want the place to look nice..."

"In all the years since my death, it has always appeared to me just as it did when I was alive," Ithaca said. "Only now, with these living eyes, can I see what's become of my home."

I led the way toward the jib door that would take us right into the necromantium, but it wouldn't budge.

"Never mind," Ithaca said. "We ought not enter like servants." She stepped through another door into the hallway, and we rolled our carts after her.

The hallway was still cluttered with wreckage, from cracked coffee tables to shattered chunks of hefty old wooden bedframes, so it took some time to navigate around the mess. It was dark and cold, with no working lights, and it grew colder as we passed along it toward the main double-door entrance to the dark temple. Our REM pods were flashing and wooing all along the hall.

The double doors wouldn't move, either. As I tried to unlock them with the keys that Earl, the custodian, had provided me, the shadows grew thicker around us.

"Let us in!" Ithaca snapped.

The strange, distorted white faces began appearing, each with a pair of red embers burning deep inside its otherwise empty eye sockets. The faces seemed clustered around Ithaca, and I wouldn't say any of them were smiling, despite the return of their original cult leader who had brought them all here in the first place. The hallway grew so cold my fingers began to turn numb.

The whispers rose all around us, loud and angry. Ithaca's haughty look began to show signs of cracking.

"Go ahead," I urged her. "Take control of the ghosts."

She raised her hand and opened her mouth to speak. All the faces vanished, leaving us surrounded in a darkness that our flashlights could barely penetrate.

Then Ithaca made a gagging sound and fell to the floor. I followed with my flashlight beam to find her writhing on the floorboards, eyes rolled up into their sockets, grabbing at her throat while spittle bubbled from her lips.

"Kara!" Nicholas shouted, clearly more concerned about his teammate Kara than the ghost of Ithaca riding within her. He dropped to her side to help her.

Something grabbed at my sleeve, and something else grabbed at my ankle. The hands felt like iron. Things were falling apart, fast.

I grabbed the ghost cannon from the cart beside me and activated it, flooding the hallway with searing, intense white light that allowed no shadows anywhere.

Unnaturally thin figures shrieked in the light, scattering from Ithaca/Kara's unconscious form like ants hit with a bug bomb. They slipped away into the walls and floorboards, but I could still hear their angry, insistent whispering all around me.

Nicholas lifted Kara's trembling, unresponsive form from the floor. Stacey helped him position her onto the cart with his gear. Then they were off, each retreating with a luggage cart. They couldn't move very quickly, though, because of all the broken furniture debris and the uneven floorboards that had popped up during the mini-quake that nobody on the lower floors seemed to have noticed.

I covered Nicholas and Stacey's exit, walking backwards and sweeping the hot ghost cannon back and forth, from one side of the hall to another, but it took much, much longer than I would have liked.

"Above you!" Stacey shouted. She was working the wheel of her luggage cart free from where it had caught on a loose, upwardly jutting floorboard.

A dark, cloudy mass was forming near the ceiling over my head. I raised the cannon, blasting it like a clay pigeon, and the mass let out a shrieking hiss as it shrank away into the crown molding.

I brought the light back down just in time to shove back a few more pale ghosts, who had approached me during the second or two that I'd swept my light toward the ceiling. They were alarmingly close to grabbing me, but the light sent them into a squealing retreat.

We worked our way around the corner of the hallway, then retreated into the service area through a jib door. The shadowy spirits passed through the wall on either side of the door, spreading out as if they meant to surround us. I had to sweep my light back and forth in ever-widening arcs, which kept me from really concentrating on any of them.

Behind me, Stacey and Nicholas rolled the carts into the waiting elevator. I backed into it after them, still struggling to keep the host of spirits at bay.

Stacey ripped the tape off the DOOR OPEN button and began furiously jabbing the DOOR CLOSED button instead. The whispering of the shadowy crowd of ghosts rose to a cacophonous roar, and then the brass doors finally snapped shut, leaving us in sudden silence.

"How is she?" I asked Nicholas, but he didn't answer. His full attention was on his fallen friend, checking her pulse, then trying to rouse her by shaking her. I took that as a sign that she did have a pulse.

The elevator shuddered as it left the fourth floor. We returned to our room in defeat, our secret weapon unconscious and drooling a little as we transferred her from the luggage cart to the bed. At least she was still breathing.

## Chapter Eighteen

"If she doesn't wake up in five minutes, I'm taking her to the hospital," Nicholas said. He'd inspected the unconscious girl and found no major wounds, aside from a small bruise on the side of her throat.

"What do we do now?" Stacey said. "Go search for Zagan's body?"

"Calvin hasn't found any information about it yet," I said. "We'll have to improvise."

"I'm afraid I haven't done much of that since the theatrical society at university," Nicholas said. I struggled to imagine him carrying out comedic skits based on suggestions from the audience.

The girl on the bed began to cough, and Nicholas touched her shoulder. "Kara?" he said. "Say something, Kara."

Her eyes opened.

"It's Ithaca," she growled, pulling away from him. She rubbed her throat as she sat up. "They turned on me. He's turned them all against me once again. They've abandoned me now, just as they abandoned me during life..."

"Ghosts do tend to repeat the same patterns again and again," I said.

"I am not some filmy residual haunting, perpetually throwing herself from the widow's walk!" Ithaca snapped at me. "We all came together after death, just as we planned. They fulfilled their oaths to return to me. *He* has ruined everything. He even brought that backstabbing Katherine back with him. We must destroy him."

"That sounds great," I said. "Do you have any specific ideas?"

Her hand balled into a fist, drawing up a lump of blanket into her fingers.

"I cannot fight them all at once," she finally said.

"Maybe it's time to recruit some reinforcements," I said. "Are you sure you can't speak to the soldiers?"

"They are loyal to Abigail."

"And?"

Ithaca didn't speak.

"You're not pals with Abigail?" I asked. "I don't get it. You bought the hotel because it was haunted, but you never communicated with the ghosts who were already here?"

"We communicated," Ithaca said. "We had a disagreement."

"Which was?"

Again, she chose not to answer.

"When our psychic spoke to Abigail, all she seemed to care about was explaining why she'd killed those men. She insisted it was an act of mercy. The soldiers themselves wanted very badly for us to speak to her," I said. "So what does Abigail want? She wants it known that she didn't kill them out of hate, or because they were on the other side of the war, but because she wanted to help them. Maybe she was misguided, but the soldiers don't seem to hold a grudge against her. You say they're loyal to her?"

"Abigail will never help me," Ithaca said, her voice more subdued than usual, less domineering.

"You still haven't explained why."

"Because I did not help her."

I nodded, seeing the bigger picture now. "You didn't want to help her, because you didn't want her spirit, or the soldiers' spirits, to move on. You wanted this hotel to remain haunted. You could have helped, you could have told people Abigail's side of the story, but you preferred to keep her ghost trapped in the house. So she hates you for that."

"We did what was necessary for our purposes," Ithaca said.

"We can't get to Zagan without help." I opened the door and

stepped out into the hall. It was easy to find the cold spots where the soldiers were lurking. I turned out the lights.

"Hey, whatcha doing there, Ellie?" Stacey asked, standing in the open door behind me.

"Do not go to them," Ithaca said, elbowing her way past Stacey to join me. Stacey stuck out her tongue at the back of Ithaca's head after she'd passed.

Ithaca's presence seemed to stir the spirits in the hallway, which I didn't mind one bit. Shadows formed along the walls, and the characteristic moaning and groaning of the amputees returned.

"Are you here to help me or not?" I asked the shadows. "Now's the time."

The temperature plunged as the bayonet-armed soldier I'd seen before appeared directly in front of me.

"If you intend to attack me, do it now," I said. "I need to get my friends and enemies lists straightened out."

He stood unmoving, unresponsive—but not attacking me, I noticed.

A scraping, shrieking rusty sound rose from the floor. A shadowy figure crawled toward me along the carpet runner, indistinct at first. As it grew closer, I saw it was another badly mangled soldier, a portion of his face burned, an amputated arm replaced by a crude and rusty iron claw. As he crawled, one of his legs dragged uselessly behind him. At first I thought his foot was enclosed in a trap or leg iron, like an escaped prisoner. As he pulled himself closer, I saw it was some kind of heavy wheel made of iron and wood. Two wheels, actually, one each screwed into the broken, exposed nubs of his tibia and fibula, then connected through the bones by an iron axle.

Not surprisingly, his face was contorted in excruciating pain. He looked up at me as he clawed his way close to my boots, and I stiffened up, ready to move if he attacked.

Instead, he melted down into the carpet like a shadowy puddle. I heard his groan of pain as he shrank away.

"I think I know what to do," I said. "Stacey, is there a late-night toy store open around here, by any chance?"

"Uh..." Stacey thumbed at her phone. "There's a Target on East Victory that's open until eleven. We might be able to make it if we disregard speed limits."

"Okay." I turned to Ithaca. "You need to go down to the second floor and make nice with Abigail Bowen. Apologize, kneel, beg and plead for forgiveness for how you mistreated her—"

"I will not beg!" Ithaca snapped.

"You will beg, or you will surrender to Zagan and let him have his way. Let him control your house and your people for centuries to come, while you exist as an outcast. You know you were wrong to refuse to help Abigail's ghost move on. Time to make amends. Otherwise, you have no allies among the dead here."

Ithaca glared at me, and I stared right back at her, until she finally gave a curt nod.

"I will speak to her," she said.

"Apologize and beg."

"If I must." Her lip curled in disgust. "Gregor must be cast out. I will not let him succeed in this new betrayal."

"That's the spirit," I said. "Stacey, Nicholas, you two stick with Ithaca for now. Keep her safe."

"And what are you doing?"

"I'm going shopping." I stepped back into the room to grab the keys to the van.

Less than an hour later, I returned to the hotel and went straight to the basement. Stacey had texted me, saying Ithaca had gone down to the second floor and was having a tense conversation with Abigail Bowen's ghost. It mostly occurred on a psychic level, ghost to ghost, so Stacey couldn't hear much of it herself.

I texted Stacey that I was going into the basement and she should come get me if she didn't hear back in fifteen minutes. Jacob had said the ghosts in the basement weren't immediately dangerous, that their main threat was causing illness over a long period of exposure. Earl clearly suffered some of that, his watery eyes and runny nose echoing the facial bleeding of advanced yellow fever.

I wasn't headed to the custodian's room tonight, though. Instead, I walked toward the mechanical thumping of the laundry room, but I didn't go inside. I opened the door to the long, dark tunnel of the laundry storage closet, where Jacob said the more adventurous child ghosts liked to hang out.

I closed the door behind me, leaving myself in complete darkness except for the display screen on my Mel-Meter. The device indicated possible presences as I walked deeper into the narrow room, with the electromagnetic readings ticking up a couple of milligaus while the temperature dropped slightly. If the ghosts were there at all, they were far from powerful.

Still, I didn't need them to be powerful. I just needed them to be present.

When I'd walked about halfway through the long room, I knelt on the floor, removed my backpack, and pulled out several items I'd purchased at Target. These included a couple of soft cloth dolls, a wooden yo-yo, a set of jacks, marbles, dominoes, and wooden building blocks. I'd wanted items that resembled nineteenth-century toys as much as possible, made of wood instead of plastic. A company called Melissa & Doug seemed to focus on manufacturing such retro toys, fortunately.

Then I lit a few candles, enough to draw the ghosts close and feed their energy. Dim, fiery light and shifting shadows now danced across the high stacks of neatly folded towels and pillowcases on either side of me.

"Okay," I said. "Olly olly oxen free. All are free, all come to me."

The first part of that phrase was an old phrase for kids playing hide and seek, a general announcement that the game was over and all the kids could emerge from their hiding places. I knew its usage went back to at least the early twentieth century, but I couldn't be sure whether kids who'd died in Savannah's yellow fever epidemic of 1876 would recognize the phrase. I hoped so, or that they at least received the intent behind it, that I was calling them out in a friendly way. "All are free" was an alternative phrase to "oxen free" in some places. I added "come to me" because that was what I wanted the ghosts to do, and hey, it rhymes.

I remained crouched on the floor, making myself as small and nonthreatening as possible, as if trying to make friends with a wary animal. I repeated my little chant.

Far away toward the end of the long room, near the door to the rarely-used and nearly forgotten stairwell, a small, shadowy head leaned out from behind a stack of blankets and seemed to look at me.

## Chapter Nineteen

"Please," Ithaca was saying, kneeling on the floor near room 208, her back slumped as though in defeat. Not a great sign regarding the progress of the negotiations. "Please."

Stacey and Nicholas stood several yards away from her, silently watching, the worry plain on their faces.

"How's it going?" I whispered to Stacey as I crept up beside her. She jumped, then turned to me.

"Don't do that," she whispered back. "Ithaca's trying, but Stabby Abby's not cooperating."

I removed the hefty thermals from my utility belt and strapped them on over my eyes. I could see the slumped, kneeling form of the girl Kara, possessed by Ithaca, glowing red and yellow. Not far in front of her, a cold blue shape levitated about a foot off the floor. A woman. Abigail.

Stepping toward the cold specter-shape, I held out my hand. My fingers tingled and grew numb as they passed through her shoulder.

Abigail's head turned to look at me.

Images burst into my mind. I saw her as she'd looked when she was alive, her ragged linen dress sopping with blood, the red-coated scalpel dripping in her hand. Soldiers lying on cots and floor pallets, their throats cut.

Her face was much clearer and more detailed than I'd ever seen it before, and now I recognized her.

"It was you, Abigail," I said. "You came to my apartment the night before I started this case. You knew I was coming. You reached out to me." I could see her clearly in my memory, peering in through my window from the darkness outside, her face white and smooth, her blond hair also a ghostly white.

She drifted closer to me, touching her icy fingers against my outstretched hand.

"I think I understand everything now," I said. "Ithaca Galloway didn't share the truth while she was alive, like you wanted her to do. But I will. I'll make sure everyone knows what really happened here. I'll tell them how you were bringing mercy and ending their pain. You must have sensed that I was the person who would finally do that. I'm not here to use you like Ithaca did. I'm here to set you free. But first I need your help. You know there's an evil man upstairs who must be dealt with. Come with us. Bring all your soldiers. Everyone's suffering will end tonight, if we work together."

Abigail's blue shape floated in place for a moment, as if she were thinking things over. Then she turned toward Ithaca, and her temperature plummeted, darkening her from blue to purple.

"I know you don't trust her," I said. "You don't have to. We all happen to be on the same side right now. After tonight, you'll never have to see her again. You won't be trapped here any longer."

I held my breath waiting for a response. None of the other people in the hall made a sound.

Then Abigail's color returned to a mild blue, and she sank down to the carpet. Her fingers touched Ithaca's head.

"Please," Ithaca said, looking up at her. "Forgive me."

Abigail removed her hand from the other woman's head, and the air in the hallway turned icy. Abigail's temperature wasn't dropping this time, though.

Behind me, blue shapes had appeared in two long rows along the length of the hall. Some of them slumped, many were missing limbs, and a few dragged themselves along the floor, unable to do more than slide and crawl. One stood ahead and apart from the others, directly in front of me, his right arm tapering to a long thin line about the size of a bayonet.

"She called in the cavalry," I said, letting myself enjoy a brief moment of relief. They were ragtag, badly battered, probably not nearly as equipped for supernatural warfare as, let's say, a group of dead psychics with a powerful, possibly demonic leader...but they were here for us, ready to fight.

"Okay," I told the others, removing my thermals. "If anybody asks, 'You and what army?' just point to these cold spots along this hall."

"Who is going to ask us that?" Nicholas said.

"Nobody. It was supposed to be like a joke. Let's just get moving, okay?" I shook my head as I led the way. Abigail and the dead soldiers followed us invisibly, freezing the air around us.

We again took the elevator to the fourth floor and pinned the DOOR OPEN button, but this time we planned to travel lighter, leaving the luggage carts in the elevator and taking only what we could carry in our arms or backpacks. Ithaca was unusually subdued, some of her haughtiness drained by her recent act of contrition to Abigail's spirit.

"We had such dreams," Ithaca said quietly, looking out into the semi-demolished service area. "They all turned to nightmares."

"Take this." I held out a tactical flashlight to her. I could see the initial look of feeling insulted cross her face, but her features quickly softened and she accepted the tool.

"I do not need it to see," she told me quietly.

"Then use it to help us see," I said. "And it's a minor defensive weapon against ghosts. It probably won't help much at this point, but it can't hurt."

She nodded.

I'd expected the psychic ghosts to be waiting for us as we emerged onto the fourth floor, but the place was silent and had an empty feeling. The ambient temperature was normal, not unnaturally low at all, at least until the cold front of about fourteen soldier ghosts plus Stabby Abby rolled out from the elevator with us. I didn't hear anything from the REM pods out in the main hallway.

"They've fallen back," I said. "They're waiting for us somewhere."

"Then let's go find them." Stacey heaved the huge ghost cannon from our luggage cart and pointed it in front of her, squinting. "Do I look like Rambo?"

"You kind of look like Elmer Fudd hunting wabbits," I told her.

Nicholas opened one of his black plastic cases and snapped

together two thin aluminum poles to form something that looked, to me, like a slightly modified floor lamp about four feet long. A convex fitting surrounded the light source at the end, as if to focus and channel the light. A trigger was built into the side.

"What you packin' there, pardner?" Stacey asked him.

"Standard high-impact light thrower, one hundred thousand lumens at a blast. And what about your comically unwieldy piece of illumination there?" He nodded at the ghost cannon.

"A million to a million and a half lumens, depending on its mood. No big deal." She smirked. Nicholas's eyebrows rose in surprise. With his detached demeanor, that was practically the equivalent of screaming and running circles around the room with his hands in the air.

"It burns out fast, though, and hasn't had much time to recharge, so let's not depend too much on it. And we also want to avoid burning our client's hotel to the ground, if possible," I said.

"Do not dare to damage my home," Ithaca said, her face darkening.

"Like I just explained, that's what I want to avoid. Okay, let's stop sitting here like ducks in a barrel. Stacey, go."

Stacey tapped the iPod on her belt, blasting a Civil War march she'd found. The fife and drums, I hoped, would help keep the Union soldiers focused on the task at hand.

I approached the jib door to the necromantium and wasn't surprised to find that it still wouldn't budge. Removing the hinges took a minute, with the military music providing an odd soundtrack to my efforts at unscrewing the rusty old things and prying them loose.

With the hinges gone, I pulled hard on the handle again. No luck. The jib door was plastered shut by psychokinetic energy.

"I guess we go around to the double doors," I said. "At least they open inward."

So far, we were still in the light of the propped-open elevator, but it began to flicker behind us.

Then I heard a small *plink*, like a pebble dropping on brass.

"Hey, was that— " Stacey said, and then the elevator doors closed, leaving us in darkness. Stacey, Ithaca, and I all turned on our flashlights, while Nicholas ignited his long aluminum wand, putting out a searing white glow. He was considerate enough to point it away from us before switching it on.

"Aren't you supposed to say *Lumos Maxima!* when you light that thing?" Stacey asked.

"Yes, a Harry Potter reference. Very amusing," Nicholas said, not looking very amused.

Nicholas had also brought a heavy-looking black box made of hard plastic, in addition to the long glowing light-thrower tucked under one arm. I reached over to grab the box for him, but he waved me off.

"Keep yourself safe, is all I ask," he said, lifting the box.

"How gallant," I said. "Which seems out of character."

"I'm quite gallant. You hardly know me."

"Right. Okay, forward march everyone, or whatever they say."

We started up the hall, four warm bodies trailed by a small host of dead men. We still encountered no resistance, except for the broken furniture all over the place. Maybe Zagan was investing all his power in keeping the doors to the necromantium closed. Or maybe he was lying in wait to ambush us.

When we reached the double doors, they once again refused to open. The key wouldn't even turn inside the lock.

Nicholas and I placed our lights aside, and Stacey and Ithaca helped to light us as we selected a painfully heavy rosewood coffee table from the scattered furniture pieces strewn across the floor.

"That's a valuable piece," Ithaca said. "It's from the Orient."

"Feels like...a good battering ram," I said, my teeth gritting with the effort of holding the thing. Stacey moved to help, but I shook my head. "Stay with Ithaca."

Nicholas and I backed up as far as the hallway would allow. An open door looked into an empty bedroom cell behind us, the slats of a broken chair heaped across the threshold.

"On three?" Nicholas asked me.

"Make it two."

"One, two..."

We charged forward, slamming the end of the heavy table into the double doors. They let out a cracking sound and sank inward an inch or so before rebounding. The lock held, but we'd bashed a deep furrow in both doors just above the handles.

Ithaca shook her head, frowning at the overall destruction of her property, but didn't say anything.

Nicholas and I charged again, then again. On the fourth try, the doors burst open and spread wide, opening onto a freezing, pitch-black space beyond.

We heaved the table into the room, to the side of the doorway, where it could help prop one of the doors open in case the ghosts tried to slam them and trap us inside.

Then we marched into the room. I have to admit, by this point the stately fife and drums had me walking a little straighter, as though I were there to represent some higher and greater purpose than clearing the way for a real estate investment group to renovate and monetize the fourth floor.

The darkness choked down even on Nicholas's intensely bright beam. My supposedly high-powered tactical flashlight was of almost no use at all. The black fog effect—when a place is so filled with hostile ghosts that almost no light can pierce the darkness—is usually a harbinger of evil things.

The white mask-faces appeared, all in a single straight line just ahead of the temple's halfway point. They had completely blocked off the center of the room where the crazy machine had once been, where Jacob said there was a crude portal enabling spirits to cross back and forth.

I looked with my thermals and saw them like a wall of ice, like the face of a glacier, a solid band of deep blue across the room. I did not see any heat to signify Zagan. I wondered where he was.

Our soldiers spread out to either side, their cold, mangled shapes arranged in a ragged line. Stacey's fife and drums thumped on, filling the moment with a weird sense of historical significance.

The psychics launched the first volley. The room filled with whispers. Mind-shattering panic filled me instantly, with a feeling of intense dread and a near-certainty that I was about to die if I didn't leave the room. I heard the gasps of the other three in my party as the wave of terrifying emotions hit them, too.

"Hold steady!" I shouted, faking confidence that I didn't feel at all. Stacey raised the ghost cannon with a questioning look on her face, but I shook my head. Better hold that for an even bigger emergency, like Zagan's arrival.

"I'll...take care of this," Nicholas managed to say. His voice trembled with fear. I wondered if mine had, too. I lifted my thermals off my eyes so I could see what he did next.

He stepped forward, slightly ahead of our group, and set his black box on the ground. I took his glowing staff when he handed it to me.

He lifted the lid and unfolded the device within. I saw a hand crank on the side. Then he raised a steel phonograph horn with a flaring flower shape and aimed it directly at the wall of whispering ghosts, who continued broadcasting their emotional attack on us.

A hand-cranked phonograph made sense—the ghosts couldn't drain it like an electrical device. It also seemed bulky, cumbersome, and easily broken to me. I hoped Nicholas knew what he was doing.

He set a black vinyl record onto the turntable, then flipped aside a lever that was set against the crank. Apparently the phonograph had previously been wound up, and the little lever had acted as a brake to stop the crank from turning until he was ready.

Stacey lowered the volume on her nineteenth-century marching music, making room for whatever he was about to try.

Nicholas picked up the needle arm and moved it to the rotating record. I felt a growing sense of terror, sure this wouldn't work, sure we would all be killed.

The needle touched the record, and the music came out at a surprisingly loud volume.

The opening strain of "Good Vibrations" by the Beach Boys filled the room.

"Are you serious?" I snapped at Nicholas. "We're all dead."

"It works every time," Nicholas said. "It's relentlessly life-affirming."

I looked up at the line of ghosts, expecting them to be charging at us with intent to dismember and disembowel. Instead, their white mask-faces were badly distended and twisted, and they seemed to back away in a scrambled, haphazard retreat.

"Every time," Nicholas said again, winking at me. "It is my unproven opinion that Brian Wilson may have functioned as a sort of divine conduit—"

I slapped the iPod on my belt, playing an authentic Union bugle charge that some Civil War reenactors in Tennessee had been kind enough to record and share with the world on their website.

Our line of soldiers charged. I felt the surging rush of energy more than I saw them—without my thermals, in the near-total darkness, there wasn't much to see but an occasional glimmer of movement.

I heard them, though, their groans raised to a general shout as they attacked.

The four of us moved forward, too, though there was no clear target for us in the dark, scream-filled room. It felt good to advance. Maybe the "relentlessly life-affirming" song was having some effect on me—more likely, it was just a relief to have the psychic ghosts' broadcast of intense, dark emotions cut off for the moment.

Crackling energy whirled around the room, raising hurricane-force winds as the ghosts fought it out. A distorted white-mask face swam up in the darkness near me, screeching so loud I thought my eardrums might burst. It vanished, its scream fading into the general melee. A soldier with rusty cables protruding from his elbows and the back of his skull fell to the floor nearby and faded.

"Gregor! Gregor Zagan!" Ithaca shouted. "I command you to appear!"

Zagan wasn't taking orders from her, though. No sign of him manifested anywhere.

I looked through my thermals, but didn't see any hellish heat source floating around. It was hard to tell what was happening—cold spots everywhere, colliding, some swelling, some fading. It was like watching a blizzard in the middle of a brisk Siberian winter, and the room's temperature was definitely below freezing and still dropping. I shivered uncontrollably, the cold air burning every inch of exposed skin on my body. I noticed the area at the center of the room seemed devoid of ghosts, as if they wanted to avoid the ethereal rip there, the ragged portal Ithaca and Zagan's machine had opened.

A ghostly blue figure with a bayonet for an arm approached, stopping directly in front of me. He remained there, stiff and unmoving, as though standing at attention.

I raised my thermals away. With my own eyes, I could see him like a sketchy, faintly luminescent outline in the darkness, a portrait dashed off in a hurry by an artist with a glow-in-the-dark pen.

He extended his bayonet arm and turned to point straight ahead toward the eye of the storm, the empty spot at the center of the room.

I took a breath and nodded, then I turned to Stacey.

"Stay with Ithaca!" I shouted over the howling voices of the psychokinetic storm around us. My hair streamed across my face, getting into my eyes and mouth. "She's the key to everything."

"Yeah, where are you going?"

"That way." I raised my flashlight and followed the barely-visible glow of Ol' Bayonet Arm as he led me past screaming white faces and fallen soldiers.

I steeled myself as I stepped into the center of the room.

The soldier's ghost continued on, not even hesitating before he stepped back into the high winds and screams on the far side. I was puzzled, but I followed him all the way to the far end of the room, all the way to the big altar there.

He raised his bayonet-arm and pointed.

I had to lean across the altar and bring my flashlight close to the wall to see the figures and glyphs carved there, but I quickly figured out which one he'd meant. One of the Egyptian-style engravings showed a bird grasping a half-circle in its feet, as though drawing up the rising sun. A cruder version of the same image had been scratched into my hotel room door the previous night—by Ol' Bayonet Arm, I was guessing.

While the wind and ghostly voices roared behind me, I boosted myself up onto the altar and rolled up to a kneeling position. I traced the bird-and-rising-sun design with my fingertip.

"*No...*" The woman's voice was barely audible, but it was very close. She stood over me, her pudgy red cheeks transparent, a look of horror on her face. She wore a simple dark dress, as if attending a funeral, not a big antebellum hoop skirt like in her portrait downstairs. I recognized Mabel Lathrop, co-founder of the hotel, whose ghost had long been an active but benign presence down in the restaurant named for her on the first floor. She repeated it again: "*No...*"

"Sorry, Mrs. Lathrop," I said. "I have to do it."

I pressed my hand against the bird and the half-sun in its talons. The entire panel of glyphs and symbols around it, about a foot square, sank back into the wall as I pushed.

A grinding and rumbling rose from within the wall, rattling my hands. Then a slab of the wall behind the altar slid back, creating a door-sized opening all the way to the floor. It emitted ear-splitting squeals the whole way. My flashlight found a pair of rusty iron tracks on the floor, indicating that the secret door was moving on unseen wheels.

I couldn't see much of the new space I'd just opened up—the slab of wall itself blocked most of my view—but the smell was horrific, even worse than the sour olfactory apparitions down among the yellow fever victims in the basement. It smelled like rotten blood. I don't know how else to describe it.

Beside me, the ghost of Mrs. Lathrop clapped her hands to her face and faded from view. Ol' Bayonet Arm was still standing on the floor, not apparently interested in accompanying me any farther.

I was reluctant to jump down from the altar into the newly revealed room. If someone were to push the slab of wall back into place, I'd be crushed against the back side of the heavy altar, destroying such valuable portions of myself as my ribs, internal organs, legs, and feet.

Still, I didn't have much choice. I hopped down, my boots punching into thick dust and crumbled rust. I moved to one side quickly, shining my light around as I entered the hidden room. I drew my shirt up over my nose to keep the smell from gagging me.

I first encountered a set of wooden shelves built into the brick walls, shaggy with spiderwebs. Bottles and jars with yellowed, illegible handwritten labels filled the shelves. A worktable in front of the shelves was cluttered with filthy beakers and vials.

Next was a set of primitive surgical tools, most of them turned to rust. Wicked-looking bone saws and long amputation knives hung from nails on the wall. I'd seen these kinds of tools in pictures while doing background research for the case, but they looked much more awful in person. The amputation knives looked like something you'd use for hacking through a South American jungle. The bone saws resembled hacksaws with unevenly serrated blades. Ouch. I even found the crude hand-cranked chainsaw, surely one of the earliest models ever built for surgery.

Just the sight of the implements made me ill, but they helped prepare me for what came next.

An array of odd mechanical items were on display in dusty glass cabinets. I opened them for a better look. Here I saw Dr. Lathrop's attempts to build prosthetics for the huge war amputee population of the 1860's. An iron claw sat on one shelf—and as I looked closer, I found it was mounted by a big screw into a broken length of human bone.

A strange cage apparatus stood nearby, with straps, hooks, and ropes around the interior. It looked as if the intention had been to place a human inside and then puppeteer his arms, legs, and head.

I found a rusty wheel with sharp spikes jutting out along the rim and bone fragments at the axle. Then I found a rusty bayonet, its base screwed to an old piece of human arm bone. I'd found a remnant of Ol' Bayonet Arm himself.

It looked as though Dr. Lathrop's medical experiments included attempts to replace amputated limbs with weapons, enabling the soldiers to return to the battlefield like some kind of steampunk Terminators. That certainly would have changed some of our images of the Civil War.

It was also apparent that his weird medical experiments would have been torturous for the soldiers involved. After suffering major injuries on the battlefield itself, they were brought to this hotel, supposedly for help, but instead the good doctor had brought some of them to this secret room.

I found what looked like a waste pail tucked under one workbench, full of bone fragments. That brought a new feeling of revulsion, the idea of Dr. Lathrop casually disposing of human parts and kicking the pail out of the way when he was done.

I'd figured it out when I'd seen that soldier apparition with the wheel in place of his foot. Grant had said Dr. Lathrop had attempted to patent a number of early attempts at prosthetic limbs and other experimental medical technology. I'd begun to wonder if Ol' Bayonet Arm wasn't psychologically projecting a weapon as a part of his body, as I'd assumed at first. Maybe his arm really *had* been replaced by an actual bayonet while he was still alive, just as the other man's foot was replaced by a wheel. Maybe Dr. Lathrop had been less of a humanitarian than his reputation had implied, I thought. Maybe he'd been a twisted man doing secretive medical experiments on wounded soldiers.

Near the back of the room lay a row of flat wooden cots, most of them holding darkly stained linen bundles the size of human beings. Three wide leather belts strapped each bundle to its cot.

I stepped toward them, weighed down by apprehension. There might well have been bodies inside when this room was last sealed. I told myself that if I opened them, I wouldn't find anything worse than bones after all these years. I did not completely convince myself, but I approached the nearest one anyway, drawing out my pocketknife.

"Okay," I whispered. "Let's see what we've got."

One of the human-sized linen bundles a few feet away let out a small grunt. It twitched back and forth on its cot, held in place by the big leather belt. I got the impression of a human face moving beneath the old bloodstained cloth.

Reluctantly, I moved toward the linen-wrapped body, raising my knife. It continued shifting under its heavy straps, and it appeared to be breathing heavily.

I stretched out a piece of rotten cloth near the head, and I curled my lip as I cut open the linen around the face, expecting to see undead eyes staring back, or maybe just a long-forgotten skull encrusted with black corpse dust.

Instead, I saw a girl, her face flushed red, her mouth tied with another dirty strip of cloth. Long brown hair, panicked brown eyes—I recognized her, though her Boy George hat was nowhere to be seen. A few sharp pins jutted out here and there, in her cheeks and around her neck, like some mad acupuncturist had attacked her face.

"Lemmy!" I said, pulling the filthy gag from her mouth. "How did you—"

"He's back!" she screamed, looking over my shoulder.

I didn't even have time to turn around. Something slammed into my side, something that felt squishy and jittery as it pressed against me. I stumbled away from Lemmy but managed to catch myself on a table full of rusty instruments. I shrugged my backpack off and let it land on the table behind me.

A hot streak of pain burned across my chest. I looked down. My jacket, shirt, and skin had been sliced open from the front of my collar bone out to the edge of my shoulder. Blood welled up from the long, narrow cut. I had a matching cut on my back.

"Dr. Uriah Lathrop," I said. "I wondered where you'd been hiding. I didn't know you had your own room."

While I spoke, I grabbed the rusty bayonet arm with the piece of bone still attached. A blade is, of course, generally useless against ghosts, but I thought this one might have some potent psychic energy attached. It had belonged to the same spirit who'd guided me here, though I couldn't help noticing that he hadn't accompanied me into the old laboratory. That wasn't a big confidence-builder.

The dead doctor who'd founded the hotel began to materialize in front of me, appearing as a white shadow in the dark room.

"This is where you brought wounded soldiers for your experiments," I said. "How many suffered here? How many died on the tables in this room? They were nothing to you. Just Lincoln's fighters, Yankees, foreign invaders. Who cares how much pain they endured, as long as you got to pursue your research?"

Now his features began to grow more distinct. His face was pinched, framed by thick muttonchops, his lips almost too thin to see. His eye sockets, like the spirits of the psychic cultists, were empty except for burning red embers deep inside. His whole body shuddered like an old film reel, as if he were overflowing with nervous energy.

He held an antique scalpel with a horn handle, its long blade wet with my blood.

"Looks like you've been feeding on Zagan, too," I said. "Why? What does he want from you?"

"They're trying to possess me," Lemmy said.

"The doctor is trying to possess you?" I asked her. Dr. Lathrop's ghost stood between me and Lemmy. I would have to deal with him before I could get back over there and cut her free.

"No. Her." Lemmy turned her head, the only part of her that wasn't strapped down. I followed her gaze to a dark corner of the room.

She faded as soon as I looked at her, but I glimpsed the waxy white face of the spirit I believed to be Katherine Moore.

"I saw you, Katherine," I said. "I finished your book, you know. I even made a little audiobook version for you. Want to hear it?"

I touched my iPod, and the robotic female began to recite Katherine's memoirs, starting with her childhood in Ireland, the death of her mother and brother, and her arrival in Savannah as a destitute girl whose family had died on the way over.

Katherine's apparition returned, clearer than before. Her waxy mask-face managed to show fascination and wonder as she floated closer to me.

Dr. Lathrop, meanwhile, was eyeing me along his scalpel, one eye squinted, like a butcher planning his cuts, his entire form still shaking and jittering.

"You stay back," I told him. "There are things you don't know about me."

Then I crushed the heels of my hands into my face, just under my eyes. I curled my lower lip into my mouth and bit down on the skin below it.

Capsules of stage blood, concealed under flesh-colored latex. After figuring out that Dr. Lathrop might have been one of the dangerous ghosts in this haunting, I'd bought the blood capsules for ten bucks from the Halloween aisle at Target—good thing major holidays begin several weeks early at those large retailers. When I looked at him again, blood appeared to streak down my face from my eyes and mouth, making me resemble a yellow fever victim in the final throes of the awful disease.

"I have yellow fever," I said. "I was sent here to infect you."

The doctor's spirit hissed and recoiled, retreating several feet from me without even bothering to move his legs. Strings of leather wormed their way from behind his head, two burrowing forward through the hair above his ears, two more coming up and around his chin and through his muttonchops.

They met at his nose and mouth and thickened, forming a mask that covered the lower half of his face, studded with little lengths of pipe that were supposed to act as air filters.

"Yellow fever killed you," I said. "Remember that? I bet you do. I bet it was miserable and terrifying, feeling your body slowly die around you." I reached into my backpack and removed a standard cylindrical ghost trap, about two feet long, made of leaded glass encased in copper mesh encased in insulating plastic.

I popped open the lid and dumped out a heap of toys onto the floor. The rush of cold was palpable as the ghosts flooded out.

Five pale children in ragged clothes suddenly stood around the room, bleeding from their eyes, noses, and mouths.

I advanced on Dr. Lathrop, brandishing my bayonet (well, I sort of wiggled it at him, anyway). The children giggled and joined in the game, closing in on the mad doctor's ghost from all sides.

"You're forgetting something," I said. "The mask never worked. It did not keep the fever away from you."

He straightened up, though, and approached me, swinging his scalpel and slicing the air, as if taking a practice run for what he intended to do to my throat.

"You're the one who's been cutting people," I said. "Did you push Valentino from the ladder, too, to keep your lab secret? Or was that Zagan and the others, protecting their temple? It doesn't really matter. You're all working together. You've accepted Zagan as your master."

I took a chance and leaped at him, swinging the bayonet at the leather strands that held his mask to his face. The mask might not have worked in real life, but he still believed in it, and his beliefs held more weight just now. For that matter, yellow fever isn't spread by human-to-human contact—and I was counting on him to still be unaware of that fact, too, so I could play into his mistaken beliefs.

Unfortunately, this particular gamble did not pay off. My bayonet swept uselessly back and forth through his semi-transparent face. I heard him chuckle beneath the mask, and then he raised his scalpel hand, ready to cut me with surgical expertise.

His hand was empty, though.

He hesitated with his arm raised, apparently confused by the missing scalpel. He'd definitely been holding it a moment earlier.

Four quick slashes appeared in his face and throat, slicing apart the leather straps. The mask toppled off, and his smirk instantly changed to a look of horror.

I saw her for just an eyeblink then, standing beside him. Abigail had taken the surgeon's scalpel from him. Stabby Abby had some experience wielding that particular tool herself.

I charged at Dr. Lathrop again, and the dead children joined in the game, surrounding him. His skin turned a jaundiced yellow, and blood poured from every hole in his head. He shriveled as he fell to the floor, his body almost skeletal when it landed.

"Stay dead this time," I told him.

The children stood over him in a ring, fascinated as his apparition shrank away to nothing. Then they scattered to the walls of the room, laughing. Their laughter lingered for a few seconds after they disappeared.

Katherine's ghost was getting clingy, standing way too close to me while listening to her own story being read back to her. I removed the iPod from my belt and set it on the worktable, deciding to let her hang around there and listen all she wanted. Keeping her busy took one of Zagan's followers out of the fight, at least.

Then I returned the ghost trap to my backpack, ran to Lemmy and cut her free. She shuddered as she looked at the filthy sheets in which she'd been wrapped. More of the strange needles and other bits of old iron were implanted around her skin, and I gently pulled each one out.

"You okay?" I asked her, helping her to her feet.

"Totally not."

"I wouldn't think so. You said they were trying to possess you?"

"Yep. What happened to you?"

"Don't worry, it's just costume blood." I wiped away some of the fake blood beneath my eyes. "I was betting that doctor guy would be scared of yellow fever, since that's what killed him."

"Is that just a costume, too?" She pointed to my slashed-open jacket and shirt, and the blood beneath.

"No, that's real, unfortunately." I was cutting open the other bundles of stained linens and felt revulsion at the smell of old decay. I thought my kitchen smelled bad when I'd been away for two days and forgot to take out the trash, but ripe kitchen trash had nothing on the smell inside those old sheets. I found skulls and bones inside them, but no more living prisoners. Lemmy was pale as she looked at the old bones, and I hurried to cover them up again.

"Is everything okay now?" she asked.

I listened to the howls and shrieks from the other room. "Not quite. What are the odds of you hiding in here until that blows over?"

"Zippity," she said.

"All right. Let's go." I led her toward the movable section of the wall. From behind, I could better see the tracks on which it sat. They were of an extremely old construction, wooden rails with iron plating on top. Rusty wheels sat atop them, and an arrangement of gears and pulleys at the back of the wall did the grunt work of moving the wall, amplifying the force applied to the sun-bird panel outside.

Metallic rattling sounded behind us. I turned to see the array of scalpels, knives, and saws jiggling on the countertop, though the counter itself was not moving.

Katherine's ghost remained where I'd left her, staring at the little device that kept telling her life story, paying us no attention.

"Get down!" I grabbed Lemmy and turned my back toward the rows of rusty implements. I brought us both to the floor as the barrage of old cutting tools flew at us. They pelted my back through my leather jacket, but I didn't feel anything stabbing into me. More of them hurtled past us and clattered against the back of the wall and the rusty machinery affixed to it.

When it was over, I turned to see another ghost had arrived—Mabel Lathrop, possibly drawn by the sudden exit of her husband. Her mouth was downturned in an exaggerated frown that reached her jawline on either side. There wasn't even a hint of rosiness in her cheeks now. Her face was white like chalk dust.

*"No one can know!"* she hissed.

"Everyone will know," I said. Then I ushered Lemmy to the opened wall and heaved her up onto the altar, getting her clear of the movable portion as quickly as possible. I placed my hands on the altar and began to haul myself up.

The wall surged forward with a metallic screech, ready to crush the lower half of me against the back side of the heavy altar.

I slung my legs up and rolled forward. I just managed to reach the top of the altar before the wall section slammed into place behind me, its outline immediately lost among the panels of hieroglyphs and occult cartouches.

## Chapter Twenty

The war raged on in the necromantium, the winds stronger and the cries and howls of the mostly-invisible combatants even fiercer. Nicholas's record player had overturned, and shattered pieces of vinyl lay around it. So much for our Beach Boys soundtrack.

A portion of the room was illuminated by Nicholas. His light-thrower lay on the floor, several feet away from me, sending out a continuous beam that lanced the darkness along a single path to a nearby wall.

Nicholas himself lay on the floor, too. His clothes were on fire, and in that flickering red light I could see Stacey beating him with her jacket, trying to smother the flames. The flames kept roaring back, though, like those birthday candles that relight themselves after you blow them out.

Gregor Zagan stood nearby, his smoldering ash-heap of a body leaking fiery red light here and there through cracks in his skin. His eyes made me think of a jack o' lantern, red flames dancing inside the otherwise empty sockets. Red embers burned in his beard and all over his face.

He held up one hand, facing Nicholas, momentarily focused on stoking the flames every time Stacey managed to put them out.

Ithaca stood at the center of the room, the silent eye of the storm, with her arms splayed out, swaying and muttering under her breath. If she was trying to gain control of the situation, it wasn't working so far.

I was tempted to send Lemmy out of the room immediately, but no path looked safe. The jib door had refused to open even after I removed its hinges. The double doors were on the far side of the room.

"Stay close," I said. I holstered my flashlight, opting to use the rusty bayonet as my primary weapon if I needed one. I adjusted my backpack, then hopped down to the floor. I didn't see Ol' Bayonet Arm himself anywhere—perhaps he was invisible, fighting with the psychic ghosts—so I'm not sure what he thought of me wielding his old arm.

I took Lemmy's hand as we hopped off the altar, then led her in a mad dash to join Ithaca at the center of the room, swiping my bayonet at a couple of white-mask faces that drifted too close. I'm not sure if I hurt them, but they didn't touch Lemmy or me.

"He can't get me here!" Ithaca said, shouting over the wind. "He's worried he'll accidentally slip through the portal to the other side. So are the other spirits. This woman's body protects me from that." She touched Kara's slender stomach.

"Can you stop him?" I looked at Stacey trying to save Nicholas from the fire.

"Not from here," she said. "And I'm too weak to step out there. All my people are still against me."

"What's going on?" Lemmy asked.

"Sorry, I'll catch you up later," I said. Then I asked Ithaca, "Is there anything you can do? We were sort of counting on you. You talked a good game before we got here."

"I am sorry," Ithaca said, looking distraught and lost.

I considered the howling whirlwind of shadows that filled the room.

"Your followers are here because they made an oath to you," I said. "They promised to return here after their deaths. Right?"

"Yes." Ithaca looked at me with something like hope.

"Release them from that oath and they can move on," I said. "Zagan won't control them anymore."

"But neither will I?" Something about how she asked it made me think of a petulant child who didn't want to share her toys.

"No. They'll be free and gone, and Zagan will be alone."

"Yes, all right." Ithaca took a deep breath and waved her hand in a dramatic gesture. "You are all free of your oaths! You may move on to the next world!"

We waited, but there didn't seem to be any results. Well, one result. Zagan turned and began walking toward us, taking notice of what Ithaca had said.

*"Be silent,"* Zagan said. His voice seemed to snarl right into my ear, as though he stood just beside me instead of several feet in front of me. Ithaca and Lemmy both winced, as though he had spoken directly to them the same unnerving way.

He hesitated at the edge of the circular area outlined by the holes in the floor.

"It's not good enough," I told Ithaca. "You have to *break* the oath."

"How?"

"You have to move on."

Her eyes widened, and she immediately shook her head. "I cannot. I have so much work left, so many plans, so much to do..."

Zagan laughed. It wasn't a merry Santa Claus laugh, either, but the derisive, soulless chuckling of a demon from a dark, smoking abyss. His jack-o'-lantern eyes flared with brighter fire, as though in amusement.

*"She will never move on,"* he said. *"It is not in her nature. She will linger here for eternity."*

Then he stepped forward into the circle, one hand extended toward Ithaca. From the corner of my eye, I noticed Stacey successfully extinguished the last flames on Nicholas's charred clothes. I worried about the extent of his burns.

Ithaca gasped a little as Zagan approached her, and then she rose into the air, just as Jacob had done right before Zagan had tried to make him into a psychic-accountant flambe.

Apparently the portal within the circle didn't worry Zagan at all—he'd only avoided it to give Ithaca a false sense of security, toying with her while he attacked Nicholas.

Ithaca screamed as she rose into the air, and her clothes began to smolder. Zagan laughed again, his jaws dropping unnaturally far. Fire licked out between his crooked, rotten teeth.

"You have to move on!" I shouted at Ithaca. "Take your thoughts and ideas with you, but go! Or he'll kill all of us!" I waved the rusty bayonet at her. "I'm going to take apart Dr. Lathrop's lab. That was the real center of the haunting, wasn't it? All the pain and torture the patients endured there. That's why you built your necromantium adjacent to it. It was the psychic battery for all your supernatural work. That ends now. There's nothing left for you. Choose to move on."

My little monologue only made Zagan laugh more. It was the sort of laugh you might hear from a sadistic hyena.

Curls of fire emerged all over Ithaca's clothes. Well, I guess they were technically Kara Volkova's clothes. Talking about possessed people gets complicated.

"You owe it to Abigail," I said. "It's the only way you can make things right."

Ithaca snarled just a little, though I wasn't sure if it was in response to my words or to the fire that was whipping up all over her.

"How?" she finally asked.

"I'm sure you already know," I said. "Imagine a trap door opening in the ceiling above you, a bright light streaming down. Then just...move into it. It will take you wherever you need to go."

Ithaca closed her eyes.

She slumped, all the steel gone from her spine, an unconscious woman floating in the air.

Nothing outwardly dramatic happened, but I felt a sense of the heavy air in the room growing a touch lighter.

Then the room fell utterly silent, and the whirlwinds stopped abruptly, as if something had happened that was so significant to all the ghosts in the area that it drew all their attention.

Zagan turned slowly, looking into the darkness around us, literally fuming as smoke and embers boiled out of his head.

"*Stop,*" he said, his whispering voice echoing all over the room. "*Stop. We have not yet begun...*"

Kara, the unconscious woman whom Ithaca had possessed, fell to the floor like a discarded toy, landing hard, trickles of smoke rising from holes in her clothes that revealed angry, deep red skin beneath. I hurried to her, towing Lemmy behind me. I shrugged off my backpack and smothered the little flames all over Kara.

The white masks appeared in the darkness above us, rising toward the ceiling. They unraveled as they rose, losing form, turning into a wispy luminescent fog that faded quickly.

The room had felt slightly different when Ithaca's spirit

departed, but when all of her followers rose and vanished, the tone in the room changed undeniably. Warmer, clearer, much easier to breathe.

"They're gone," I told Zagan. "Every one of them. You can choose to move on, too."

"*I have already moved on,*" his voice whispered in my ear, in that creepy and annoying way of his. "*To worlds you cannot imagine.*"

"I've seen *Star Trek*," I said. "I can imagine a lot of worlds."

Stacey was easing up toward us, her eyes dancing between Lemmy and me on one side of the circle and Zagan smoldering on the other. I was trying not to show my fear of him, but my stupid knees wouldn't stop trembling. I'm pretty sure he noticed.

The darkness around him seemed to stir. Faint outlines of limping, damaged men moved toward him, converging from all sides. They grew clearer as they approached, staring at him with dead or missing eyes, raising the hooks and blades mounted in place of their hands. They looked in worse condition than I'd ever seen them, but they weren't moaning and groaning now. I caught a glimpse of Abigail among them, her scalpel and dress wet with blood.

"My friends have *not* moved on," I said. "Gregor Zagan, you are now a prisoner of the United States Army."

Stacey brought up the Civil War march on her iPod again.

"Your penalty is execution and exile," I said. "In that order." The fife and drums made it sound almost official.

The soldiers bellowed and closed in tight around the smoking figure of Zagan. I could only hear his howls as they tore into him.

"Whoa," Lemmy said.

"You might want to avert your eyes," I said. "Stacey, how's Nicholas Nickleby doing over there?"

"Mostly alive." She went back to check on him.

"What is happening?" The woman on the floor, Kara, stirred, then hissed, touching small coin-sized burn spots all over herself.

"I'll have to explain later," I said, kneeling down beside her.

"She says that a lot," Lemmy told her.

"No." Kara sat up, touching her chest, then her head. "Where is she?"

"Oh, Ithaca Galloway? She went, you know..." I pointed toward the ceiling.

"You took her from me." Kara's petite supermodel face looked seriously angry. I noticed she spoke with a faint East European, possibly Russian accent. As previously mentioned, I'm not well-traveled and don't really know accents.

"Well, it was more of a choice on her part—"

"You have caused me to fail my assignment." She got to her feet, slapping away the hand Stacey offered her. Kara stepped close to me, her pale blue eyes simmering, her hands balling into fists at her hips. For a second, I seriously thought she was going to punch me right in the face. "This is unforgivable."

"Really sorry about that," I said. "Hey, on the bright side, we exorcised a whole pack of troublesome ghosts from this hotel, I mean some really dangerous ones—"

"This has nothing to do with me!" She threw up her arms in frustration. "We agree to help you, and you betray us."

"Excuse me? I was basically just trying to survive, because your pet ghost turned out to be not very helpful at *all* until I convinced her to move on—"

An angry roar surged from the mob of spirits. The floor shook like an earthquake.

Union-blue blurs flew out in every direction, turning to faint traces of fog at the edge of the room.

Zagan rose up like a pillar of ash and fire, swelling in every direction, reaching a height of eleven feet. His roar shook the room. He was really trying to intimidate us, and it was really working.

We ran back from his swelling form to avoid being enveloped by it. I don't even want to know what that experience might have been like.

His appearance was only crudely human now, fire licking from his eyes and jaws, more flames peeking out from beneath his charred, flaking flesh.

I'd really hoped that someone would have dragged Zagan off to the other side with them by this point—Ithaca, their cult followers, or maybe Abigail and her soldiers, *somebody*. He looked as tough as ever, though, and I had just one last-ditch desperate move to try.

I grabbed the ghost cannon from where Stacey had left it on the floor, near Nicholas's overturned record player. I switched it on and pointed it straight up. The powerful beam glinted off the grimy pressed-tin ceiling and spread out, flooding the entire room with white light. No shadows, nowhere to hide.

Zagan watched as I drew the ghost trap from my backpack. I hoped he didn't have any idea what it was.

"You like fire, don't you?" I asked him, using a firestarter to light the candles mounted along the interior of the trap. I'd packed it with extra candles in advance, in case I needed to try luring Zagan with it. I gave this gambit about a two percent chance of working. Maybe one percent. "It seems like the demonic entity you met packs a lot of firepower. So how does it work? You summon him, he kills you, then you're like his servant for eternity? Sounds like a raw deal."

*"You know nothing,"* he said.

"What was your plan? Have the crazy doctor develop some kind of streamlined possession technique? Place your psychic friends network into the bodies of hotel guests as they came and went? Mass possession to bring your cult back to life, back to the flesh? Do I still know nothing?"

*"I do not need them."* As he spoke, I rose off the ground, levitating as Jacob had just before Zagan torched him. Yikes. Giant unseen hands seemed to stretch out my arms and fingers to either side of me, like a mockery of the Crucifixion. The ghost trap dropped from my fingers and rolled away across the floor. *"You have done nothing to harm me. I could turn this world to cinders if I wished."*

"I bet that's an exaggeration," I said. I certainly hoped it was. "I think you can only act under the command of the demon who consumed you. I think you are a slave. Or more like a...pet." I winced and hissed in pain as spots all over my body began to burn, as though someone had shoved hot coals underneath my clothes, next to my skin. I forced myself to hold it together, rather than do the natural thing and scream and kick in pain. I could do nothing to put out the fire, except to hold my focus on Zagan and keep talking. I spoke faster, using the words to distract me from my pain.

Zagan's black-ashy surface boiled and bubbled, emitting larger flames. Maybe I was making him angry.

Smoke curled from my sleeves, my shirt, and my jeans as I began to burn.

"You can still be free," I said. "Your true soul can move on. You can always choose. Let go of the power the demon gives you. Let go of your plans and desires. Move on! Be free!" I was screaming in pain, not because I felt like I was reaching the crescendo of some great speech.

More fire erupted all over him, so that he looked like a walking mass of lava, little veins of fire cracking open here and there. An awful roasting heat rolled out of him.

I did not get the sense he would be moving on. I kept talking, not because I thought it would help at this point, but because if I didn't talk, then one hundred percent of my attention would have to focus on the fact that little flames were popping up all over me.

Stacey, Kara, and Lemmy lay on the floor, struggling, as if he'd simply pinned them there with brute psychokinetic energy. Only Nicholas wasn't struggling. He was either unconscious or dead.

This really wasn't going well.

"I have my own relationship with fire, you know!" I shouted, because when you're literally on fire, it's extremely hard to keep your voice cool and controlled. "I hate it. I hate it. I'm afraid I'm going to die in a fire like my parents. Like, especially right now. That's why every time I go into one of these huge old buildings, I'm always noticing the fire safety situation. That's why I'd already noticed the fire hose in the hallway. And that's why I noticed that what you have up here is a standard automatic sprinkler system. It looks pretty old but it must be up to code or the hotel wouldn't pass fire safety or insurance—"

Then it finally happened. Between the incredibly unsafe levels of heat pouring out of the ghost cannon, pointed directly at the ceiling, and the heat rolling off Zagan as I goaded him about connecting with his higher self or whatever and moving on, the sprinkler system was finally activated.

Gushers of water erupted from the ceiling, pouring down into the room. I didn't think the water actually hurt Zagan, but it certainly annoyed him, and had seemed to have scrambled him for a minute on our previous visit.

Hot steam filled the room, blinding me, and I heard him roar. I tumbled down from the air, slamming into wet marble tiles.

Alarm bells clanged all over the hotel.

I scrambled back to my feet and nearly collided with Stacey, who was running in my direction, her hand over the ghost trap to protect it from the downpour. A few candles still burned inside.

"There's an umbrella in my backpack!" I shouted at her as she passed me the trap.

"You thought of everything." She opened the umbrella and passed it to me. It was just large enough to shield me and the burning candles inside the open trap from the sprinklers. Mostly the trap. I got soaked.

I held the trap out in the direction where I'd last seen Zagan. My thinking was that if he hated water, he would move toward the light of the burning candles, the only spot in the room that wasn't cold and wet. Any port in a storm, I hoped.

A dense, scorching cloud of steam rolled across me, so hot that I had to squint my eyes and turn away from the sting. Gooseflesh all over my body told me I was in the presence of a supernatural entity.

A searing gout of flame roared from the mouth of the trap as the candles within it exploded like a knot in a bonfire. For a second, it looked as though I held a bazooka under my arm.

Then I clapped the lid on top of the flames, gaining painful new burns on my fingers for my trouble. I just hoped the trap wouldn't melt.

Inside the airtight container, the dense red fire turned to black smoke. A moment later, a pale, distorted image of Zagan's face appeared against the glass, the cartoon-simple eyes scowling and mouth open in an apoplectic rage.

"Gotcha," I said.

Then I figured we needed to do something about turning off the sprinklers before they flooded the hotel, if they hadn't already.

## Chapter Twenty-One

The fire alarm meant the hotel was evacuated, so we soon joined the hotel guests and staff out in the street. Frightened and confused people huddled together in their pajamas and bathrobes. Sirens approached, growing louder.

Lemmy spotted her parents, who looked utterly panicked, standing with Madeline and Conrad, the security chief. They shouted and pointed as Lemmy ran over to them.

"What happened to you? Where did you go?" her mother asked.

"Ghosts kidnapped me and tried to possess me," Lemmy said. "It was super not fun."

"What kind of hotel are you running here?" Lemmy's dad snapped at Madeline.

"A haunted one, just like you wanted," I said. "If you want to keep your daughter safe, you might consider safer vacation destinations. Isn't there a big botanical garden back home? She might like that."

The parents scowled a little, but Lemmy smiled. Then Madeline stepped closer to Stacey and me, looking furious.

"What happened up there?" she asked me. "Is there a fire?"

"There was, but it didn't last long," I said. I helped Stacey ease

Nicholas to the ground. We'd managed to rouse him enough to walk, but he was in pain. Kara sat down with him while we faced Madeline. "The worst of the ghosts are gone, but...you may have a small flood on the fourth floor." I adjusted my backpack. It was like I could feel Zagan wriggling in there.

"A flood?"

"The sprinkler system. The ghost was a hot one."

Fire trucks arrived, and Madeline spoke with the officials while we turned Nicholas and Kara over to the EMT's. They examined Lemmy, too. Michael was among them and hurried over when he saw me.

"You came," I said, smiling and reaching out to embrace him.

"I knew you were here. I was worried you were hurt." He hugged me very lightly and stepped back to inspect my burns and cuts, all business. "Also, I was in the response radius."

"You know how to melt a girl's heart."

"What happened? Is there an active situation up there?"

"No, just a very wet passive one."

"How can I help?"

"Stay close to me. I know I'm going to spend hours trying to answer questions here, and I really just want to collapse."

"Okay." He put an arm around my waist as Madeline approached with the fire chief and a uniformed police officer to whom she'd been talking.

Soon we were all back upstairs—Michael, Stacey, the fire chief and the cop, and me. I was doing most of the talking. I didn't hold back for the sake of the authorities. I just told the truth, even though the fire chief, a tired-looking guy with thin white hair, just looked incredulous. At least he was quiet. The cop was a middle-aged woman, and her face remained placid, giving me no idea what was happening inside her mind.

"Dr. Lathrop's hotel was used as a hospital all through the Civil War, for Confederates and then Union soldiers," I reminded them as we squished our way among shattered furniture and uprooted floorboards along the fourth-floor hall. Madeline was gaping, shaking her head at the destruction. "After the North took over—and maybe even before that, I don't really know—Dr. Lathrop started bringing certain soldiers up to this hidden room for medical experiments. I'm sure a lot of them died in there."

"What hidden room?" Madeline asked.

"Right through here." I let them into the necromantium, where a shallow layer of water still remained on the floor. "When Abigail Bowen killed those soldiers, she was freeing them from a long, slow death at Dr. Lathrop's hands. He turned her over to the occupying forces for execution. We're not even sure whether there was a proper trial.

"Of course, Dr. Lathrop goes down in history as a saint for his work with the war wounded and then the yellow fever victims, while everyone thinks Abigail's just some crazy psycho killer. You know, Stabby Abby. Abigail and the soldiers have stayed here ever since, waiting for justice, or at least waiting for the truth to be known.

"When Ithaca Galloway bought the hotel in 1895, she must have discovered this secret room during her renovations." I climbed up on the altar and pressed the bird-and-rising-sun symbol. The section of the wall repeated its scraping, shuddering retreat, opening an entry into the old laboratory.

Madeline, the cop, and the fire chief all murmured in surprise. The cop and fire chief had already been trading looks about the bizarre temple room with its columns and hieroglyphs.

"Ithaca covered it up and kept it hidden," I said. "She wanted a very haunted house, because of her interest in ghosts and séances. She refused to help Abigail's ghost get free of the house and move on. She kept Dr. Lathrop's secret in order to keep the house as a major center of supernatural activity. Ever since Ithaca and her followers died, they've haunted the fourth floor, driving away anyone who came up there so they could protect the secret room from being discovered. It kept them powerful as ghosts, I suppose, to have a place like that in their domain. And Ithaca may have felt some guilt for covering up Dr. Lathrop's crimes, almost acting as his accomplice decades after the fact. The laboratory had become her secret as much as his."

I explained that Ithaca's ghost had left the house one month earlier, and her old partner Zagan had immediately returned to assume control of the cult. "It takes a powerful ghost to possess a healthy living person," I said. "I think Zagan recruited Dr. Lathrop's ghost to develop a technique to make it easier. All of the ghosts up here were going to possess living people, guests of the hotel. It seemed like they intended to go after children in particular."

"Makes sense," Stacey said, and everyone looked at her. "What? Kids have more life ahead of them. If you're going to all the trouble of possessing someone, why not buy new instead of used?"

"This doorway isn't safe," I said. "Last time I used it, someone tried to slam it shut on me. Michael, could you grab some of that broken furniture out there?"

He nodded, and soon we were placing shattered tables and chairs in a heap inside the laboratory. Hopefully it would slow down the wall if someone decide to push it back into place.

"Everyone wait until I give the all-clear." I jumped through the gap into the room, landing near the front corner, away from the movable portion of the wall. Then I took a hammer from my utility belt. I'd borrowed it from a hotel maintenance closet.

I repeatedly struck one of the rusty wheels on the back side of the wall, until it cracked and broke loose. The wall lurched to one side with a heavy thud.

"Ellie?" Michael called. He jumped into the room with me, not waiting for an answer.

"I'm fine." I swung the hammer again and again, smashing the wheels and gears on the back of the wall, hopefully locking it open.

"This is...awful," he said, looking around at the old tools and pieces of bone. "Really sad."

"It was worse than that a few minutes ago." I walked to the counter and picked up my iPod. The battery was dead. There was no sign of Katherine's ghost.

Then the weeping began.

I turned, expecting to see Katherine. I was surprised to see Mabel Lathrop instead, faintly visible in the corner, dressed in one of her big hoop skirts and crying softly, like an antebellum lady who'd become emotional and had to run off to be by herself. Her hair was immaculately styled with braids that must have taken hours to set. Jeweled rings and bracelets glittered at her plump fingers and wrists.

"Mabel Lathrop," I said, to get her attention. She stopped weeping and looked up at me. She made no move to resume her very recent attacks on me, but I stayed on guard.

*"What will they think of me?"* she whispered.

"I suppose they'll think the truth," I said. "Your husband was a monster...and judging by how you're acting, you knew and covered up for him."

*"I can never face anyone again,"* she said.

"That's right. The whole town will know what your husband did. There's no stopping that now. If I were you, I'd move on. Leave town and never come back."

*"But this is my home..."* She resumed her sobbing, covering her face with her hands.

Michael stood quietly beside me, watching. I heard footfalls behind us. Madeline, Stacey, the fire chief, and the cop were entering the room.

"You should go, Mabel," I said. "Unless you want to watch as your reputation is torn to shreds."

She let out a loud, piercing wail. She turned toward the wall and faded into a thin mist, then vanished.

Madeline and the officials stared at where she'd gone.

"Did you see that?" Madeline whispered to the fire chief.

"This town never fails to surprise me," he replied, shaking his head.

I pointed out the artifacts of Dr. Lathrop's medical experiments, as well as the pieces of bone still attached, and the pail of bone fragments under the counter. "Once you clear out these implements and bury these body parts, that should put your ghost troubles to rest. This room was the core of the haunting."

"We won't be able to keep a lid on this, will we?" Madeline said. "Everyone will know the hotel is named after a man who...who tortured wounded soldiers..." She looked in disgust at the rusty claw and hook hands, and the wheels attached to a piece of leg bone. "Americans aren't going to like that much at all. Surely the bigwigs won't like it. There's so much to do before they arrive..."

"Maybe you can get out ahead of it," I said. "Start thinking up possible new names for the hotel."

"This is too much," she said, shaking her head.

I'm glad she was shocked. It was better than being furious at me for flooding her hotel...though I was sure that would come later. Perhaps after she got chewed out by her bosses, those infamous bigwigs of Black Diamond Properties. She'd called them "bigwigs" so many times, I'd begun to imagine them as a committee of cranky old-man Muppets with gigantic powdered wigs larger than their heads.

Still, Madeline would be able to do what no one had done since Ithaca Galloway more than a century earlier, and remodel the fourth floor without fear of ghosts running off the workers. Ultimately, the hotel would be more profitable with more rooms to rent, and her bosses would be pleased, and she would forget about how she had to scramble to get the water cleaned up and pumped out. That was my hope, anyway.

## Chapter Twenty-Two

Two days later, Stacey and I returned to the fourth floor with Nicholas, Kara, and a couple of others from Paranormal Solutions who'd brought down some specialized gear. The entire level of the hotel looked different—the broken furniture had been carted away, and huge portions of the floors and walls had been ripped open to let the innards of the building dry.

Stacey and I had buried Zagan's trap in the "bad ghost" cemetery, located in the ruins of an old churchyard in the virtually inaccessible Appalachian ridges in northwest Georgia. If Zagan's spirit ever broke free of the ghost trap, he would still be trapped within the cemetery's rock walls, an area ruled over by the ghost of a long-dead crazed preacher named Mordecai Blake and his followers.

Some unfinished business remained at the hotel, though, so we now carried equipment into the necromantium and closed the door. I hopped up on the altar and looked into the secret lab room behind it. It was nothing but bare bricks and floor, everything else had been removed. The pieces of bone were taken for forensic examination before disposal. The Savannah Historical Association had accepted the collection of Civil War-era medical instruments, as well as my written report on what had really happened with Dr. Lathrop's torturous experiments and Abigail Bowen's desire to free the wounded soldiers from their pain.

Kara was still furious with me for convincing Ithaca to leave her body and move on. She was extremely curt with both Stacey and me. Oh, well.

Nicholas was just as chatty as ever. Like Kara, he had a number of first-degree burns and a few second-degree ones, but it didn't stop him from working.

We had to set up some of the gear designed by Ithaca, arranging things like a positive ion pump and electromagnetic field generators, tuned to certain frequencies, around the circular area at the center of the room.

"You think this will really work?" I asked. The idea was to shut down the rip between worlds that Ithaca had apparently torn open long ago while trying to create her machine.

"It is a reversal of the process that punctured the hole," Nicholas told me. "It should be sufficient to patch things up and prevent unwanted beasties from slipping in and setting up shop in your newly ghost-free hotel."

"We haven't made our final inspection, so we're not sure it's one hundred percent ghost-free just yet...but thanks, Nicholas, for helping us mop things up. For all your help. You too, Kara. I'm sorry you both got hurt." I didn't mention that they'd more or less caused the problems in the first place, but our client had received good value beyond fixing the problems Nicholas and company had caused. We'd removed a pile of ghosts, including the two most dangerous with Zagan and Dr. Lathrop, and we'd completely liberated the top floor of the building.

Kara kept her eyes on the generator in front of her, pretending not to hear me. I wondered how long she'd bear a grudge against me, and whether that was going to affect my life in any way.

"We're pleased to help," Nicholas said. Kara heard *that*, judging by the brief, angry flick of her eyes in his direction. "I hope all of this has changed your mind about combining with the Paranormal Solutions fam...corporation. You can see we're not monsters. We're all in the same line of work, with the same goals."

"Are we?" I asked. I looked at Kara and the technicians from their company, who were starting to break down and pack up the hefty gear. "How much of this was a set-up?"

"I'm sorry?" Nicholas asked.

"We followed a short trail of fat bread crumbs right to your secret research facility," I said. "Why would you go to the trouble of creating that fake film company to hide who you really were, but then give out a phone number tied to the physical address of your ghost lab? Why not get a burner cell phone for the Metascience Productions business card? Seems like a no-brainer."

"I shall forward that advice to our Director of Operations," he said.

"Come on," I said. "You knew removing Ithaca Galloway, the master of the house, could cause problems and chaos. It's like snatching away the alpha wolf and leaving the rest to fight it out for dominance."

"An interesting comparison, though we are discussing electromagnetic remnant personalities of humans, not live wild canines—"

"You knew the hotel would probably hire Eckhart Investigations if there were problems. And you made it easy for us to find you—but you disconnected the phone so we'd have to drive all the way to your facility."

Kara let out a derisive snort, without looking up from her work as she finished packing away the gear.

"That's an elaborate conspiracy theory," Nicholas said. "Have you heard the one about the aliens who built the pyramids?"

"Yeah, from your logo designer." The emblem of his company was a pyramid with a tilted, Saturn-like ring near the top.

"You've got us there," he said. "We are all secret aliens—"

"Stop. What was the idea? Impress me with your dazzling ghostly experiments? Force me to come to you for help?"

"We were having such a friendly conversation a moment ago," he said, looking entirely unruffled by what I was saying.

"Am I right?" I asked. "I'm only asking to measure how honest you're being with me."

Nicholas held up his right hand, as though being sworn in at court. "I solemnly swear there was no manipulation or hidden agenda here. Unless you're free this evening and not opposed to dining with a horrific burn victim." He raised his arm, showing me the swollen red spots on the back of his hand.

"I don't...did you just ask me on a date?"

"I will not be leaving town until tomorrow," he said. "And I should be back and forth over the next several weeks—"

"Trying to buy my company."

"After which, we'll have many more occasions to see each other," he said.

"Right. Many more occasions," I said. "You know I have a boyfriend, right?"

"And yet, mysteriously, my offer stands," he said. "You would have the choice of venue, as it's your town. You could be my tour guide."

"I'm a little busy," I said. "Maybe next time?" Why did I add that?

He smiled just a little more, the only sign that my weak rejection had irked him at all.

"I will look forward to next time, then." He rejoined his co-workers.

"You know, if that were me, you'd be all, 'Oh, you have a *boyfriend*, Stacey,'" Stacey said.

"Why does your impression of me talk like Mr. Snuffleupagus? Anyway, I'm not going out with him. All I'm doing is getting out of here as fast as possible so I can prepare an invoice for Madeline. How much do you think we should charge for wrecking the place?"

"A lot," she said. "We took some heavy hits on our equipment. It'll take some spending to restock."

I nodded and led the way out, eager to see the hotel in my rearview mirror.

## Chapter Twenty-Three

I can tell you the exact moment that Abigail Bowen's spirit moved on. It was 2:47 in the morning, and my cat woke me by jumping on my face, yowling, claws extended.

After a delicate feline-removal procedure, I sat up and looked at the door to my balcony, which was where my cat's anger had been directed. Bandit scrambled under my bed and resumed hissing and growling down there, like a Paleolithic lion guarding its cave.

Her face looked in at me—not strangely smooth and lifeless like before, but a lifelike face with detailed features. She was so transparent that most people would have tried to dismiss it as a reflection, a trick of the eyes. I knew better.

I climbed out of bed and crossed my narrow apartment. By the time I reached the glass door to the balcony, the face was gone, but I opened the door and stepped outside anyway.

The night was clear and cool. The street outside lay deserted, streetlamps glowing under the low canopy of old, intertwined tree limbs.

I didn't see her again, but I could feel something in the air, a sense that things had changed. A follow-up investigation of the hotel, including a walk-through by Jacob, would confirm that all the spirits had gone, even the yellow fever victims in the basement, who might have been trapped there by the overall haunted atmosphere of the place where they'd died. Jacob pronounced the hotel "whistle-clean." The thick layers of residual hauntings had vanished, too. I hope that didn't cost Madeline too many tourist dollars.

My future might have been filled with questions and uncertainty, but at the moment, the world felt a little more right, as though some giant scale had shifted, however minutely, away from senseless suffering and toward justice and compassion.

Whatever happened in the future—whether I was pushed into joining with Nicholas and company, or whether I decided to take Michael up on his idea and leave town before I had to work for those people—I knew that I would always pursue the same calling, doing what I could to make the world a little bit less dark and dangerous. I would always be a ghost trapper.

## From the author

Thanks for continuing to read Ellie Jordan's stories. I had a lot of fun researching this one, and several actual ghost stories from Savannah served as inspiration.

If you're enjoying the series, I hope you'll consider taking time to recommend the books to someone who might like them or to rate or review it at your favorite ebook retailer.

The sixth book in the Ellie Jordan series is already in the works, and should be available around August or September of 2015. I can say that it will involve a family farm with a corn maze, and takes place around Halloween.

Sign up for my newsletter to hear about the new books as they come out. You'll immediately get a free ebook of short stories just for signing up.

If you'd like to get in touch with me, here are my links:

Website (www.jlbryanbooks.com)
Facebook (J. L. Bryan's Books)
Twitter (@jlbryanbooks)
Email (info@jlbryanbooks.com)

Thanks for reading!

Made in the USA
Lexington, KY
22 October 2016